A BUTTERFLY IN PHILADELPHIA

Also by Bruce Hartman:

Perfectly Healthy Man Drops Dead

The Rules of Dreaming

The Muse of Violence

The Philosophical Detective

A BUTTERFLY
IN
PHILADELPHIA

a novel

Bruce Hartman

Swallow Tail Press

Published by Swallow Tail Press
Philadelphia, PA, USA
www.swallowtailpress.com

Front cover photo courtesy of Shutterstock.com

ISBN-10: 0988918145

ISBN-13: 978-0-9889181-4-6

Author's Note: This is a work of satirical fiction. Any resemblance to actual persons, places or organizations, or even to the known universe, is entirely coincidental

PART I

1. The Puzzle Factory

You can blame me, if you've got to blame somebody, for the train wreck that started at the puzzle factory. It wasn't Charlie's fault or Audrey's or even Jeff Pangborn's, though he hired Stupid Butchie who set the whole disaster in motion. And why does it got to be somebody's fault if things don't fit together exactly the way they're supposed to? I didn't make this world, or those puzzles either. All I did was jumble up the pieces.

The place was called Artistic Puzzles Inc. and it was in South Philly near Passyunk and Washington. I took the bus down there every night, listening to hip hop tracks through my headphones which the driver, if he was white, would make me turn down so low I could hardly hear them. Believe it or not that shop ran twenty-four hours a day like the world needed those Masterpieces of Western Art jigsaw puzzles more than food or clothes or TVs or anything else you could think of. Every night it's the same routine, just me and a swarm of retarded cats with seven or eight toes on each foot that scratch and hiss and try to climb my leg when I run the die press. Old Mr. Pangborn shuffles in every morning but his son Jeff, who wears a suit and tie and shows up maybe once a month, seems to make all the decisions. Audrey the bookkeeper sits in her glassed-in booth, way too old to be hot but she's still working on it with her long fingernails that click over the keys of her computer. From midnight to eight it's just me running the die press until Charlie comes in for the day shift and we work together a couple hours sorting out the puzzles and setting up the next run. Charlie looks like a 300-pound white styrofoam Mr. Potato Head with the ears stuck on too low and a few tufts of orange hair on top. He has some blotchy spots on his left hand where he got it caught in the die press trying to save one of the retarded cats.

"Spencer," Charlie tells me my first day, "you just spent the night chopping up the Masterpieces of Western Art into 1000 pieces."

"Get out of here," I tell him.

"See this?" He shows me his hand with the blotches on it that looks like some girl's face. "This was supposed to be the Mona Lisa."

The whole job I learn in about fifteen minutes. First you glue the prints on the cardboard in the glue press and then you run them through the die press and a thousand little pieces drop in coded bins so the Vietnamese ladies at 6th and Tasker can put them in boxes with the right labels on them. In the morning after Charlie gets there we make coffee and joke around until Audrey starts making eyes at me.

"Don't look now," Charlie says one morning, "but the cougar's getting ready to pounce."

"No way I'm going in that bookkeeper booth."

Audrey calls to me from the doorway. "Spencer! Could I talk to you for a minute?"

"I've got your back, buddy," Charlie whispers, and we march together toward her office.

"Charlie," she says, "you better get out on the loading dock to help Stupid Butchie before Jeff sees you standing around."

Stupid Butchie's a college boy hired by Jeff, who's his uncle. He don't wear a suit and tie but he looks like he's aiming for one. Mr. Pangborn and Jeff call him Stupid Butchie but we're not allowed to call him that because he's a member of the family.

Mr. Pangborn's about a hundred years old and when he cracks a smile you can hear it across the room. He don't do any work but sometimes he'll stand and watch me like he's trying to learn the job. One day we're taking our coffee break and Stupid Butchie asks him where to find the broom.

"I don't know," Mr. Pangborn says. "Ask the colored kid."

He means me. "I'm African American," I tell him.

Mr. Pangborn looks blank as a slice of white bread before you put the peanut butter on it.

"He's African American," Charlie explains.

Mr. Pangborn stares like he never seen me before. "What part of Africa are you from?"

Everybody laughs except me. They're racists, naturally, like all white people, and I know they'd lock me up in chains and throw away the key if they could make me work for nothing. But besides the chains, what've they got worth talking about? All they've got is the Masterpieces of Western Art cut up in 1000 pieces, and what's Western about them I don't know, I don't see no cowboys and Indians, just naked white women and babies that look like little old men and piles of fruit like you can see every day in the produce department.   They call them masterpieces because if you mess with them long enough you end up with the same picture you started out with, and that's the best these people can come up with after two thousand years. It reminds me of my cousin Shawn, who just turned 16. Shawn burns CDs about pimps and ho's on his laptop and sells them to old ladies at church suppers, then on Sunday he sings in the choir about Jesus. His mother, my Aunt Lorraine, says he's really a con artist, because the old ladies think the CDs are about Jesus too and he knows they don't have CD players to listen to them on. But one way or the other he's creating something, not just chopping something up that already exists. It bothers me when he says I've got no gifts or talents and nothing to contribute to the world. That's what my teachers used to say too. I was a waste of their time. Nobody noticed when I stopped going to school, not even Aunt Lorraine, though she was mad when she found out later. Aunt Lorraine likes to say that everybody's got a little spark in him no matter who he is, even if he's got no job and no money, even if he's a killer on death row, he's got a little spark in him that could make the world a better place. A little spark of what I don't know, but mine was burning so low by the time I got that job at the puzzle factory even Aunt Lorraine agreed I had nothing to contribute to the world. I was almost 20.

"Why'd you quit school, Spencer?" Charlie asks me one morning while we're taking a break on the loading dock, feeding the retarded cats.

"They said I'm my own worst enemy," I tell him. "I've got such low self-esteem it gives me a too high opinion of myself. I'm a know-it-all who don't know anything."

"I graduated over twenty years ago but a lot of good it did me," Charlie says.

"And they were always treating me like I'm a victim of something. I'm a victim of poverty and the welfare system, discrimination, miseducation, low expectations, the ruling class, the underclass, crime, the cops, the Republicans, the Democrats, lead poisoning, budget cuts—and finally, it dawns on me, I'm a victim of *them,* the people who're always telling me what a victim I am. And you know what? It's not just me. They want everybody in the world to think they're a victim, like it's one big prison you can't escape from, so they can keep guarding the doors. Well, I'm tired of all that. I'm going to stop being a victim."

Charlie rolls his eyes around in his big potato head, thinking it over. "How you going to do that?"

"I'm going to stop being an effect and start being a *cause.*"

Charlie takes a minute to think that one over. "Good luck."

"How about you?"

"I'm not a victim of anything," he says, shaking his head like he's sorry to admit it. "Except myself."

Every morning Stupid Butchie goes in the van to take the puzzles to the Vietnamese ladies at 6th and Tasker who put them in boxes and stick the stickers on the boxes and he brings back what they did the day before to be shrink wrapped and stacked on the pallets until the truck comes to pick them up. But one day something goes wrong. Mr. Pangborn starts pacing around like a guard dog, squinting his eyes at everybody like we're some kind of criminal, his son Jeff in the suit and tie comes in and yells at Audrey back in her walled off glass world like we're not supposed to notice. I hear it all. The licensing company that owns the masterpieces says we're missing hundreds of them. Can't account for them, they say, even though we log out all the puzzles like we're supposed to. They hire a detective and after about a week he begins to suspect Stupid Butchie. He follows him one morning and Stupid Butchie stops the van in front of a garage at 8th and Reed and unloads about half the load—puzzles, boxes, lids, labels—and stashes it in the garage, then he goes on and delivers the rest to the Vietnamese like nothing happened. When he comes back Mr. Pangborn calls the cops and they search the garage and find Stupid Butchie set up a whole operation in there, a regular puzzle factory of his own. Gotta hand it to the dog, though it was the beginning of the end for the rest of us. Stupid Butchie assembled the boxes, poured in the puzzles, stuck on the lids and the labels and even had his own shrink wrap machine in there to make it look official. Then he went around selling his own puzzles to stores and collecting his own cash like he owned the business. The licensing company had him arrested but Jeff got him a lawyer and they dropped the charges. For the rest of us, things don't look so good. The licensing company's threatening to take back the masterpieces and put us out of business.

Now Jeff Pangborn's in Audrey's bookkeeper booth yelling at her all morning long while me and Charlie listen at the door. "The bank's got a lean on all our asses," he tells her. "If we lose the license we won't be able to pay the bank and we'll have no choice but to sell our asses to the Chinese." I sure hope my ass ain't included.

"You think the licensing company might back off?" Audrey asks Jeff.

"It'll take a miracle," Jeff tells her.

"Don't give up hope," she tells him. "A butterfly in China can cause a hurricane on the other side of the world just by flapping its wings."

Those Chinese, I'm thinking. Is there anything they can't do?

The door flies open and Jeff sails out, glaring at me and Charlie like we're the ones who just wrecked his business.

"Try to look like you're working," he says. "Even if you're not."

I'm listening but not listening, my mind's on the die press that I forgot to turn off. Corner of my eye I can see one of the cats squatting on Whistler's Mother.

"You! I'm talking to you." He's talking to me. "You got attention issues? Maybe you've got ADHD."

"Not yet," I tell him. "Just regular cable."

Audrey and Charlie start to laugh so I laugh too. Jeff don't think it's so funny. He looks like his necktie's choking him and his face swells up red as a plum. "You think this is funny?" He pokes his finger at me. "Pretty soon your job will be going to China. Let's see how funny you think that is."

That night I'm chopping up a piece of modern art called Chaos Scape 19 by Armand Brigantine and I'm wondering, did this dude spill his paint set before he got around to painting the picture? The first time I look at it I think it must have got screwed up in the glue press, but no, Charlie says, that's the way it's supposed to be. By the second or third time I chop it up, I start to understand why this Armand dude might have painted it the way he did. Maybe he's tired of always doing what the man wants him to do, tired of being called stupid, tired of being an effect instead of a cause. He wants to break free, cause a ruckus, like that butterfly in China. Tell people that butterfly don't have to be in China—it could be anywhere, could be right here in Philadelphia. Or maybe, I'm thinking, he's trying to paint something that can't be painted at all. He's trying to understand something much bigger than himself and this is all he could see of it.

After a long night on the die press I feel like I'm just part of the machine. When I stop and close my eyes that machine keeps running inside my head. By the time Charlie comes in at eight I'm delirious from lack of sleep because it's always a hundred degrees in my house on account of Aunt Lorraine's sick bird. So when we collect the puzzle bins to be boxed and labeled by the Vietnamese ladies at Sixth and Tasker, I get a sudden urge. It just comes over me, I don't know why. I guess I just don't want to be part of the machine anymore.

I take a handful of puzzle pieces from one bin and drop them in another bin, and then a handful from that bin and drop them in another bin—they're mostly from the same masterpiece, Chaos Scape 19, by Armand Brigantine, but I mix a few others in too—and so on down the line, till they're all jumbled together, one big puzzle spread through a hundred bins, soon to be in a hundred boxes. If it's a masterpiece, it's my masterpiece now and nobody else's.

Charlie sees what I'm doing and tries to stop me. "Why in hell are you doing that, Spencer?"

"Do I got to have a reason?"

He looks at me like he might be sick, his eyes darting over his shoulder in case Mr. Pangborn or Audrey is watching. "Sure you've got to have a reason," he says. "You wouldn't do something like that—"

"You think that butterfly in China's got to have a reason before he flaps his wings? No, sir, he just flaps them, and that's it!"

I wish I'd listened to Charlie and tried to unscramble those puzzles before we sent them out. It never occurred to me that anybody'd have a heart attack or go bankrupt or lose their house or go crazy just because of what I did, and even if I'd seen that coming I probably wouldn't have considered it my problem, any more than that Chinese butterfly, flapping its wings some summer morning in Shanghai, could imagine a hurricane blowing down houses on the other side of the world.

The first sign of trouble comes about six weeks later. The licensing company agreed to back off but put us on probation. "No more screw ups," Jeff warns me and Charlie one morning, as if it's us instead of his nephew Stupid Butchie who robbed the place. "Or it's all over."

I nod and keep my mouth shut and so does Charlie, though we both know a Class 5 hurricane is on its way. We keep our fingers crossed but sure enough the puzzles start coming back. First by ones and twos, then cartons full, then whole shipments of Chaos Scape 19 are being dumped on the loading dock. Audrey calls Macy's and they tell her they sent the puzzles back on account of customer complaints. They don't want any more of our masterpieces.

We can hear Jeff yelling at Audrey over the phone. "What the hell are they complaining about?"

"Nobody can put the puzzles together."

When Audrey's not looking, Charlie and I have to laugh. "Naturally they can't put them together," I tell Charlie. "You can't put any of them together if you don't have all of them."

That makes Charlie stop laughing. "Jeff's gonna fire our ass and sell everything to the Chinese. And you know what? I could care less. I wasted enough of my life in this place."

He picks up one of the puzzle boxes and shakes it. "This is all I accomplished in life. A million jumbled up pieces of crap like this one."

Two weeks later Jeff calls us together outside Audrey's bookkeeper booth and tells us the licensing company pulled the plug. The business's been sold to the Chinese, who made their own deal with the licensing company. We've got three days to finish what we're doing and hand the whole lot, equipment and inventory and all, over to the Chinese. We work like dogs and before you know it that last night arrives.

It's three A.M. and we're all there, me and Charlie and Audrey and Mr. Pangborn and the retarded cats. The cats know something's wrong, they're all racing around and howling like it's the end of the world. Mr. Pangborn don't look much better. Charlie and Audrey feel a little sentimental about shutting down. Audrey's got a big bottle of vodka and a couple six packs and we pull up some folding chairs and take turns drinking shots and washing them down with beer, the cats crawling all over our laps and jumping away when we try to push them off. Charlie wiggles his left hand like a puppet and tells dirty jokes in a squeaky voice that's supposed to be the Mona Lisa, and he and Audrey sing a few old rock and roll songs but they end up laughing too much to sing. Then Audrey starts to cry, thinking about the old times when she started working there and they had about ten people on a shift. "I can find another job," she tells Charlie, "but it's never gonna be the same." She says that over and over again until Charlie wraps his fat white arms around her and almost falls off his folding chair trying to comfort her. Then he joins in with the crying. "I don't know what I'm gonna do," he tells Audrey, sobbing and wailing like it's his mother's funeral. "I don't know how I'm gonna feed my kids." He pulls out a picture from his wallet and shows us. He has four kids and from the picture I can see why he's worried about feeding them. The smallest one weighs about three hundred pounds.

Mr. Pangborn don't laugh or cry or take a drink. He just sits on his folding chair staring at Audrey and Charlie and me like he never seen us before. Audrey tries to include him in the conversation. "How's Mrs. Pangborn doing in the nursing home?" she asks him. He shakes his head like he don't understand the question.

"Mr. Pangborn's afraid his son's going to stick him in the nursing home with his wife," Audrey tells me.

"Why would he do that?" I ask.

"To get rid of him."

"Jeff is evil," Charlie explains.

"He has no redeeming social value," Audrey says.

Mr. Pangborn looks at me like he's hoping I disagree. "Everybody's got a little spark in him," I tell him. "No matter who he is. Even if he's a killer on death row."

"You don't know Jeff," Audrey tells me.

Mr. Pangborn stares back like he's thanking me for saying something good about his son. Then he stands up and reaches in his pocket and pulls out three brand new $100 bills and hands them to us. "I want you to have these," he tells us. "Whatever you do, don't tell Jeff." Then he steps in his office and shuts the door behind him. Mr. Pangborn's a good man.

Audrey and Charlie stop crying when they see the $100 bills and Audrey celebrates by pouring some more shots. The money makes me happy too—there's some new shoes I've been wanting to buy. Audrey holds up her shot glass like a toast and catches my eye. "For old time's sake," she tells me, peeking across the rim of her glass. "We'll probably never see each other again." She gives me a little wink and points with her eyes toward her bookkeeper booth, where the lighting looks softer than usual.

When Charlie heads for the bathroom, Audrey tugs me into her booth and pulls down the shades, then throws herself on me, digging her long fingernails into my back like fish hooks.

"You go for younger guys?" I ask her, trying to pull away.

"A little younger," she giggles. "I'm not exactly old."

Not exactly, I'm thinking. Just sort of a ballpark estimate.

"I prefer to call it experience," she says.

She glides closer and I stumble against her desk, knocking her knickknacks and pictures on the floor. She pushes me farther until I'm backed against the wall.

"Well, if you go for younger guys." I tell her, "you came to the right place. I'm so young, this here is my first pair of long pants."

She wraps her arms around my neck and pulls me closer.

"I've still got my baby teeth."

She stands on her toes and kisses me on the mouth.

"Hey, want to see my collection of Star Wars figures?"

I'm thinking about how to escape when I see Charlie peeking in one of the windows where the shade don't go all the way down, grinning like a dog. I jump away from Audrey and catch up to him and pin him face down over the die press with the conveyor running. He's about six inches away from becoming a masterpiece of western art and he knows it. "How'd you like to have your ass chopped up in 1000 pieces and stuck in a box so some 12 year old girl can spend her summer vacation trying to put it back together?"

"Easy now"—he sounds worried—"just let me go."

"Because if that's what you want, just tell me and I can take care of that for you."

"Spencer, please! You feed me to that machine, who's gonna feed my kids?" And he starts crying again. This time it's serious, it goes on for about ten minutes after I turn off the die press. I have to hug Charlie like he hugged Audrey to calm him down, only Charlie's not like Audrey, he's like a big slippery side of beef you can hardly get your arms around to reach the other side.

"Here, Charlie," I tell him when he stops crying. "Take this $100 bill Mr. Pangborn gave me—"

"No, I couldn't do that."

"It's just a loan. So you can feed the kids until you find another job. Then you can pay me back."

"What you gonna do?"

"Keep on living with Aunt Lorraine. She don't charge me nothing."

"OK." He snatches the bill out of my hand. "I'll pay you back."

"You're damn right you'll pay me back," I tell him, "or your ass's gonna be the fattest, ugliest masterpiece that ever hung on a wall."

We both laugh and Audrey laughs too. She's out of the booth now and still a little hot in the face but trying to show me and Charlie that nothing happened between us, just some fun like a game of hoops because she knows she'll never see me again. Only I can tell she's disappointed we stopped when we did. She says maybe we ought to get together again sometime, just the two of us, for old time's sake. I'm too young for old time's sake, I want to tell her. But I just smile and let her talk. I know I'll never see her again.

It's eight o'clock and we're expecting Jeff and the Chinese in an hour. Audrey drives out in the van to pick up the last of the finished boxes from the Vietnamese, which, I can't help noticing, happen to be Chaos Scape 19 by Armand Brigantine. When she brings them back she takes her calculator into Mr. Pangborn's office and shuts the door.

Mr. Pangborn comes out of his office with Audrey, his face looking green and heavy. He takes one of the boxes off the pallet and hands it to Audrey. "Here," he tells her. "I want you to have this." Then he hands one to me and Charlie. "And you too, fellas. Take one of these for yourself."

"Why?"

"For good luck."

Then he sort of gags and his eyeballs roll up in his head and he topples over clutching his chest. I throw myself down and pound his chest and breathe in his mouth like they do on TV but it don't do any good. I move his arms around but they feel limp as a couple of ropes. I beat his chest and blow every breath of air I have inside me into Mr. Pangborn until I don't have any left for myself. And then I see that look, that look I'll never forget—suddenly Mr. Pangborn opens his eyes and smiles like he caught a glimpse of something far, far away and I realize he's dead, but that look stays on his face. I fall over and curl up on top of him gasping and shaking like a baby.

Audrey kneels down and lays her hand on my head and the other one on my shoulder, crying until the ambulance arrives. Charlie brings the EMTs through the front door at the same time as Jeff and the Chinese pull up at the loading dock in back.

"What's going on?" Jeff stomps in. "The Chinese are here to pick this stuff up. Where's my father?"

"Mr. Pangborn's dead," I tell him.

"Now? He had to die right now?"

"Your father saw his world coming apart," Charlie tells Jeff.

Jeff's face looks red as a cherry bomb about to explode. "You're fired! All of you! Get the hell out of here!"

For two months I take it easy, collecting unemployment and sweltering in front of the TV with Shawn. Then Charlie calls and keeps me on the phone a long time. "I still can't find a job," he says. "Nobody wants to hire a guy who spent fifteen years in a puzzle factory. It's like being an ex-con. How about you? What're you doing?"

"Moving on to bigger things," I tell him, on purpose a little vague. I'm thinking of going back to school for my GED but I don't want to tell Charlie that.

"Like what?"

"Better things, anyway."

"What're you talking about?"

He keeps asking and I keep stalling him off. Aunt Lorraine asks me the same question about ten times a day and I don't answer. I'm keeping my little spark to myself until I decide what to do with it.

"I still owe you that hundred dollars," Charlie says, like I need reminding. "But you know," he says, "I gotta feed the kids."

I think back on that picture he showed me of his kids grinning like a row of pumpkins in their Eagles jerseys, bulked up to about the same weight as the offensive line and probably just as dangerous if you don't feed them. I feel sad when I picture those kids going hungry, but the situation's not hopeless—maybe I can help set it right. "You can pay me back when you find a job," I tell Charlie, "or when the kids stop eating. Whichever comes first."

"Thanks, Spencer. I'll never forget this. Hey, you heard about all the lawsuits being filed against Artistic Puzzles?"

"I thought they went bankrupt."

"They did, but there's still lawsuits. Audrey told me about it."

"What're they suing about?"

"Chaos Scape 19. Audrey says there's people going berserk all over the world from trying to put that puzzle together."

"You believe that?" I ask him. "That's just some lawyer telling a story so he can make a million dollars suing somebody."

"You don't think it has anything to do with... you know, the puzzles being scrambled up?"

"No way, man. Something bad happens, they just find somebody to sue. And you know what, Charlie? As long as that somebody is Jeff Pangborn, they've got my vote."

Charlie laughs, but he's still worried. "What if you're wrong?"

"Don't blame me," I tell him. "I'm only the butterfly."

2. Jeff Pangborn

Jeff Pangborn sat in his Renaissance Florentine bedroom goggling at the computer screen. Shaved and showered but still a little wasted from Monday Night Football, he was able, with a few clicks, to learn the depressing news about his bank balance (negative), his investments (in the toilet), and his day's schedule (potentially annoying 3:00 o'clock meeting with an insurance investigator named Erik Anselmus). Kellie—his young, hot, but increasingly mercenary live-in—had gone downstairs to get the kids off to school, leaving him a few precious minutes to himself. He sent a playful text message to Alex, the drop-dead gorgeous (judging from her picture; admittedly he'd never met her) 25-year-old exotic dancer he'd been flirting with on his phone, and powered off to keep Kellie from seeing it. Standing in front of the mirror, he adjusted his suit and tightened his tie, then slipped downstairs in hopes that he could escape from the house without being bitten by the dog or cursed by his kids. He avoided the breakfast table, which meant avoiding the kids: 14-year-old Lindsay, who had an eating disorder and talked incessantly about how nauseated she was by everyone else's food, and 16-year-old Zachary, who would chomp through five bowls of cereal in one gulp as scenes of mayhem and carnage played across the screen in front of him. (Just a healthy teenage boy with a tendency toward psychopathic nihilism, the guidance counselor had assured hm.) Jeff's life had been a parade of horribles since the demise of Artistic Puzzles three months before: foreclosure, divorce, claims for alimony, child support and so-called equitable division of property (which meant he would be lucky to keep forty percent of everything he'd saved in a lifetime of hard work), and now these far-fetched lawsuits coming in from all over the world, bringing lawyers and investigators in their wake. How had he been so quickly overtaken by disaster? For years he'd made every sacrifice to keep the family together, and look at him now—angry, broke, depressed, scorned by his wife, his kids, his sister, even the dog. His wife Roberta: a kleptomaniac on her best days, in rehab and spoiling for a messy divorce. His son Zachary: withdrawn, hostile, cynical beyond his years. His daughter Lindsay: moody, resentful, almost bipolar. Cupcake (the dog): a spoiled throwback who had to be kept in a cage like Hannibal Lecter. Two hundred thousand dollars of home equity squandered on dude ranches in Wyoming, wine tours of Italy, shopping sprees in London and Paris, and when all else failed, on Roberta's therapists, Roberta's defense attorneys and now Roberta's divorce lawyer, the slithering Morton C. McMonigle, Jr., Esq. Losing his biggest customer, payments falling behind on the Mercedes and the Land Cruiser, foreclosure looming on the house, forking over his last dime to that Quaker Oats academy the kids hated with their only passion. Dad—betrayed by his coke-snorting nephew, the aptly named Stupid Butchie—filing for bankruptcy at the age of 89 and having to close the puzzle factory and sell out to the Chinese, then dying of a heart attack, face up on the factory floor, lips blue, eyes wide, surrounded by his last three incompetent, thieving employees, the very day the Chinese came to haul out the equipment and ship it to China (still warm when Jeff found him, as warm as he'd ever been, smiling up at Jeff, as if he'd made a point of dying just before he arrived). Mom simmering in a vegetative state in that nursing home in New Jersey, devouring his inheritance through a feeding tube at the rate of five hundred dollars a day, ill-tempered and spiteful to the end, yet—through some neurological or bureaucratic glitch—viewed by the nursing staff and even the chaplain as the next Mother Teresa. His sister Jane, off in Sedona, meditating by day over an energy vortex and by night over a prickly pear margarita, never, after either experience, displaying the slightest inclination to come to the aid of their dying parents. The only good news in Jeff's life was that things couldn't get any worse.

Arriving in the kitchen with a cheerful hello, he earned a snarl from Cupcake, a nauseated grunt from Lindsay and sociopathic silence from Zachary. From Kellie he received a chaste, not-in-front-of-the-kids peck on the cheek. (Officially she was still sleeping in the guest room.) Kellie did a good job with the kids, helping them with their homework, chauffeuring them to their activities, offering the love and affection their mother had never been capable of. But lately she'd shown signs of catching Roberta's kleptomania, with Jeff rather than Nordstrom's or Bloomingdale's as the victim. It was the same disease—a compulsion to acquire fabulously expensive designer clothes without paying for them—but Kellie's version involved the use of Jeff's American Express card. And when she wasn't spending money he didn't have (he still hadn't told her about the foreclosure and the near certainty that by Christmas they'd be sleeping in the Greyhound bus terminal)—she'd been making alarming noises about Commitment, with a capital "C," even marriage when the divorce from Roberta became final. Poor Kellie didn't seem to realize she was only a temp. She was a woman with a past as long as a stretch limousine—barmaid, masseuse, and God knows what else Roberta's attorney would bring to light in the custody battle that lay ahead.

Lindsay sat at the table, dressed for school or a Victoria's Secret modeling session (he couldn't tell which), her face green from food-induced nausea, tears streaming down into her granola as if Cupcake, fortunately secured in his crate, had been gnawing on her ankle. Jeff would have liked to sound sympathetic, wise and loving, like a TV Dad, but it never came out that way. "What's the matter with her?" he asked Zachary.

"She doesn't have any friends."

"Neither do you."

"Yeah, but I don't want any."

Zachary, with his black T-shirts, his piercings and plugs, his music that sounded like the machinery of Hell, was clearly from another planet, and probably fated to return there if Jeff didn't intervene. But no, Kellie had told him the night before, Lindsay was the one he should worry about. She was so moody, so volatile, she so desperately wanted to live down the humiliation of what her mother had done to her.

"Moody? Volatile?" Jeff had laughed. "Isn't she just a typical teenage girl?"

"A teenage girl is hopelessly unpredictable," Kellie said. "Take it from me. Lindsay could do anything."

"What do you mean, *anything?*"

"You know what I'm talking about."

That morning, as he shaved, Jeff had given some thought to Kellie's advice. What was he going to do about his daughter? Some possibilities had been suggested by Ms. Stebbins, the guidance counselor, who believed Lindsay needed more physical activity and—if she wanted to attend even a mediocre college— some opportunities to show leadership. When he walked into the kitchen and found her crying over her unmunched granola, he realized that the time had come for a bold initiative. "I'm going to talk to the rowing coach about getting you on the crew team," he told her.

"I'll kill myself," she said, between sobs.

3. My Dad, by Lindsay Pangborn

I was so grossed out when I found out my Dad was a
pervert!

When my Mom went into the rehab program and Dad's
girlfriend Kellie moved into our house, I was basically OK with
that. My Mom's crazy, I mean really crazy, like she takes all sorts
of pills and steals stuff and needs to be locked up sometimes.
Kellie seems a lot nicer than my Mom and she's way younger
and cooler. She used to be a waitress at a bar downtown when
my Dad met her. She was also a dancer and a masseuse, which
is somebody who gives massages. Now she's going to school to
learn to be a massage therapist. My Mom hates her even though
she's never met her. She won't even say her name. "How's the
whore doing?" my Mom asks me when I visit her in the rehab
center. "Don't worry," I told her one day. "Dad's not going to
marry her, even if you get divorced. He told me that. 'No way
I'm going to marry that whore,' he said. 'Not in a million years.'"
Actually my Dad never said that. I just told it to my Mom to
make her feel better.

Every morning Kellie drops me and my brother Zachary off
at school after we take Cupcake to Wagsmore Manor. I have to
go along because I'm the only one in the family he won't bite.
Cupcake, I mean, not Zachary, though Zachary should be kept
in a cage too. He dresses Goth and says he's a nihilist. He has a
picture of Dylan Klebold over his bed. He stays in his room for
hours with the door locked and when he comes out there's a
funny smell on his clothes. We go to a Quaker school and

Zachary hates it. He says the Quakers died out because they never had sex and now they're trying to recruit normal people as breeders. "I feel like a freak going there," he tells my Dad.

"You should feel like a freak," Dad says. "You are a freak."

"What do the Quakers have to offer? Oats? Granola bars?"

"Peace," Dad says. "What do you have against peace?"

It makes me sick to my stomach just hearing about Quaker oats and granola bars. The whole idea of food makes me sick to my stomach. "Stop it!" I tell them. "Stop talking about food! Or does that make me a freak too?"

"You have an eating disorder," Dad says calmly.

"Eating is a disorder."

"You need more physical activity."

Every day Dad makes Kellie pack my lunch and every day I throw it in the garbage outside the cafeteria. All the girls have so-called eating disorders so I don't know what the big deal is. It's not like we're starving or something. After school or between classes I'll meet one of the other girls in the stairwell or in one of the stalls in the girls room and maybe she has some Tastykakes she'll share with me, we just shove them down, two or three at a time. Sometimes I'll be sick half an hour later and have to throw up. But I'm not exactly wasting away, am I? So what's the big deal?

"I spoke to the rowing coach and he's adding you to the crew team."

Getting sent to the galleys is what Zachary calls it, like in the Middle Ages, he says, when rowing on one of those boats was your punishment for stealing a loaf of bread or chopping somebody's hand off in a sword fight. But at least it was for something serious, not just for throwing your lunch in the garbage. Ms. Stebbins, my guidance counselor, says being on the crew team will help me get into a good college. Having top grades isn't enough, she says, you've got to swim or play field hockey or lacrosse or basketball or row on the crew team to get into the really competitive schools, unless you're Asian and then you can learn to play the violin. Zachary says the crew team is just a way to get money from alumni, who like the idea of students being treated like slaves for their amusement, like the gladiators in the Roman Empire.

So now every afternoon I have to sit sliding back and forth in this fake boat for two hours building up my back muscles and my legs so I can get into a good college unless I decide to be a dancer or a massage therapist like Kellie. I take the late bus with Zachary, who's on the boys lacrosse team, but we still get home long before Kellie or my Dad. Even so, in October it's practically dark when we get home. Zachary locks himself in his room and does whatever he does in there and I usually sit on my bed texting my friends, or at least I would if I had any friends. Most of the girls at school won't even talk to me, which actually suits me fine since they're a bunch of snobs anyway.

Sometimes I get bored, and that's what got me into trouble. One Saturday afternoon when my Dad was out cleaning the pool, I was messing around with his phone and I decided to take a peek at his text messages. Of course I didn't know the password, but I took a wild guess and typed in "Lindsay" and sure enough the screen opened up like a magic door in a fairy tale. I could see all his messages, which were typed out in sentences, if you can believe that, with no abbreviations or hashtags, so you could hardly read them. I found a long string of messages between Dad and a girl named Alex that he met on Craigslist. She said she was an exotic dancer, I guess that means she's from Turkey or someplace like that, though in her picture she looked totally American, blonde with blue eyes and a great figure, and the funny thing was that Dad called himself Steve, though his name is really Jeff. That made me go back and read through all the messages from the beginning and I wished I hadn't done that. I mean, Dad and Alex didn't really do anything, they were just sending messages back and forth, flirting and saying how crazy they were about each other, but the temperature kept rising until finally Alex came right out and said she wanted to have sex with him and she described exactly what she wanted to do to him, which almost made me throw up. And he agreed and asked her when they could get together.

Then, before I could read any farther, I heard a little beep and a new message from Alex hit the phone:

> *Steve, there's something I need to tell you. I'm a little younger than I said I was, though everyone says I'm very mature for my age. I was afraid you'd stop messaging, so I exaggerated just a tiny bit. Hope you won't hold it against me! Love forever, Alex.*

A little younger? In her picture she looks about 25, and my Dad is 45, so what's the big deal, even if she was 22 or 23? But what if she was 18 or 19—what would people say about that, especially Mom and her sleazy divorce lawyer? I felt all tingly and excited, like when I went with Mom on one of her shoplifting expeditions to King of Prussia. I hit the button and typed out a message the way I thought my Dad would write it:

> *Dear Alex, I understand and forgive you, of course. You don't need to be afraid, it doesn't bother me if you're younger than you said you were. All that matters is that we love each other. Love, Steve.*

A minute later there was another beep and another message:

Steve, I'm so relieved! You've known this all along, haven't you? That's why you said you felt like a kid again! But I'm still afraid to tell you my exact age.

My heart was racing but I texted back to reassure her:

Alex, love, stop worrying. I'll never stop loving you, no matter how old you are. I promise.

It seemed like a long time before she replied, though it was probably only a minute or two:

OK, I trust your love. I look 21, though actually I'll be 15 in March. But all that matters is that we love each other, right?

Oh my God! She's only 14! My age! I felt the way a crazy person must feel—dizzy, queasy, sick to my stomach. Dad's messing around with a 14-year-old and she says he's known it all along! They're going to put him in jail! Without thinking, I deleted all the messages between Dad and Alex—well, I forwarded them to my phone first, then I erased and deleted them from his phone, along with the message where I forwarded them, and then I ran into my room and sat on my bed and cried as I read them again. I must have read them about twenty times before I stopped crying. Some of the stuff Dad said to Alex, stuff he told her he wanted to do to her, I didn't even know was possible with the human body. It made me feel really creepy to realize this was my Dad talking to a girl my own age.

I had to do something. If I just kept quiet, he'd send her more messages, she'd answer them, and who knows where it might end up. So I set up a new account on my phone under the name "Steve" and texted back to Alex from that address. I couldn't just text the way I'd do to one of my friends, if I had any friends, even though she was my age. I had to keep writing like my Dad wrote, in old fashioned English sentences with punctuation and spelling and grammar and everything, without "u" for "you" or "2" for "to" or anything like that:

Alex, my dear –

Yes, our love is all that matters, but please listen closely: For reasons I'll explain later, I had to stop using my old phone. I've set up this new account on a different phone. From now on we have to use ONLY the new phone number. DO NOT send any messages to the old number, and if you get any messages from there, don't answer them!

What the two of us have is very special, as pure and beautiful as the first blush of Spring, and I'm not going to let anyone spoil it just because they can't see beyond their own petty, narrow-minded prejudices!

Love always,

Steve

I was proud of that last sentence—I mean before the 'Love always, Steve' part—and I thought Mr. Siegal, my English teacher, would approve.   Mr. Siegal encourages style and eloquence in writing, and I guess I was trying to add a little style and eloquence to a nauseating situation. Literature can do that, Mr. Siegal says. Literature can transform the revolting and banal (I'd better look that word up) into something extraordinary and beautiful, just through the power of language. That's what I tried to accomplish in my next few messages to Alex. I kept the dialogue on a high level and tried to appeal to her nobler qualities. Deep down, I think I was hoping that if I wrote in a better style, more like what you'd find in a book, I could turn my Dad back into a hero, which he always used to be, and make his relationship with Alex something pure and beautiful instead of corrupt and ugly, which is what it really was.   Not to blame Mr.

Siegal, but I wouldn't have even tried that last year when I had
Mr. Murphy for Standard English and all we read were little
articles from *People* magazine about athletes and celebrities. Mr.
Murphy never said the kinds of things Mr. Siegal says about the
power of language and literature, but now I'm in Mr. Siegal's A-
Level College Prep, which Ms. Stebbins said I had to take if I
want to get into a good college. We're reading *A Midsummer
Night's Dream* by Shakespeare and it's about some mechanics
who get lost in the woods and turn into animals. Later in the
semester we're going to read *Romeo and Juliet*, which is also by
Shakespeare. Mr. Siegal encourages us to write journal entries
every day (that's what this is, my first journal entry). He said we
could write about one of the Shakespeare plays if we wanted to,
or we could write about our own lives, friends and families—
that's what I decided to write about, starting with my Dad—and
then at the end of the semester we're going to collect all our
writings into something called a chapbook, which we have to
hand in for a grade. I guess that's one reason why I tried to
write my messages to Alex with style and eloquence, which
might have been a mistake. Anyway I was afraid that if I didn't
write back to Alex she'd start using the old phone number again
and Dad would find out that someone was messing around with
his phone. I felt sort of trapped.

Alex must not have been in A-Level College Prep because
she totally missed the idea I was trying to get across. Her
messages got dirtier and dirtier, to the point where I'd get all
sweaty and out of breath just thinking about them. I couldn't
help myself. I'd hurry home from crew practice and hide in my
room with my phone and read them over and over again. This
must be how Zachary feels, I thought, being a porn addict. I
was incredibly impressed that a girl my age even knew any of this
stuff. She teased and tempted poor Steve mercilessly, waiting

for him to make the first move.   It was exciting until I remembered that it was my Dad she was writing to. That made me sick to my stomach, even sicker than I usually am. I couldn't sleep, I couldn't eat—not even Tastykakes in the girls room— and finally I decided the whole thing had to stop. One day after school I slipped into my room and wrote what I thought would be my last message:

> *Alex, I've also got a confession to make. I'm not really the sexy and understanding man you think I am. My name isn't Steve and I'm not a man at all. I'm a 14 year old girl named Lindsay. I know this must be hard for you. I don't want to hurt your feelings but our relationship has to end.*

Before I sent it, I felt a pang of conscience. What was I doing to this poor girl? Just breaking up like that in a text message? Maybe she was miserable like me and with this message I'd be pushing her over the edge. What if it made her want to slash her wrists or jump in front of a train? I had to soften the blow, show her she still had a friend if she needed one, so I added another line at the end:

> *P.S. If you want to talk about it, just text back. We can still be friends. Love, Lindsay.*

I think that last part might have been a mistake.

4. A Schmuck With a Fountain Pen

After a bracing lunch at Hooters, Jeff Pangborn fired up the Mercedes and headed back to the suburban office park where his company, Win/Win Solutions, occupied a top-floor suite. Checking his iPhone, he discovered an unpleasant reminder: At 3:00 o'clock he was scheduled to meet with an insurance investigator named Erik Anselmus about the ludicrous lawsuits which had sprung up around the ruins of the puzzle factory. The precise nature of these lawsuits remained obscure. The plaintiffs couldn't sue his father, who was dead; they couldn't sue Artistic Puzzles, which had been liquidated; and so they were suing Third Millennium Bank, which had foolishly loaned three million dollars to Artistic Puzzles, secured by a lien on all its assets and—even more foolishly—by the personal guarantee of Jeff Pangborn. When the assets were sold, all the money went to the bank; Jeff was happy to see the bank paid off so his guarantee wouldn't be called. But now, according to his lawyer, if Third Millennium had to pay any money to the plaintiffs, it would come back against him on his guarantee. Thank God the puzzle factory had been fully insured! Still, something told him that no good could come of this meeting with the insurance investigator, whose mission was undoubtedly to find a way to avoid covering the claims. But then again, something, or someone—in fact it was his father, the old fool, who'd let the hired help destroy the business—had told him it would be a good idea to guarantee the bank debt. Too late, he'd learned the definition of guarantor: A schmuck with a fountain pen.

5. Sweating It Out

Spencer Casey

Aunt Lorraine's got a parrot named Dewey who's been hers since she was a little girl and that bird probably means more to her than her own son Shawn and definitely more than me. Last year Dewey caught beak and feather disease, which is about the worst thing that can happen to a bird. His beak shriveled up and his feathers started falling out and now he's skinny and cold as a chicken neck, with slimy blue skin and no feathers at all except a droopy little clump on top of his head. He huddles in his cage shivering and whimpering and he would've died in July if Aunt Lorraine didn't turn off the AC and move an electric heater next to his cage. Now it's October and we've got the thermostat set at 100 and the heater going full blast and we even boil pots of water on the stove to keep that bird from freezing to death. It's not so bad for Aunt Lorraine who goes to work during the day but for me and Shawn it's like living in a Navajo sweat lodge. You've got to spend all day in your boxer shorts and the whole night sweating like a pig. In the morning you wake up soaking wet and twenty pounds lighter.

Most days Shawn pretends to go to school but comes home as soon as Aunt Lorraine leaves the house and sits on the couch watching TV or playing video games for the rest of the day. On weekends he spends his time flirting with that skinny girl from church named Rochelle who works at McDonalds. He can't decide whether he wants to be a minister or a hip hop artist.

Aunt Lorraine don't like hip hop music one bit. She's the church secretary and her father was a deacon and an English teacher and she reminds us about ten times a day that in her house *certain standards must be maintained.* That's how she puts it, *certain standards must be maintained.* She don't allow cursing or smoking or bad English inside the house or out of it if she catches us. When she catches Shawn listening to hip hop on his ear buds she says it's making him stupid. You don't need hip hop or ear buds to go stupid in this hothouse, I'd like to tell her (though I don't). Just look at Dewey, who used to talk all the time. All he does now is shiver in his cage—his teeth would be chattering if he had any. And Shawn's not much different, sprawling on the couch in his boxer shorts, fanning himself a mile a minute with the Daily News to keep from melting down.

One night we're watching TV while Aunt Lorraine works on a crossword puzzle in her two-piece bathing suit. "What's a five-letter word for stupid?" she calls out.

"Spencer ought to know this one," Shawn says.

"Thick," I tell her. "Dense. Dopey. Dumb."

"Dumb," Dewey croaks in his quacky voice. "Dumb."

Shawn and me, we laugh out loud. Dewey don't talk as much as he used to, but sometimes he can't resist jumping into the conversation.

"'Dumb' is four letters," Shawn points out.

"How'd you expect Dewey to know that?" I hit back. "You think he can count?"

"OK, Spencer," Aunt Lorraine says. "Try this: The eighth avatar of Vishnu. Seven letters."

"Krishna." I don't know why I knew that. Probably something I read on a cereal box.

"Have you been memorizing my crossword puzzle dictionary?"

"He's studying to be an idiot savant," Shawn says.

Aunt Lorraine slides her glasses down her nose and stares at me across the top. "You've got a good head on your shoulders, Spencer. Why aren't you using it for something? I saw Monique when I was getting my hair done at Brenda's. That girl's going places. She can help you get with the program."

"Maybe I don't want to get with the program." I grab the remote off the coffee table and click it at the TV. "Maybe I want to change the channel."

When I'm not sweating my brains out with Shawn in the living room, I'm shivering with a smoke out on the front porch, thinking about Monique. Monique's a smart, sassy chick who thinks she's headed for great things and maybe she is. She's finished two years of college and works in her mother's hair styling salon part time so she can stay in school and someday be able to start her own business. Her mother Brenda is an important person in the neighborhood. She's President of the Philadelphia Beauticians and Cosmetologists Association and owns Brenda's Hair Styling Salon where Aunt Lorraine's been going every Saturday since before I was born. It was on the bulletin board in that hair styling salon where Aunt Lorraine saw the job posting for the puzzle factory. I always wondered why that job was listed on that particular bulletin board in this neighborhood, but Aunt Lorraine didn't stop to ask. She wrote down the phone number and brought it home and told me to call it, which I did, hoping my life would be a little more connected to Monique's if I got a job from the bulletin board in her mother's hair styling salon.

Not that I'd ever say any of this to Monique. She don't like it when I point out the ways our lives are connected, like living on the same block since we were born and Aunt Lorraine going to Brenda's Hair Styling Salon all these years and both of us singing in the same choir back when I used to go to church. All this has the ring of fate to me but to her it must seem more like a curse.

"Spencer, what're you going to do with your life?" she asked me once.

"I've got a future," I told her. "I just don't know what it is."

That made her laugh. "If you don't know what it is, then you don't have one."

We were supposed to go downtown but she wouldn't even get on the bus. All we did was walk around the block a few times and sit on the stoop in front of her house. "You need to expand your horizons," she tells me. "Get out of this neighborhood and see the world."

"How am I ever going to get out of this neighborhood," I ask her, "if you won't even get on the bus with me?"

"Don't you get it, Spencer? You're never going to get out of here unless you turn your life around."

"I'm going back for my GED."

"Did you even start yet?"

The answer was no but I didn't want to admit it. "How about you?"

"When I finish college I'm going straight to graduate school to get my MBA." She smiled but there was something hard in her look. "You won't be seeing much of me after that."

There's a lot more to Monique than meets the eye. Aunt Lorraine says she's got a secret boyfriend even Brenda don't know about, who drives a black BMW with tinted windows and racing tires. That's what the other hair stylists told Aunt Lorraine one Saturday when Brenda was taking the weekend off.

They didn't see the boyfriend but they saw his BMW glide up and Monique slip out of the house, which is right next to the shop, and climb inside in a dark gray suit and high heel shoes. It made me wonder, what kind of a boyfriend is that, who wants you to dress up like you work in a bank?

"Look," I tell Monique the next time I see her, "if you've got a boyfriend—"

"What makes you think I've got a boyfriend?" she asks me.

"Well, you were seen climbing into a certain black BMW with tinted windows that pulled up in front of your house."

She laughs like I'm some kind of fool. "Curtis isn't my boyfriend. That's strictly a business relationship."

"The two of you starting a bank together?"

"I can't tell you about it yet. It's a business deal, that's all I can say right now. It's going to be big."

I've read a little about these big business deals. "What is it? Some kind of internet bubble? Social networking?"

She glances around to make sure nobody's listening, then whispers: "Franchising."

"You starting a hamburger chain?"

"Don't be an idiot."

"OK," I tell her, trying to get back to where we started, "if you've got a boyfriend—"

That makes her mad. "I don't have a boyfriend," she says, "and I don't want one. Look at Lyla." Lyla's her little sister, who's got a baby daughter and a boyfriend who drops by once a week with a bag of groceries. "You think that's how I want my life to end up?"

Shawn gives me a lot of advice about women, even though I'm 20 and he's only 16. "First you need a sharp haircut," he tells me, propping himself up on the couch. His ear buds are squawking on his lap but at least he doesn't have them in his ears. "And some better clothes. Then all you've got to do is flash those eyes and give them that little smile."

"What little smile?"

"The smile that says it all. You know what I mean?"

I know what he means, even if he don't. "You don't know Monique," I tell him. "This is a girl who don't care about having a boyfriend."

"You believe that? What's she care about then?"

"Franchising."

"Like McDonalds and KFC? That kind of franchising?"

"What other kind is there?"

That stumps him for a while. "That's just her way of reminding you she's got to eat," he says. "You need to start flashing the cash."

"I'm broke since I lost my job."

He reaches for his ear buds and stuffs them in his ears like he hopes to find the answer on the radio. "OK, then, you've just got to start playing hard to get."

Hard to get? Is that what Shawn's playing when he lays around all day in his boxer shorts in front of the TV while his skinny girlfriend Rochelle dishes out french fries at McDonalds? And how's that going to work out with Monique? How can you play hard to get with a girl who's already told you how glad she'll be—soon as she gets rich—if she never sees you again?

6. A Messenger of Fate

Erik Anselmus worked for Assurance Suisse, of Geneva, Switzerland, one of the oldest and most successful insurance companies in the world. It was founded in 1627 on strict Calvinist principles, including, most significantly, a belief in predestination. In a universe created and sustained by an omniscient, omnipotent and benevolent God (as the Calvinists of the seventeenth century believed), everything that happens is subject to divine foreknowledge and control. There are no accidents. If man suffers evil, it can only be the result of his own depravity. For this reason the company, from its earliest days, had adhered to a strict policy of denying all claims.

Erik was of Scandinavian nationality and appearance—six feet four inches tall, pale almost to the point of invisibility—and his habits of mind recalled the austerity of the subarctic landscape. Trained as an actuary, his job was not to judge but to understand, to piece the facts together into a chain of causes and effects. Though not an adherent of Calvinism or any other religion, he believed in predestination, which he called destiny or fate. He did not believe in chance occurrences, any more than he believed in miracles. He conceived the universe as a vast machine of causes and effects, whose motions could be studied, mapped and predicted with scientific accuracy. Accordingly he supported his company's policy of denying all claims. His job as investigator was to document and explain the basis for that denial in each individual case.

He saw himself as a messenger of fate.

Jeff Pangborn sat sweating at his conference table after Erik Anselmus left the office. He daubed his forehead with a paper napkin and then wadded up the napkin and crammed it into his styrofoam coffee cup. His early morning optimism had been cruelly misplaced: things could have been a lot worse, and now they were. As if Third Millennium Bank and Morton C. McMonigle, Jr., Esq., weren't enough to keep him awake at night, he now had this hulking, steely-eyed, albino Viking zombie to haunt his dreams. The insurance investigator had informed him that Assurance Suisse did not believe in chance occurrences, and moreover did not insure against misfortunes that people brought on themselves.

"If your father or his company let something happen that could have been prevented," Erik Anselmus had explained, "or—I hesitate even to suggest this possibility—if someone who worked there deliberately sabotaged the puzzles, that would be malfeasance at the very least, which is a specific exclusion from the policy. Criminal charges might even be involved."

Fiddling with his yellow tie, Jeff wondered if he would ever run through his bad luck—or would it be infinite, like the number of habitable planets in the universe? He'd read an article about that recently. It said there's an infinite number of planets that are more or less identical to Earth, populated by beings more or less identical to ourselves. Why couldn't he be on one of the planets that's just a little better than this one? Why couldn't he be one of the almost-identical Jeff Pangborns whose life is just a little less screwed up than the one he had? He tried to maintain a positive outlook and stay cheerful in the face of adversity, but frankly, being stuck on this particular planet as this particular version of Jeff Pangborn, with his life going down the drain faster than a sinkful of dirty dish water, it was hard not to ask himself why he was bothering to fight on. He could think of only one bright spot at the moment, and ironically it involved Stupid Butchie, the depraved nephew (son of the Sedona vortex worshipper) whose thievery had all but destroyed the puzzle factory. Stupid Butchie had offered to make amends for his defalcations by cutting Jeff into his latest money-making scheme, a long-term investment in America's biggest industry that was sure to bring in millions. The deal was a little sketchy, not the sort of thing Jeff would've gone within a mile of in better days, and it required him to put even more money at risk (luckily he still had control of the kids' college funds) as a silent partner. But that was the beauty of it—it would be off the books and nobody would ever know he was involved. The plan had to be kept secret from Roberta and her scheming attorney McMonigle, and from Lindsay—he suspected her of spying for Roberta— and from Kellie or she'd blow his profits at Bloomingdales before they got the deal closed, and probably (not to be overly paranoid about it) even from Cupcake, who'd probably demand a personal chef and a live-in groomer. And with the arrival of Erik Anselmus there was another nemesis who had to be held at bay.

Jeff pulled out his fountain pen and jotted down a note to himself: "Call Audrey, Charlie and Spencer. Keep them away from this lunatic at all costs."

7. From the Journal of Erik Anselmus

October 24: Jeff Pangborn, son of owner. Untrustworthy. Claims no involvement in business. Bankruptcy records show two machine operators, Charles Quill and Spencer Casey, plus a bookkeeper, Audrey Scalzo. Good place to start.

8. Whistleblowers

Spencer Casey

Monique came over last Sunday night to watch the Eagles game. Before the kickoff she sits close beside me on the couch so she can tell me her troubles. She's working twenty-five hours a week in the hair styling salon while she goes to college, but it's not for the money because her Mom stopped paying her. Between the shop and being President of the Philadelphia Beauticians and Cosmetologists Association, Brenda's in over her head and the bank's making rumblings about foreclosure. Monique helps with the bookkeeping and her friend Curtis from business school, the one with the BMW who's supposed to be a financial wizard, is trying to find a solution. He's not her boyfriend, she says, she don't need a boyfriend. If you want to get anywhere in life, you've got to focus on strategic partnerships, not on personal relationships—they just inhibit your entrepreneurship when you should be developing your brand. That's the way she talks now, ever since she went to business school. I can hardly understand her, and it's a good thing Aunt Lorraine's not home. "In this house we speak English," Aunt Lorraine always says. "We don't curse or say 'ain't' or say 'I got' when we mean 'I have.'" If she heard Monique talking that business talk she might throw her out of the house.

But Monique's not done with me yet. "You see, Spencer," she says, "the world doesn't stand there waiting until you're ready to hop on it. You've got to reach out and take what's coming to you. You'll learn that if you ever grow up."

"Right," I tell her, wishing the game would hurry up and start.

"When is that going to be, by the way?"

Later, after she goes home, I'm wondering why she keeps asking me when I'm going to grow up. Isn't that like asking a tree if it's as high as it's going to be? You've got to be careful asking questions like that. Maybe you're talking to a mighty oak but you just don't know it yet.

I feel a lot better now that I started my new job. Nobody thought that would ever happen, especially Aunt Lorraine, who prayed for a miracle and predicted I'd find a job after Michael Jackson came back from the dead. It just goes to show, some miracles take longer than others. There were sightings of Michael Jackson almost every day, but for the longest time no sign of Spencer Casey finding a job. And then all of a sudden it just fell out of the sky.

Last Sunday morning Charlie calls and says we need to drive out to the suburbs and talk to Jeff Pangborn, which was the first time I thought about that jackass since he fired us from the puzzle factory. Jeff's not so bad, Charlie says, maybe he can help us find new jobs. So he picks me up in his van and we cruise out to where the rich people live, winding along on the hilly roads until we find Jeff Pangborn's mansion, set way back so you can hardly see it in the trees. Charlie parks in the driveway and Jeff runs out to greet us before we're out of the van, shaking hands and hugging us like he just found Jesus. He leads us around the house to a patio by a big swimming pool, where there's a table with refreshments already set up, and sits us down on some plastic lounge chairs. This would be like a resort in the summer, I'm thinking, but it's October, maybe 50 degrees, and I'm used to living in a sweat lodge. There's a little dog inside the house barking like he wants to bite us in half.

Jeff and Charlie trade some small talk about how beautiful Jeff's house is, but before I can say anything a girl in a halter top, mini-skirt and high leather boots parades in front of me and smiles in my face. "Hi," she says. "I'm Lindsay." She looks like a hooker but I figure out pretty quick she's Jeff's daughter. She looks about 15.

"Hi. I'm Spencer."

"Lindsay!" Jeff puts on a little show so Charlie and me won't get the wrong idea. "Where do you think you're going in that outfit?"

The girl rolls her eyes. "Duh! The mall?"

"You know what you look like in that outfit, don't you?"

She pokes her tongue in her cheek and sashays into the house, laughing all the way.

Jeff acts like he's in on the joke. "Kids! What can you do?"

There's more small talk and before long Jeff comes to the point. An insurance man named Erik Anselmus is prowling around investigating what went wrong at the puzzle factory, and for some reason Jeff is all worked up about it.

I'd like to listen but I need to use the bathroom, so I ask Jeff where I can find it and his head spins around with a sort of crazed look, like he's afraid to let me in the house or that's the whole reason he brought me out here—looking back I can't decide which it was—but anyway I stand up and follow his demented stare to the door his daughter went in.

I never been in a rich people's house before so I stop and take a good look around. White walls, white carpets, white furniture, even a white wood stove, and more junk than you could truck home from a flea market. Planters, vases, clocks, statues of dogs and cats, glass cases full of knick-knacks, figurines, Barbie dolls, and Eagles bobbleheads that looked just like Charlie's family. Pictures on the wall—the Mona Lisa, Botticelli's Venus, Van Gogh's Starry Night—that were glued together from Masterpieces of Western Art jigsaw puzzles and shellacked over, even a whole room dedicated to the Three Stooges. OK, I'm thinking, this is America. If this is what rich white folks want to do in the privacy of their homes, who's to say there's anything wrong with it? In some ways you've got to hand it to them. They've got flat screen TVs in every room and more bathrooms than a hotel, one about every ten feet, with floor to ceiling mirrors and a hot tub where the shower's supposed to be, all stocked with books and magazines for if you get bored with what you're doing in there. Must take them a long time to get that out of the way. When I step out I come smack up against a hot blonde in a white tennis dress and almost scare her out of her skin. She shrieks and runs away.

"Hey, it's OK!" I follow her through an open door into the kitchen, which is about the size of Aunt Lorraine's whole house. "I'm Spencer. I'm here to talk to Jeff."

She crouches behind a stone platform in the middle of the room that looks like a sacrificing block, waving a knife with about a ten inch blade. "Don't take another step!"

Behind me I hear a snarl and the little dog runs up and sinks his teeth into my pants leg. I couldn't take a step if I wanted to.

The teenage hooker I met in the driveway wiggles up next to the sacrificing block. "This is what I'd call an awkward moment," she says, rolling her eyes. "It's OK, Kellie," she tells the blonde. "This is Spencer. He's here to meet with my Dad."

"Spencer?" The blonde holds her knife in attack position. "Are you sure?"

"I'm sure. I saw him coming in with the fat guy who worked at Grampa's puzzle factory. They're back by the pool with my Dad. Right?"

"Right," I tell her.

"Cupcake! Let him go!"

The blonde lays her knife down on the sacrificing block. She runs her hand through her hair and laughs. "I'm sorry," she tells me. "You scared me."

"It's not just because you're black," the girl adds.

"No, of course not," Kellie says.

"I came in to use the bathroom," I explain, trying to smile.

"I'm not a racist," Kellie says.

"No, sure. I know that. I mean, why would I think that?"

Lindsay—that's the girl—pries Cupcake away from my pants leg and gives me directions back to the patio. But at the patio door she blocks my way and grabs my arm, pulling me toward her as she tosses her head back and gazes up at me through her fake eyelashes. She's cute, I'm thinking, but not that cute. Jail bait, no more than 15, plus she's Jeff's daughter, and even though she looks like a hooker I doubt if Jeff wants me to see her that way. But then again, maybe he does, maybe there's more to this puzzle factory business than meets the eye. Maybe he set her up to wait for me and grab me before I can get back out the door. All sorts of crazy ideas are running through my head, making me a little dizzy.

"What do you think of my Dad?" she asks me.

"Your Dad's all right," I tell her. "Going to help me and Charlie find a job."

"I mean, does he seem normal to you?"

"Normal?"

"You know, about sex. Did he ever say anything about, like, being interested in young girls?"

Now I'm really feeling dizzy. Or maybe queasy is the right word. "Young girls?"

"How well do you know my Dad?"

"Not too well, I guess."

I try to pull away but she just tightens her grip. "You can tell me what you know," she says. "I won't go to the police."

Before I can think of what to say, Kellie's standing beside me, prying Lindsay's hand off my arm.

"Lindsay," she says, "please get ready to go. I need to talk to Spencer."

"I am ready to go."

"Change into your jeans. You look like a hooker."

"You ought to know."

Lindsay stomps down the hall and now Kellie grabs my hand. "Spencer, I hope I didn't make you feel unwelcome."

"No problem," I tell her, pulling away. "It's like a family picnic."

"You surprised me, that's all."

"No problem." I'm half way out the door.

"Maybe you could surprise me in other ways."

"I've got to go."

Out by the pool I'm suddenly looking at Jeff Pangborn in a whole new light. What kind of joint is he running here? Is he a pervert like the daughter says? Or some kind of pimp, setting his girlfriend Kellie, and maybe even his daughter, in my path? He's stretched out next to the pool blabbing on in his usual dumbass way, trying to find out from Charlie if he knew why nobody could put those puzzles together.

"Technical malfunction, it could have been," Charlie tells him, sipping his Dr. Pepper.

"Technical malfunction? When the puzzles come off the die press one at a time?"

"Human error, then," Charlie says. He holds up his hand that's got part of the Mona Lisa stamped on it. "Like this."

Jeff turns away like he can't stand the sight of the Mona Lisa. "That's what I'm assuming. Human error, just the kind of thing my Dad had insurance for. And the only two humans who could have made that error are sitting right here."

He squints at me and Charlie like he's accusing us of something. I don't know about Charlie but I don't like being squinted at by a pimp, let alone a pervert. So I shift on my lounge chair a little and when he glances my way I give him just the hint of an evil look.

"It was just a mistake, right?" he says. "An accident. Simple negligence, right?"

He's glaring at me like a cop and my look is getting eviler and eviler. "Don't worry," he tells me. "I want it to be an accident."

Worrying about what he wants is the farthest thing from my mind. "Why's that?" I ask him. "Why do you want it to be an accident?"

"Don't you see? If someone who worked there deliberately sabotaged the puzzles, that could void the insurance policy—"

"Void it?"

"It wouldn't be effective. The insurance company wouldn't pay. And then my guarantee to the bank—well, I won't go into the details, but let me just say this: It could cost me an enormous amount of money."

I'm no expert on money but it seems to me that if something costs Jeff Pangborn an enormous amount of it, maybe that's not such a bad thing. It might even be just what a pimp and a pervert deserves. And if he's got to spend some of that money on me and Charlie instead of paying it to the bank, maybe it's time to send the bank a message that they should stop making loans to pimps and perverts in the first place.

"If you want my opinion," I tell Jeff, "I doubt it was an accident."

He lowers his voice, just in case the insurance man is snorkeling up behind him in the pool. "Are you saying it was sabotage?"

"That depends on what you mean by sabotage," I tell him. "If somebody did it on purpose, but for no reason—"

"Spencer, you better keep that to yourself," Charlie says.

"I mean, if somebody just got a notion in his head—"

"What?" Jeff looks like what's left of a balloon somebody just popped and tossed on the patio. "Are you saying you deliberately scrambled up those puzzles?"

"I didn't say that," I cut him off. "Charlie, did you hear me say that?"

"Nope. You definitely didn't say that."

"Then what did you just say?"

"I said *if* somebody did that, what he might've done. Not that he did it, but what he might've done, if he did it. And what he done might've been to take a handful of pieces from each of those Chaos Scape 19 boxes and drop them in a different box, and then take a handful of pieces from that box—"

"Why the hell did you do that?"

"I didn't say I did it, I—"

"All right! Why *might* you have done that?"

"I might've done it—*if* I done it—because I'm tired of being called stupid, tired of being a victim, tired of being treated like part of a machine. I'm working in a damn puzzle factory chopping up the Masterpieces of Western Art into 1000 pieces and all of them were made by men like me. Why are they any better than me? I'm about to lose my job, it's going to China along with everything else and Charlie's losing his too—"

"Keep me out of this!" Charlie tells me.

"And I've got one last chance to flap my wings so the world can be a little different because of me, and here comes the last puzzle, Chaos Scape 19 and they say it's a masterpiece no matter what it looks like. It's already a jumbled mess as far as I can tell but I can jumble it up even more and make it my own, and all those puzzles, they're one big masterpiece now, spread through a hundred boxes and they're my masterpiece and nobody else's."

By this time Jeff is sitting up in his lounge chair covering his face with his hands and making a noise almost like he's crying. "Did my father know anything about this?" he whimpers.

I can't resist pulling his chain just a little bit more, even though I've already got him trussed up like a pig. "Sure, your Dad was in on it," I tell him. "Wasn't he, Charlie?"

"Afraid so," Charlie nods.

"In fact it was Mr. Pangborn's idea, wasn't it, Charlie? He gave me and Charlie and Audrey each $100 not to tell anybody about it. Ain't that so, Charlie?"

Jeff rolls over and curls up face down on his lounge chair. "This is way worse than I thought," he moans. "Intentional vandalism, aided and abetted by the owner! No insurance company is going to cover that!"

Maybe you're just going to have to belly up and pay that bank, I'm thinking. But I don't say that or anything else. Believe it or not, I feel sorry for the dog.

"Listen," Charlie says. "There's a way out of this."

"There is?"

"Spencer and I don't necessarily have to tell anybody. Do we, Spencer?"

"Not necessarily," I agree.

"I mean, we don't even have to talk to this insurance guy, do we? And then how's the insurance company ever going to find out?"

"That's right!" Jeff sits up and beams at me like a bird dog. "Will you do that? Will you do that for me?"

"Well, it could get expensive," I tell him. "If the man comes around asking questions—"

"This Erik Anselmus isn't a cop. He's just an investigator for an insurance company."

I pucker my lips and take my time answering. "Could still get expensive, though. Couldn't it, Charlie?"

Now Jeff's face is red and ugly and he's gasping for breath like he just choked on a bone. He's a dumbass but I think he's finally catching on. "I can't believe this!" he explodes. "Are you trying to blackmail me!"

"Oh, no, no, no!" Charlie laughs. "We're not trying to blackmail you. Are you trying to blackmail him, Spencer?"

"No way," I tell Charlie. "No way I'm trying to blackmail anybody."

Charlie's smiling at Jeff, not a nice smile, though, sort of sly and ruthless, like a gangster in a movie making an offer you can't refuse. I never knew Charlie had it in him. "You see, Jeff," he says, "you've got it all wrong. If we were trying to blackmail you, we'd ask for money. A lot of money. Wouldn't we, Spencer?"

"Damn right we would. Enough to retire on."

Jeff leaps out of his lounge chair and pounds his fist down on the table, shaking all the cups and soda bottles onto the cement. "You could go to jail for this!"

"You still don't get it, do you, Jeff?" Charlie says. "We're not blackmailers."

"What the hell are you then?"

"We're whistleblowers."

"Whistleblowers?"

Jeff stands with his mouth hanging open like he don't know what Charlie's talking about. Luckily I just saw a TV news show about whistleblowers so I can fill in the gaps. "There was some bad behavior going on in that puzzle factory," I tell Jeff, "and we're blowing the whistle on it."

"But you're the ones who did it!"

"That don't matter. We're still entitled to back pay."

"Back pay from what?"

"Back pay from the jobs you fired us from."

By now Jeff's going berserk, stomping around on the cement kicking soda bottles and beach balls and rafts and even a couple of lounge chairs into the pool. "The factory's closed, you morons! You want to move to China, you can have your jobs back!"

That one throws me but Charlie don't miss a beat. "No," he says, "we want new jobs. High quality jobs. Not the kind you sent to China."

"Jobs?" Jeff is quiet, motionless. He suddenly forgets about all the stuff he wanted to kick into the pool. "Is that all this is about?"

"How else am I going to feed my kids?"

Jeff comes toward us and we both stand up. "If I get you new jobs will you stay away from Erik Anselmus?"

"Absolutely."

"Slam the door in his face?"

"Kick him in the teeth."

"All right, then." He shakes Charlie's hand, then mine. "I know a lot of people in this town. All I have to do is pick up the phone and you'll have better jobs than you ever dreamed of. It's a deal, right?"

That's how Charlie and I got started on our new careers, both in the health care field. Charlie's at GastroPlonix Corp. selling surgical equipment for stapling fat people's stomachs together. I'm the all-night security guard at Frankford Testing Labs, where they test out hospital beds to see if the people in them are going to get bedsores. I like the job all right but I'm afraid the nights are going to be long and lonely with nothing to do except sit at my desk and watch the surveillance monitors. The place looks like an insane asylum with all the beds lined up in little rooms with windows so you can peek inside, and sometimes I feel like running away even though I'm supposed to be the security guard. When they hired me they explained all my rights, how they could fire me at any time if they felt like it, only they couldn't fire me on account of my race, which they already knew, or my disabilities, which I don't have, and they couldn't hold it against me if I wanted to have a sex-change operation, just let them know and they'd make all the necessary arrangements—I didn't like the way the HR dude looked at me when he said that—and then they told me about my vacation days and my sick days and health insurance and life insurance and the pension plan and all the deductions they planned to take out of my paycheck so I wouldn't end up keeping any of it, but there was one thing, one big thing, they forgot to tell me about.

They didn't tell me about Naked Dave.

9. Mean Kampf

Lindsay's online girlfriend "Alex," when not exchanging erotic fantasies with child predators, was a 26-year-old rookie cop named Dennis Gilboy. In addition to his regular duties he had volunteered for a special assignment supporting the Child Abuse Prevention Task Force. His supervisor, a big, red-faced detective named Bob Kampf (called "Mean Kampf" behind his back at the District 41 station), was initially impressed with his dedication to ferreting out child predators on the internet. But when he made his first arrest—it was a 47-year-old optometrist from Swarthmore who thought he was meeting a girl named Cherry at King of Prussia Mall—Gilboy went nuts. He frothed at the mouth and took a sadistic delight in roughing the optometrist up in the back seat of the squad car. Kampf favored a more humane approach. He would have driven the suspect to the nearest ATM and accepted a handsome cash settlement in lieu of delivering him into the maws of the legal system.

"It's what I call due process," Kampf explained when he saw the optometrist crumpled in the back seat. "You've heard of that, right? It's in the Constitution."

"Due process is too good for this animal," Gilboy spat. "I'd like to throw him in a ditch."

Detective Kampf disapproved of Gilboy's excessive zeal, though not entirely on Constitutional grounds. It made him look bad, it made the whole District look bad, as if this self-righteous kid had something on them, like they didn't care as much as he did about putting these perverts in the can. Why would Gilboy get so emotionally involved, other than to show them up, make them look like a bunch of corrupt incompetents who were content to let child predators run wild? Unless—and this, in Kampf's mind, was the clincher—the rookie cop had some issues of his own.

"I've seen it before," he told Gilboy one day as they sat in the lunch room sipping their coffee, "even in some of the more experienced cops. Your typical male police officer doesn't feel comfortable spending his days pretending to be a 14-year-old girl named Alex or Tiffany, especially when that girl is doing everything this side of entrapment to seduce another guy."

"Not a problem for me," Gilboy grunted, stirring his coffee. "I just want to hammer those scum buckets."

"Frankly, it's unmanly and humiliating, a little like dressing up in a bra and panties, isn't it? I don't blame you for feeling that way."

Gilboy looked away. "I told you it's not a problem. If that's what it takes to get the scum off the street—"

"Like I said, I don't blame you one bit. You know what happens to some guys? They feel uncomfortable pretending to be girls—like I said, perfectly understandable—and then, because of that, they start to identify with the guys they're pursuing—or the guys who are pursuing them—and they find themselves fantasizing about the girls they're pretending to be. Sort of like the Stockholm syndrome. Happens all the time."

Gilboy turned his dark eyes on Kampf. "I've got a daughter."

"Who doesn't?" Kampf grinned.

Gilboy gulped the rest of his coffee and crushed the styrofoam cup in his fist. Then without another word he stood up and stamped out of the lunch room.

Definitely a weirdo, Kampf thought. And a menace to the District, with his overzealous, holier-than-thou attitude, implying that every cop who skimmed a little off the top was voting to put perverts back on the street. Someday he'd crash and burn, and Kampf wanted to be there when it happened.

A few days later, Kampf was standing behind Gilboy, watching his computer screen, when "Alex" received the unexpected message from "Steve" confessing that "Steve" was really a 14-year-old girl named "Lindsay."

"Holy Christ!" Gilboy muttered. "Now what?"

"Typical pervert," said Kampf, eyeing Gilboy for his reaction. "Gives him a thrill to pretend he's a girl."

"You think this Lindsay's really a girl?"

"No way. Steve all the way. And he thinks you're Alex."

"You ever seen this before?"

"Happens all the time. Just keep the dialogue going. Act like it turns you on."

"I don't know, I—"

"Don't you want to nail this scumbag?"

10. Free Food

"The Free Food Principle stands at the heart of all business and commerce. Some would argue that it is the basis of civilization itself."
— *Austin Ivey III*

Charlie Quill sat across from Bill Symonds, his new boss at GastroPlonix Corp., in a booth at P.J. O'Hooligan's in Northeast Philadelphia, gnawing into a double French dip sandwich while Bill Symonds initiated him into the art of salesmanship as expounded in the New York Times Bestseller, *The Free Food Principle*, by Austin Ivey III. Charlie had just embarked on a new career in sales and was anxious to learn everything he could about the subject. At the moment, however, he couldn't enjoy his lunch or concentrate on what Bill Symonds was saying—in fact he felt a little nauseous—because less than an hour earlier he'd realized that his wife Penny was having an affair with a real estate broker named Jim Grillo. His eyes felt moist, his skin clammy, his breathing choppy and asthmatic. He felt like he might burst into tears or stand up and start shouting obscenities, but he couldn't do any of those things in front of his new boss. GastroPlonix was his big opportunity, compliments of Jeff Pangborn, who seemed to know everybody in Philadelphia. If he had any chance of hanging on to Penny, this was it. He dipped his roll into the tiny cup of au jus that was buried in his double order of french fries and swabbed out the last remaining drops.

"Just read this book, it's all in here," Bill Symonds said, poking the book's dust jacket with a pudgy forefinger. "First you buy a cup of coffee for a customer. Then a nice lunch. You need some more au jus, by the way?" He gestured to the waitress with a twirl of his hand. "And the next thing you know—there's a sort of three-date rule for customers, you don't want to move too quickly or you'll scare them away—it's dinner at Ruth's Chris Steak House!" Bill Symonds winked obscenely. "They can't get enough of that thick prime beef!"

The image—conjuring a vision of Penny with Jim Grillo—almost made Charlie lose his lunch. Instead he clamped his lips together and forced a smile. GastroPlonix was a leading manufacturer of bariatric surgical devices ("bariatrics" being the branch of medicine that deals with obesity and its treatment), and when he applied for the job he assumed that his overweight appearance would be a disadvantage. Now, lunching with his new boss, he realized it was the reason they'd hired him. At 5 feet, 10 inches, weighing in at just under 300 pounds, he looked as though he'd been blown into his new polyester suit like foam insulation. But until that morning he thought Penny liked him just the way he was. She was a big girl herself—always had been—and the whole family, including Penny and himself and the four kids, tipped the scales at over 1,200 pounds. He'd been following the Free Food Principle all his life without knowing it. What went wrong?

Bill Symonds seemed confident that Charlie would have a quick grasp of the underlying science. "All the studies—they're all in this book—all the studies show it's an infallible principle. You give people free food and you literally have them eating out of your hand. The government knows this—what do you think food stamps are all about? And look at Halloween! Millions of parents pimping their kids up in costumes so they can go around begging free food from the neighbors!"

The mention of Halloween gave Charlie's stomach an unpleasant turn, as he remembered Jim Grillo materializing at the front door of their row home with his two daughters—who even in their princess costumes looked like underfed escapees from a refugee camp—and Penny running to the door and shoving half the candy he'd bought into their greedy loot bags, giggling with Jim about fattening them up. Charlie'd had to leave his Hungry Man turkey dinner, which he'd just pulled out of the oven, on the kitchen counter—"You can heat it back up in the microwave," Penny said—and run out to the Seven Eleven for a couple more bags of Snickers and Reese's Pieces; he'd had to leave Penny there with Jim, skinny smartass Jim Grillo from the eighth grade who cheated on all his tests and never did a day's work in his life, and who now, while Charlie was gone to the Seven Eleven, sent his emaciated princesses on down the block with their loot bags so he could stay behind and make time with Penny. It all seemed so innocent, just so much holiday fun, but in retrospect Charlie should have known there was something going on between those two. His own kids were out trick-or-treating somewhere in the neighborhood—he didn't escort them around like Jim Grillo did; if they wanted candy they'd have to work for it, he told them—and so nobody else was home for those fifteen or twenty minutes while he ran out to the Seven Eleven, leaving Penny alone with Jim Grillo in their living room. At least he hoped they'd stayed in the living room. Anything could have happened while he was gone.

"It all goes back to evolution," Bill Symonds went on. "What's the only instinct stronger than sex? Biologists will tell you—and this is a fact—that the animal that gets more food with less effort is the one who wins the race."

"People need to eat, don't they?" Charlie ventured. He wasn't disagreeing but he thought he ought to say something.

"This goes way beyond needing to eat," Bill said. "In the modern world, most people have plenty to eat. We're talking *free* food here. Not just any food, but *free* food."

Bill Symonds set his laptop on the table and opened it to YouTube, where he found a video from a recent GastroPlonix sales meeting. "Team building for the sales reps," he explained. The idea was to run up and down a simulated supermarket aisle as fast as you could, urged on by pulsing music and a frenetic DJ, grabbing food off the shelves and shoving it into your cart at lightning speed until a buzzer went off. The person who grabbed the most in retail value was the winner. "Great stuff," Bill Symonds said. "I wish you could've been there."

"Looks like a lot of fun."

"It's not about fun." Bill Symonds eyed him sternly. "It's about the work ethic."

Charlie knew all about the work ethic. It had been stamped into him by his second-generation Irish parents the same way he'd stamped the Masterpieces of Western Art into thousands of pieces of cardboard at the puzzle factory—indelibly, hydraulically, at risk of life and limb. He'd worked at the puzzle factory for fifteen years, twelve hours a day, six days a week, and since it went broke and he was spending more time with the family he realized that the work ethic applied only to him. Penny (under the spell of Jim Grillo) was obsessed with real estate, the kids with rap music and video games and smart phones. They were like an army of elephant-sized ants, consuming everything in their path and everything he could throw in front of them, even if it meant running up the Discover Card balance to the limit and putting another mortgage on the house. Yet he would do anything for his family. All he really wanted was for his family to know how much he loved them. Listening to Bill Symonds he realized that he'd spent most of his life in something like a GastroPlonix sales meeting, scurrying up and down the aisles of an enormous simulated big box store grabbing armfuls of food, soda, health and beauty aids, pet supplies, school supplies, toys, clothes, electronic gadgets and everything else he could pile into his cart, with the goal of acquiring as much, measured in retail value, as he possibly could without ever having to pay for it. And what was wrong with that? People need to live, don't they? When he looked at Penny, he used to think: This is my wife, who I love more than anything in the world. And now suddenly the buzzer had gone off.

At home that night everything seemed the same as usual. Fifteen-year-old Bridget sprawled on the couch murmuring into her smart phone and a can of Pepsi, as her sister Megan, texting in front of the TV, commandeered an armchair and a jumbo bag of potato chips. The two boys, Sean and Brian, bounced off each other like bumpo cars as they took turns raiding the potato chips. Penny, in her Eagles jersey, stood in the kitchen sliding a frozen pizza into the oven.

The normality of it all infuriated Charlie. On the counter beside Penny he saw the makings of a salad: a head of lettuce, some carrots and three ripe tomatoes. Without a word he stepped over and swept all the vegetables into the sink. Then he flicked a switch and started pushing them down into the garbage disposal.

Penny shoved him aside and tried to save the vegetables. "Are you nuts?"

"We don't need this crap anymore," he said. "We don't need any more of Jim Grillo's organic crap."

"I think you *are* nuts."

Since the puzzle factory closed, Jim Grillo had been bringing groceries to the real estate office for Penny to take home. He was an organic food nut and must have thought her family should eat nothing but grass, even though Charlie had never eaten a salad in his life outside of a restaurant. "When I was out of work, that was one thing," he said. "But now we don't need his organic salad crap."

"Did you get paid yet? Where's your paycheck?"

"I get paid on Friday."

"So in the meantime the kids can gnaw on the rug? I can't believe you're throwing away food."

"I can't believe I saw you walking down Cottman Avenue arm in arm with Jim Grillo."

Penny straightened up and laughed in his face. "Is that what this is about?"

"You tell me what it's about."

She handed him a wad of soggy lettuce from the sink— "Here, you feed the kids"—and fled upstairs.

Later that night, when the kids were up in their rooms, Charlie broke the unwritten pact of silence he and Penny had been living under for the past few years. She sat in her chair in the living room immersed in some stupid TV show like the ones she watched every night. He watched Monday Night Football by himself on the small screen TV in the bedroom. At half time he came downstairs and stood behind her.

"We've got to talk," he said.

He felt like a corny TV character when he said that, and she must have thought so too. "We've got to talk?" she mocked him, without turning around. "I didn't know this TV had surround sound."

He thought about heading back upstairs.

"Go ahead and talk," she said. "What do you want to talk about?"

"Your thing with Jim Grillo."

"Charlie"—she turned to face him—"There isn't any *thing* with Jim. We're friends, that's all. He's helping me get started in real estate. It's a tough market right now. He gives me the kind of support I don't get much of around here."

"That's it, huh?"

"That's it. Trust me, we're not having an affair. I'm not attracted to Jim."

Charlie remembered what Bill Symonds had told him. "You're just in it for the free food?"

"The food helps."

Charlie saw a million years of evolution in her eyes. It's stronger than sex, Bill Symonds had said. Even a skinny geek like Jim Grillo can get a girl if he gives her enough free food.

"Are we in any position to turn it down?" she asked. "Or throw it away, for God's sake?"

"His kids don't look like they get enough to eat," Charlie insisted. "His wife looks like she just got out of a concentration camp."

"They eat healthier than us. They have a healthier lifestyle in general. Maybe that's why they look thin to you. They belong to the Cheltenham Swim Club."

"So what?"

"Our kids have to go to the city pool. It's filthy."

"You never said that before."

"And our kids have to live in this dump."

"This dump is where I grew up."

"I know that."

Another million years of evolution flickered past, unearthing an even more ancient instinct: She began to cry.

Charlie wasn't ready to give up. "I don't get what the problem is," he said. "Haven't I always put food on the table?"

"There's more to marriage than food."

He saw the opportunity for a possible inroad into what had been an impenetrable swamp. "Sex? Isn't there supposed to be sex?"

"There doesn't have to be sex. At least not all the time."

"OK, just checking, because if that's a necessary ingredient, then once every six months—"

"You've got to reduce everything to the crudest level, don't you?"

What's more crude? he wanted to ask. A husband thinking about sex or a real estate salesman currying favor with organic vegetables?

"Like we're animals or something. Jim doesn't think that way."

"No, he just tries to buy you with free food."

"Jim is a gentleman."

There was no instinct to account for it, but Charlie felt like crying too. He knew he'd never cry in front of Penny but he felt his throat tightening, his eyes clouding over.

"What's the matter?" she asked in a soft voice.

"I was hoping with the new job maybe I could, I don't know, save some money, provide a little better future for the kids—"

"Charlie." She squeezed his hand. "You're doing fine—we're doing fine, you know what I mean? Just keep hanging in there, OK?"

He forced himself to smile. It made him feel normal and important to be talked to like somebody on a TV show. Maybe there was hope after all.

11. My Mom, by Lindsay Pangborn

I love my Mom but I'm glad she doesn't live here anymore. She can be sort of strict and militaristic sometimes, like Baron von Steuben who came over from King of Prussia to help George Washington at Valley Forge. One time she threatened to have me horsewhipped if I didn't clean my room, another time she said she was going to send me to boarding school in Iraq. I guess that's why Kellie calls her the Queen of Prussia, or maybe it's because she got arrested at the mall, on the second floor of Nordstrom's where the guy plays old songs on the piano. I was with her when it happened but I try not to think about it. They took me to a children's shelter and kept me there for eight hours until my Dad came and bailed me out. It was like being in jail even though I didn't do anything. I remember a bridge near the mall—we drove over it in the police car but you could walk there from the Gap—where I could hear the cars and trucks roaring and pounding on the expressway, all going about eighty miles an hour, and there's a sidewalk over the bridge that hardly has a guard rail. Mom never came back to the house except to pick up her stuff. She knew about Kellie by then and already had a lawyer who got her into a rehab program so she wouldn't have to go to jail. I can visit her along with Zachary but I hate it so much I throw up on the way home. All she does is ask questions about Kellie and what kind of clothes she's wearing and where she bought them. Sometimes she asks about Cupcake. She hopes to get custody as soon as she gets out but Dad says there's no way he's going to let that happen. Kellie tries to say things to make me feel better but Zachary always throws in one of his quotations from Kurt Cobain or Dylan Klebold's diary. Not that Kellie or my Dad are listening. Zachary's like one of those fools in a Shakespeare play. He can say anything because nobody pays attention to anything he says. Mr. Siegel says those fools are actually the smartest people in the plays, but that doesn't apply to Zachary. He really is an idiot.

My Dad's been having a rough time in the past few months. His Dad—my Grampa—died of a heart attack practically in front of him after his jigsaw puzzle factory went bankrupt and had to be sold to the Chinese. This was after my Grandma, who was always sort of demented, got dementia and had to be sent to a nursing home. Then these lawsuits got started claiming the puzzles were defective, which they are—Zachary's been trying to put one together for the last two months—and Dad's company lost its biggest account (whatever an account is). I know this because one afternoon when I was bored I peeked into his desk drawer and found a little notebook where he writes all his passwords. Now I can read all the stuff on his computer as well as his phone. Mom's lawyer hounds him for support payments, medical bills, rehab charges, even her legal fees, and she's suing to get custody of Zachary and me. Dad's got Kellie but I don't think the two of them have been getting along lately. He hardly talks when she's around. After dinner he tries to help me with my homework but he's always in a bad mood and I can't stand him hovering over me, especially after I found out what he wanted to do to Alex.

Our school is a sore point with Dad, because it costs so much and we both hate it. "I want you to have the opportunities I didn't have," he explained to Zachary this morning for the ten millionth time.

"So"—Zachary gave us his triumphant know-it-all look—
"you didn't have the opportunity to be a dorky, tree-hugging,
granola-gnawing, Birkenstocks-with-your-socks-on all-purpose
Quaker dweeb?"

"Like you," I added.

"That's correct," Dad said.

Zachary held his ground. "We had the Junior Olympics
yesterday. You know what they had instead of the Tug of War?
The Pull of Peace!"

"Nothing wrong with peace," Dad said. "You should try
holding yours."

"Instead of what you've usually got in your hand," I added.

At school Ms. Stebbins is leaning on me hard about getting
into college. Without asking, she signed me up for Girls' Crew,
Field Hockey, Concert Choir, African Dance, Habitat for
Humanity, Morning Yoga, Navajo Sign Language, Mandarin
Chinese, Islamic Civilization I, II and III, Organic Chemistry,
Organic Gardening, and String Theory, and that will only take
me halfway through my junior year. "Will I be able to go to
college if I take these courses?" I asked her.

We sat across from each other at her desk in the Guidance
Office, where she had just shown me my schedule for next year.
Sometimes Ms. Stebbins's eyes have a weird glow like she's a
character in a horror movie. She told me once, when she was
trying to get me to sign up for physics, that a UFO had landed in
her back yard and brought her on board to give her an IQ test.

She nodded brightly. "If you take these courses, you won't
be able to do anything but go to college."

"Maybe I don't care that much."

"What did you say?"

"About college, I mean."

She seemed to be hyperventilating, even turning a little green, the way I do when I think about eating. "You're jeopardizing your future!"

"But it's *my* future, isn't it? I can jeopardize it if I want to."

She glanced around with her horror-movie eyes to make sure the other guidance counselors weren't listening. "There's something you need to understand," she said with her teeth clenched. "If you don't get into college—a good college—that will make this school look bad. And people will say, 'Don't go to that school, you won't get into a good college if you go to that school.' And donors—we're dependent on donors for our very existence—will say, 'Why should I donate money to a school that can't get a girl of average intelligence'—I assume you have an IQ of at least 100—'into a good college?'"

I tried to stand up but she reached over the desk and grabbed my wrist. "So for you to put this simply in terms of yourself—although typical for a person of your age and maturity—is monumentally selfish and irresponsible. It's unfair to the school, unfair to me, to your teachers, to your parents and most of all to your classmates, who will suffer for years to come as the reputation of the school goes down the drain. Getting into a good college is your destiny. Do you understand?"

By the time I got home from school I felt like locking myself in my room and eating a Tastykake. I always check my text messages to see if there's one from Alex. She sends them every day except Sundays, even after I told her I'm a girl. She seems really nice but very needy—I almost feel sorry for keeping her away from my Dad. It's funny because we've never met, but I've started thinking of her as a friend, a really good friend. Does she think of me that way? I guess that's sort of a dumb question, since she still thinks I'm my Dad, even after I told her

I wasn't. What I'm actually wondering is: if she believed I was who I am, would she still want to be my friend?

I spend a lot of time thinking about Spencer, the cute black guy who used to work at Grampa's puzzle factory. Dad says he's stupid, but I don't believe it. There's a lot going on in his head, just like there is in mine—maybe he's even thinking some of the same thoughts—only he's too smart to say any of them. Like the day he and the fat guy from the puzzle factory were talking to Dad out by the pool, I think Spencer was a little grossed out by the way Kellie sicced Cupcake on him and threatened him with her French chef's knife when he came inside looking for the bathroom. I tried to smooth things over, but Kellie got really jealous and chased me away as soon as she noticed how cute he was. Later she warned me not to go near him again. It was sort of pathetic. Kellie won't say how old she is, but she must be about thirty or forty. Spencer looks about twenty, though you can't really tell with black guys. It shouldn't matter that I'm a little younger than him. I'm the same age as Alex, which my Dad doesn't seem to have any problem with.

One night I tried to ask my Dad about Spencer but he just got mad. "You can't imagine the grief I've suffered because of that moron!"

"I think he's kind of cute."

"Cute?" he yelled. "Don't even think of going near that idiot! That's all we need!"

I know it's mean, but I sort of like the idea that Spencer caused my Dad a lot of grief. It's what I'd do if I could think of a good way to do it. And Dad telling me to stay away from Spencer just makes me want to see him more. So I copied his number out of my Dad's phone when he left it on the table.

Then I erased it so Kellie couldn't get her hands on it.

12. Audrey

Audrey Scalzo stood in front of her mother's house in South Philadelphia. It was one of those tidy row homes with lawn chairs on the stoop and garbage cans blocking the curb in case anyone was crazy enough to think they could park there. Her mother—who liked to boast that she was a direct descendant of Lucretia Borgia, the Renaissance princess famous for poisoning her enemies—spent most of her time settling old scores with neighbors and relatives of her late husband. An atmosphere of vendetta permeated the house like the pungent fumes of her marinara sauce, a pot of which simmered on the stove day and night like a witch's cauldron. She had taught her daughters that of all the basic instincts—hunger, sex, greed, power—the strongest is the thirst for revenge. Audrey, taking after her father, had always rejected this teaching, but since moving back under her mother's roof she found herself succumbing to temptation. Though short on cash and starved for sex, she spent her waking hours fantasizing about Jeff Pangborn and the revenge she intended to exact for the many indignities she'd suffered at his hands. Luckily for the state of her soul, her little sister Diane, who'd fled to California years before, had been enticing her with a more wholesome future in the land of the lotus eaters, where she could find a new job, start a new life, and consign Jeff Pangborn to the dust bin of history where he belonged. "Revenge is sweet," her father used to say, "but you can't put it in your coffee."

Her wizened mother hovered beside her, shooting her garden hose at a car trying to park along the curb. "Get the hell out of my parking space!"

"Mom," Audrey said, "you don't have a car. You don't even know how to drive."

"I know my rights."

The driver rolled up his window to keep from getting wet, then gave up and drove away.

"You let people walk all over you, Audrey," Mom said. "Run over you. Drive over you. Then you wonder why you're covered with tread marks."

"Thanks, Mom."

"Lucretia Borgia poisoned her enemies. That's what you should do to that Jeffrey Pangborn."

Audrey stepped off the stoop and started to walk away. "I'm going over to Plato's Cave for a drink."

"There's plenty of older men—men in their fifties and sixties—who wouldn't mind your looks."

"My idea of getting lucky with guys that age is when they can't get it up."

After dark Audrey dreamed of younger men. She'd been angry once when her friend Cathy called her a cougar. She hated the word, but (she had to admit) it sounded wild, fierce, ravenous—all the things she wished she could be. She'd gone to bed with plenty of older men, but as a cougar she remained a virgin, never having bedded any of the younger men she fantasized about. She tried not to think too much about Spencer Casey, whose rebuff of her advances that last night at the puzzle factory had left her feeling humiliated and ashamed. Every night she fled her mother's house of horrors and sought refuge in one of the local bars. Her favorite was a Greek place called Plato's Cave, near the corner of Broad and Passyunk. There one night she met Cathy for a drink, triggering a string of three momentous meetings—which, had they been as accidental as they were made to seem, would have been a coincidence bordering on the miraculous. The first of these encounters was with Erik Anselmus.

13. From the Journal of Erik Anselmus

November 3: Pinocchio's—Restaurant across from former puzzle factory (now a garage). Images of Jiminy Cricket, Gepetto and Monstro the Whale on the walls. Waitress: Cathy. Cute blonde: sharp, friendly eyes. Wears a small Tyrolean hat and a Pinocchio apron. Long painted nails, several rings but none on ring finger. Nice smile. Says she's a friend of Audrey Scalzo's. Expects to see her tomorrow night.

November 4: Followed Cathy after work to a bar called Plato's Cave to find Audrey Scalzo—evasive, but hates Jeff Pangborn with visible intensity. Be sure to tell Administration: whereabouts of other two employees unknown.

14. Girth of a Nation

Charlie's first week at GastroPlonix consisted entirely of compliance training. Evidently the company had been guilty of some crime that was either too trivial or too heinous to mention—Charlie was told only that it had to do with the way they promoted their products—and as a result, according to Bill Symonds, they were under the corporate equivalent of house arrest. "It's like trying to do your job in a strait jacket," Bill complained, "with one of those sensing devices duct-taped around your ankles. And they wonder why all the jobs are going to China!"

After completing his compliance training, Charlie sat in Bill Symonds's office listening to a barrage of long-winded downloads about GastroPlonix and its products. "GastroPlonix is America's No. 1 manufacturer of bariatric surgical devices," Bill told him. "Luckily, the one thing people are still allowed to do is eat."

Bill Symonds peppered his monologues with joking asides—pitched an octave below his usual voice, as though he were talking through a ventriloquist's dummy—that poked fun at what he was saying, usually at the expense of the people who used their products. "We sell to bariatricians—fat doctors, but don't ever call them that—and sometimes to general surgeons. We refer to the patients—and for once it's a euphemism that fits—as 'consumers.' And by the way, don't ever call them fat."

"Obese?"

"Are you kidding? These are our customers you're talking about!"

Charlie had to think fast. What would he prefer to be called? Or—more to the point—what would he let someone call Penny or the kids? Not fat, certainly, or even obese; his boss was right about that. "Overweight, then?"

"Look"—Bill squinted at him as if noticing his body build for the first time—"whether you weigh 200 or 600 pounds, it's a lifestyle choice, isn't it? So who's to say whether it's over or under? But if you're dissatisfied with your weight for any reason, GastroPlonix can do something about it."

"You mean, like stapling my stomach shut?" That idea, which Charlie had read about in a magazine, filled him with the sort of dread a violinist must feel watching a butcher slice roast beef.

"Yes, we do that," Bill said. "But there's a lot more to GastroPlonix than staple guns. When a consumer has open-heart surgery, for instance, the surgeon needs special tools. Did you ever try to find a pork chop or a wrapped-up hamburger in the bottom of the freezer? Well, just imagine what it's like to replace somebody's heart valves when you've got to reach in through two feet of fat! It can get mighty slick in there, let me tell you!"

The explanation left Charlie a little uneasy, but fortunately Bill chose that moment to stand up and announce that it was time for him to meet Dr. Patel, the company's Medical Director. Dr. Patel, a serious man in a dark blue suit, occupied a spacious office in the executive suite that was decorated with pictures of ducks and geese. He greeted Charlie with a firm handshake and sat back down at his desk, in the middle of which, next to a plastic model of the human stomach, was a shiny metal object resembling a staple gun which Charlie recognized as the company's leading product, the popular Tummy Tweezer™. "GastroPlonix is not one of your greedy, heartless corporations that only cares about the bottom line," Dr. Patel told Charlie in his clipped Indian accent. "We put people first. We actively support farm subsidies, food stamps and other government programs to feed the masses."

"And when we say 'masses,'" Bill chuckled in his ventriloquist voice, "we mean masses!"

"We support free health care—and in particular free bariatric surgery—for all Americans who need it. And that, sad to say, is a great many Americans. Today the morbidly obese are the fastest growing segment of the population."

"No pun intended!" Bill added.

"By 2025, fully 41% of the US population will be obese."

"I could retire on that!"

"And GastroPlonix will be there."

Bill picked up the Tummy Tweezer from Dr. Patel's desk. "Here, Charlie, try out one of these hummers."

"I don't know, I—"

"They're just like the Black and Deckers you get at Lowe's," Bill said. "Just pull the trigger and let 'er rip!" He aimed it at Charlie's stomach and pulled the trigger. "Gotcha!"

"But I'm not a surgeon," Charlie objected, taking a step backwards. "Why would I need to know how to use these staple guns?"

"Come on, Charlie! If you want to be a salesman"—Bill Symonds winked at Dr. Patel—"you've got to be able to demonstrate the products, don't you?"

At home the situation had gone from bad to worse. Jim Grillo kept bringing his organic hamster chow to the office and Penny kept hauling it home by the bagful. Then he started delivering food directly to the house: first it was Girl Scout cookies (which his daughter was supposed to be selling) and then loaves of bread, fruit, gourmet soups and even cheese steaks—cheese steaks! as if Charlie would let his family go without cheese steaks!—and before long the man was showing up with donuts (how could donuts be organic?) and a chocolate cake. That did it, as far as Charlie was concerned. With no commissions, only compliance training, he'd barely made enough in his first paycheck to cover the tax withholding. There was no way he could compete when it came to chocolate cake.

"This isn't the Food Bank," he told Jim Grillo, blocking his way at the door. "We don't need this crap."

"Hey, just being neighborly," Jim smiled. "Just showing a little appreciation for Penny's efforts down at the office."

"Why don't you try paying her if you want to show your appreciation?"

"Whoa!" Jim stepped back. "It's a little premature for that, isn't it? I mean, when she gets her license—"

"Get out of the way, Dad!" The kids surged around him like a flash mob, tore the bags out of Jim's hands and retreated to the kitchen. "We're starved!"

In the kitchen, after Jim had yelled good-bye, Penny stood blocking the sink in case Charlie tried to throw the food away. "You're a piece of work," she said. "Truly unbelievable."

"I don't want that jackass coming around here."

"What's the big deal? He's just being friendly."

"Friendly? Yeah, he's being friendly, all right." Charlie knew, now that he'd been through his salesmanship training, what Jim Grillo was up to. It was the Free Food Principle, in all its irresistible Darwinian brutality. He was taking advantage of Charlie's temporary weakness in bringing home the bacon to move in on Penny and the kids, who seemed more voracious and demanding than ever. What's the big deal? she wanted to know. Charlie could tell by the way she purred at Jim, cozying up to him like a cat to the one who feeds it, what the big deal was. They were a lot cozier together than she and Charlie had been in a long time. He felt like crying again, desperate to save his marriage. He wanted to love her, wanted her to love him, wanted the kids to love him, but he felt them slipping away— lured away, ridiculous as it seemed, by another man's groceries.

Is she really sleeping with him? he wondered. Or just thinking about it? If not, why doesn't she just come out and deny it? "I don't want you hanging around at that office any more," he told her. "There must be another place you can work for nothing."

"I'm going to work there until I get my license," she said. "And then I'm going to keep working there, unless things improve around here."

"What does that mean?"

"Where's this great new life we were supposed to be having when you started this job? Did I miss it when I blinked or something?"

"We just need some quality time."

"Quality time?"

"Things could improve around here for me too, you know. Things could be a lot better."

15. Naked Dave

Spencer Casey

The owner of Frankford Labs is a white lady named Ms. Killebrew. She calls me Spencer but I've got to call her Ms. Killebrew. She's about the size of my Aunt Thelma's pit bull with the same sly smile that says someday she just might bite my head off. My boss is a redneck from the New Jersey pine barrens named Lester Blount. He used to be a cop but he had to retire because he has every disease known to man. Diabetes, asthma, allergies, migraine, high blood pressure, ulcers, kidney stones, psoriasis, emphysema, arthritis, heart disease—you name it, he's got it, in fact you don't have to name it, he's got it anyway and he'd love to tell you all about it. He's also an alcoholic but he don't talk about that one. He plays country music on the radio and has Bible verses tattooed on his arms. Sometimes he calls himself the Chief of Security but usually he just calls in sick.

My first day Ms. Killebrew made me come in at three in the afternoon so I could get disoriented and meet Lester Blount but usually I don't start until 10:30 at night. What we do here, Ms. Killebrew tells me, is clinical trials on hospital beds. All I can see is a few old ladies laying around in floppy nightgowns, wearing themselves out tossing and turning and cranking their beds up and down with a remote control, sitting up and laying back down, rolling over, cranking up and cranking down, until I can't stand the sight of them anymore. Ms. Killebrew looks at me with her pit bull smile and tells me, over and over again, we've got to do this right, we file government reports with the FDA and they've got to be done right or we could go to jail. "Isn't that right, Lester?" she says. Lester Blount agrees in his twangy voice, repeating what she said and throwing in a few stories about when he was a cop, but before long he's coughing and losing his voice, like he's coming down with one of his diseases. This talk about jail scares me a little but I can't see why the cops would care about a bunch of old ladies in nightgowns cranking their beds up and down at three in the afternoon. And I'm thinking, out of all the things I could be doing, I'm not going to worry too much about this one landing me in jail.

At night after Lester Blount and Ms. Killebrew go home the place looks like an insane asylum, all dark and spooky with dim lights and high ceilings and cobwebs in the corners, but no strait jackets or padded cells, just the testing rooms with hospital beds in them, and what's called the control room in the middle, which is where I sit. Each room's got a little window in the door so you can look in and see how the subject is doing—"subjects" is what they call the folks testing out the beds—and make sure they're not getting out of bed except to go the bathroom. On the night shift all the old ladies are gone home and there's just me and one subject named Naked Dave—that's not his real name, his real name's Dave Brunner but everybody calls him Naked Dave. He's the subject in what they call a long term clinical trial. His job is to lay in bed all day and night with nothing but a blindfold on, not getting up or moving a muscle, to see if he's going to get bedsores in that bed like somebody in a coma. I asked Ms. Killebrew could I apply for that job but she say no, you need a college degree. Naked Dave himself's got a Ph.D., in what subject I don't know, and it just goes to show, like Aunt Lorraine says, you can't have too much education. I want to ask Ms. Killebrew, if I go back for my GED, could I get paid for just taking a nap? Naked Dave tells his friends he works in research and I guess he does. It's harder than it looks, laying there perfectly still like that—I tried it at home and couldn't do it more than five minutes, though Shawn might have the knack if he ever finishes high school. And it would be hard work even for Naked Dave if he ever actually did it. But that first night, after Ms. Killebrew and Lester went home, I found out his secret. Peeking in the little window to his room, I see him sitting up in his bed without his blindfold on, so I bang on the door like I'm supposed to and the next thing I know he's standing in front of me stark naked, a 60-year-old white man, skinny and slimy as a chicken neck. In fact he looks a lot like Aunt Lorraine's sick bird Dewey, if Dewey wore glasses.

"What you doing out of bed?" I ask him, reaching for my pepper spray in case he takes a notion to jump me.

"Relax, kid," he tells me, pulling on his bathrobe. "You think I'm going to lay there all night like some stiff in a morgue?" He says *dere* and *mawwwg*, like he's one of the gangsters in Goodfellas.

"That's what Ms. Killebrew told me you'd be doing."

"That broad is nuts. Follow me."

He leads me down the hall to the computer room and behind the big xerox machine he slips his hand into a crack and off comes a piece of the wall big enough to drive a truck through. Inside there's a space about the size of a garage where you could live in style for about a year and nobody'd be the wiser. He's got a stash of booze and magazines and porno movies and a lot of fancy clothes hung up on hangers like it's his closet. He's even got a little refrigerator in there for making ice cubes and keeping his drinks cold.

Back in the control room we lounge around sipping ice cold vodka tonics and eating popcorn and flashing through porno movies on the computer screen while Naked Dave tells me the story of his life. "I used to be a profes*sah*," he says, "back in New *Yawwwk*. Frankly it wasn't a whole lot different from this. You've got your days free and plenty of time to think about whatever you want to think about."

"So why'd you quit?" I ask him, just to be polite.

He laughs like a crazy man. "They wanted me to teach two classes a week!"

After awhile he runs back to the computer room and comes out dressed to the nines in the weirdest outfit I ever saw, like something from outer space. "I'm going out," he tells me, heading for the door. "I'll be back before six."

"Where you going dressed like that?"

"*Awgies,*" he says.

"Awgies?" I never heard of awgies and from the look in his eye I don't think I ever want to.

"That's right. You do your job and someday I'll take you along with me."

"My job?" I didn't think he meant security guard. "What job?"

He pulls a $10 bill out of his wallet and hands it to me. "All you've got to do is freeze the surveillance camera while I'm going in and out." He reaches over to the control panel and shows me what buttons to push. "The recording freezes on whatever the camera happens to be looking at when you push that button down—until you push it again. Understand?"

"Sure." It looks like a pretty easy ten bucks to me.

"If anybody asks, I never got out of that bed except to take a leak. Understand?"

"What about the bedsores?"

"Bedsores? You think I'm going to lay around in this dump till I get bedsores?"

Every night it's pretty much the same thing. Naked Dave gets up a half hour after everybody else leaves. Sometimes we watch movies, sometimes we play cards, sometimes we just pop some corn and drink vodka tonics. Then at midnight he goes out to his awgies, slipping back in before the day shift arrives. Not too bad a job if you've got the education for it.

One night Charlie and I go to a bar in Chinatown to meet Audrey, who told Charlie she needed to talk to us about something important. She looks paler and saggier around the eyes, like she spends most of her time crying, but after a few drinks—she drinks something called a Cosmo—her face gets bright red and her eyes bug out like they used to and she looks normal again. I've got to work that night so I'm drinking Cokes and wearing the fancy blue uniform they gave me at the testing lab. At first there's a lot of hugging and kissing and laughing, Charlie guzzling beer and carrying on about the Free Food Principle, which is how he plans to sell stomach staplers to fat people (I just hope he gives them the free food before he staples their stomachs shut) and win back his wife from the real estate agent she's sleeping with (I can't see how free food's going to solve that one), and Audrey describing how she's living with her crazy Mom in South Philly while she looks for a job. If she can't find one soon, she tells us, she's going to head out to California to visit her sister and see what turns up. Finally she comes around to the reason she wants to talk to me and Charlie.

"Wait'll you hear this," she says. "Remember Cathy, the waitress at Pinocchio's?"

Pinocchio's is the Italian place across the street from the puzzle factory where we used to go for pizza. The waitresses— one of them was Audrey's friend Cathy, who I didn't remember—wear pointy hats with feathers in them and aprons that make them look like they've got on red shorts and a yellow shirt and a blue tie, just like Pinocchio.

"Well, one night I met her at a bar I hang out in, Plato's Cave on Passyunk near South Broad, and she starts telling me about this weird insurance guy who's been hanging around Pinocchio's, and all of a sudden her jaw drops and she says, 'Oh my God, don't look now but there he is!' This creepy giant albino in a black suit, staring at the two of us from across the room. And when he sees us looking at him, he stands up and comes over like we're old pals. 'Are you stalking me?' Cathy asks him, trying to make a joke of it, and he's like, 'Aren't you going to introduce me to your friend?'"

"Meaning you?"

"Meaning me." Audrey empties her Cosmo and orders another one from the Chinese guy behind the bar. "The next thing I know, Cathy scoots out the door and he starts picking my brain about Artistic Puzzles—there's something very weird about that guy—and then he asks me if I know Charlie Quill or Spencer Casey and where could he find them."

"Meaning us," Charlie mutters, dribbling beer out of the side of his mouth. "I hope you didn't tell him anything, because we can't talk to that insurance guy."

Audrey blinks her eyes like she can't believe what Charlie just said. "You mean you know about the insurance guy already?"

Charlie nods sheepishly. "We're sort of working with Jeff on this."

"Working with Jeff?"

"Yeah, he found us our new jobs—they're good jobs, right Spencer?—and we're not supposed to talk to the insurance guy."

"That's right," I chime in.

"We pretty much promised that to Jeff, didn't we, Spencer?"

"Sure did."

"Because if we talk to the insurance guy," Charlie goes on, "Jeff could lose a ton of money—don't ask me how—and that wouldn't be good for us either."

"It's money he don't deserve," I tell Audrey, "him being not only a jackass but a pimp and a pervert—"

"You don't have to tell me that," she says, and there's sort of an evil gleam in her eyes.

"—but still we don't want him to lose it, cause if that happens we lose our jobs."

She squints at me cross-eyed, like she's thinking hard about something. "Are you blackmailing Jeff?"

"Absolutely not!" Charlie says.

"We're whistleblowers," I explain. "And we told Jeff, we won't blow the whistle long as we have a job."

She gives me a deep, meaningful look, like Aunt Lorraine gives Shawn when she asks him if he stayed in school all day. "What is it that you aren't blowing the whistle on?"

"Exactly what happened to those puzzles that makes them so hard to finish."

"And exactly what did happen?"

"Beats me," Charlie says.

"Might've been something we ate," I admit. "Who knows?"

Audrey starts to laugh. "This is priceless!" she says, clapping her hands together. "You're blackmailing him for something you guys did! Priceless!"

We all have a hoot over that, without agreeing or disagreeing on whether we're blackmailing Jeff, which Charlie keeps saying we're not, or what we'd be blackmailing him about, in case we were. Then out of the blue Charlie asks, "Hey, remember that last night, Mr. Pangborn gave us each one of the puzzles? For good luck? Right before he died?"

"Chaos Scape 19," I tell him. "I've got mine in a safe place."

"So do I," Charlie says. "And it's going to stay there. How about you, Audrey? What'd you do with yours?"

"Oh," she giggles. "I gave mine to Cathy."

Audrey orders another Cosmo and Charlie tosses some money on the bar and leaves me alone with her and before long she's talking about for old times sake and stroking my hand like she's petting a cat. The last time I saw her with that look in her eyes she was dragging me into her glassed in bookkeeper booth and I don't really want any more of that, not on my way to work all night at the testing lab. Luckily I've got my uniform on and my pepper spray canister on my belt so I'm pretty sure I can defend myself if I have to. I stand up and tell Audrey I've got to go to work.

"I love your uniform," she says, running her hand over my chest. "What are you, a cop? A doorman? A train conductor?"

"Night security guard," I tell her. "I work all night, every night. Hardly have time to breathe. Leaves me so weak I can't lift a finger."

"You must have a little energy left over."

"You don't know what Naked Dave is like in that bedroom. Keeping him happy for eight hours is about all I can do."

Her face turns redder than if I'd shot it with my pepper spray. "Spencer, I'm so sorry!" she says. "I didn't realize!"

I tried to tell Monique about my new job (except the part about the awgies) but she's not impressed. "Sounds like the perfect job for you," she says. "Laying around all night."

"I don't lay around all night," I tell her. "There's a whole lot more to it than that."

"Oh, exc-*u-u-u-u-se* me!" she laughs. "I've got it all wrong. Your job is *watching somebody* lay around all night."

Every time she sees me going to work she makes fun of my uniform, calls me the Generalissimo or the Last King of Scotland or asks me where I left my marching band. Now I can hardly set foot on the block in that uniform without getting bricks thrown at me, so I'm switching to gangsta gear—cargo shorts and airbrushed hoodies and rope chains like Shawn puts on when he's practicing his hip hop act in the living room. That outfit gets me out of the neighborhood and onto the bus for the long ride up to the Northeast and then when I get to work I've got to put my uniform on in the men's room. There's a sensor in there that's supposed to turn the lights on when you walk in but usually it don't notice me—I'm the invisible man until I hop around and puff out my chest and rattle my bling and then suddenly the lights flash on and there I am, caught in the mirror, half gangsta, half cop, wondering how I fit into this picture and how would Monique feel if she could see what she drove me to?

16. From the Journal of Erik Anselmus

November 5: Dinner at Pinocchio's. A lucky break: Cathy has one of the puzzles, given to her by Audrey Scalzo. Chaos Scape 19 by Armand Brigantine. She says I can work on it in the back corner booth where nobody sits. Should be a simple matter to put together.

November 6: Picture on the box shows Chaos Scape 19 as a meaningless jumble of lines and colors, no discernible form or pattern. 1000 pieces. First hour—only three pieces matched. Cathy says I can leave it on the table overnight (will spread a tablecloth over it). This could take a couple of days.

17. Trust Me

Audrey had three encounters at Plato's Cave: the first with Erik Anselmus, the second with Jeff Pangborn, and the third with Roberta Pangborn's divorce lawyer, Morton C. McMonigle, Jr., Esq.

She'd expected Erik Anselmus to be weird—Cathy had warned her about that—but she wasn't prepared for his gargantuan size, his near-albino coloration or the oddly vacant look in his eyes. He was all smiles, polite in the condescending European fashion. "I heard all about you from Jeff Pangborn," he said.

"He warned me not to talk to you."

"And yet that's what you're doing."

"Every woman has her price. Mine is in the mid six figures."

There were times when his voice faltered in the middle of something that sounded like a threat and then he cut himself off with a shrug followed by a shy, self-conscious smile. She played it coy and denied knowing anything about the puzzles. Charlie and Spencer? Why would she stay in touch with those two losers? But when it came to Jeff she left her options open, fostering the impression that, given the right incentives, she'd toss him to the dogs. Erik handed her his card with his hotel phone number written on the back. On the front he'd drawn a big question mark and circled it: would she help him out? Before she could answer, she'd need to know a lot more—for one thing, what was in it for her? And for another: what was in it for her?

"I'll think about it," she told him.

The other two meetings ended in a similar fashion. Jeff Pangborn, wearing a pink shirt, a plaid sports coat, and a yellow tie, his hair looking thinner than before, his eyes more sunken, his jaw more slack, tried to persuade her to work for him in his new business venture ("Exciting new project—top secret, can't tell you what it's about—need someone with a strong financial background, not full-time yet, just consulting for now, but trust me, this could turn into something big") and begged her not to talk to Erik Anselmus ("Looks like a Viking-Nazi psycho from outer space, six and a half feet tall, white as a ghost, ice blue eyes like a Siberian husky's"). Audrey hated people—men, they were invariably men, stupid, insinuating, untrustworthy men like Jeff Pangborn—who said "trust me." It was a sure sign (unnecessary in Jeff's case) that they were about to tell you a lie. But wasn't there some way she could cash in on this?

"I've just got two questions," she told Jeff. They were the same two she always had. "One, what's in it for me? And two, what's in it for me?"

"I can make it worth your while," Jeff said.

"I'll think about it."

The next night Audrey was back at Plato's Cave, hoping to relax a little. Living with her mother was driving Audrey to drink and desperation. At the bar she ordered a shrimp salad and tried not to think about Erik Anselmus or Jeff Pangborn.

In the mirror over the bar appeared a man with a speckled complexion and cold, hooded eyes. He wore a shiny greenish suit under a half-open raincoat, as if the fashion statement he wanted to make was a little obscene. He ordered a ginger ale with plenty of ice. Audrey recoiled instinctively when he turned toward her with a crooked, insinuating smile.

"I noticed you in here last night," he said in a dry, croaking voice. "Talking to a friend of mine. Jeff Pangborn."

She studied his reflection out of the corner of her eye. He looked about sixty, though he might have been a few hundred years older. "Jeff doesn't have any friends," she said. "If he was really a friend of yours, you'd know that."

The man chuckled and took a tiny sip of his ginger ale. "Well, then let's say I'm a friend of his wife's."

"Roberta?"

"Her lawyer, in fact."

"Her divorce lawyer?"

"Precisely." He pulled a business card from his jacket pocket like a magician releasing a dove from his palm and laid it down in front of her, taking pains to align it perfectly with the edge of the bar.

"Morton C. McMonigle, Jr., Esquire," Audrey read. "Well, not to rain on your parade, Mort, but Jeff considers you about ten levels below pond scum."

McMonigle winced. "That's harsh. Though I can see why he might hold that view. I represent a woman he abused and deceived for twenty years before tossing her out, bringing a prostitute into her bed and doing everything in his power to alienate her from her children."

"A lunatic, he calls her—"

"That's an exaggeration."

—"who sicced the dog on him and tried to decapitate him with a butcher knife."

"It was a French chef's knife," McMonigle admonished. "And let the record reflect that the dog is only about six inches high."

"The record? You wearing a wire?"

"Just a figure of speech."

After some further repartee, McMonigle cut to the chase. His client had reason to believe that her husband was diverting money out of the marital estate—their joint assets—from which she was entitled, under applicable law, to an equitable distribution. Evidently he had found some devilishly clever way to do it, which so far had evaded detection. If Audrey could see her way to renewing her business relationship with Jeff, gaining access to certain confidential information such as banking records that could be used in the divorce proceedings, then "hypothetically" (McMonigle stressed), a good deal of money might be headed her way.

Eyeing her salad fork, Audrey was sorely tempted to pluck out the attorney's eyes and stomp them into the classical Greek tile floor. Instead she swiveled to her feet, slipped on her jacket and flashed her deadliest smile. "I'll think about it," she said.

Audrey had a lot to think about. Should she chose sides in what was shaping up as a titanic struggle between a jackass, a sleaze bucket and a psychopath—in this lineup she almost felt sympathetic to Jeff, though in fairness he might have qualified in any of those categories—or sit on the sidelines and watch his adversaries hammer him into the ground? Should she throw him to the dogs—his wife and her lawyer—to have his bones picked clean? Or leave him to the tender mercies of the insurance industry, to be processed, adjusted, appraised, arbitraged, assessed, collateralized, denied, reinstated, reinsured, subrogated, surcharged and in the end, ground painstakingly into dust? It gave her a delicious thrill to contemplate the serendipitous position she found herself in, the sense of freedom and power she couldn't have hoped for in her wildest dreams.

18. Quality Time

Charlie began the day with the same dumb joke he'd blurted out every morning for the past sixteen years: "Penny for your thoughts?"

Penny turned away in disgust. Shuttling between kitchen and dining room, she was mustering the resources needed for the day's first major onslaught—plates, cereal bowls, juice glasses, silverware, coffee cups for herself and Charlie, milk, butter, orange juice and creamer from the fridge—while Charlie manned the Great Wall of Cereal, a six-foot barricade of cereal boxes arrayed on an island separating the two rooms. It was almost 7:30. The school bus would arrive at the corner in less than twenty minutes.

"Hey, c'mon!" he tried again. "What are you thinking?"

What am I thinking? About the life I could've had if I didn't let myself get stuck in this rut, and maybe I still could if you'd stop complaining and let me get my real estate license, not that it's just about money, no, just the opposite really, what I think about most of the time are the people I'd meet and the places I'd go if I could break out of this zoo and lose about fifty pounds and have a little money to spend on myself, join a gym, take care of my hair and be able to buy some decent clothes for a change... "Nothing," Penny said.

Breakfast at the Quill home was a serious business. There were calories to ingest, thousands of them, and no time for idle chatter. The kids, mouths working furiously in a race against time, observed a rule of silence, except for unavoidable grunting, gasping, chomping, gnawing and belching, which, in any case, perfectly expressed their innermost thoughts. Penny stood aside sipping her coffee, intervening occasionally to help someone cut their sausages or mop up their spilled orange juice.   Her innermost thoughts were a skein of sarcasm, complaint, self-pity, taunts and recriminations, and thus better left unsaid. Charlie, as always, was completely lacking in innermost thoughts.

"More pancakes!" Sean shouted as he gulped down the last of his Cocoa Puffs.

"Me first," said Bridget, holding out her plate.

"Butter," said Megan. "Syrup."

"Whoa!" Charlie laughed. "Didn't you miss something?" He'd stopped at Costco the night before for a two-pound slab of thick-sliced, maple-cured bacon, which Penny had just finished frying up. He held up the frying pan piled high with bacon slices. "How many slices can everyone eat?"

"Ten!" shouted Sean.

"Twelve!" countered Brian.

"Going once! Going twice!"

"Fifteen!" yelled Bridget, elbowing Brian off his chair.

"Sold!" Charlie declared. "To the lady in the orange Flyers shirt. How's that for survival of the fittest!"

He tipped the frying pan in front of Bridget, then pulled it back. "Wait a minute! Mom gets first dibs. Honey, how many for you?"

You just don't get it, Charlie, you think if you feed us that should be enough, like we're still at the Neanderthal stage, but you ought to know better, you never stop talking, even in front of the kids, about Darwin and evolution, as if we're a bunch of monkeys who should worship you and greet you at the door with our tongues hanging out in hopes that you'll feed us, which you never do anyway... "None for me, thanks," Penny said.

"What's the matter? Not organic enough for you!"

Half the time we'd starve if it wasn't for Jim Grillo, who really likes the kids and wants to see them get their weight under control so they don't have heart attacks by the time they're thirty-five, but you, when you're not thinking about food, are so obsessed with sex you've got it in your head that Jim and I are sleeping together and I don't mind letting you think that, if you want to, let you squirm a little if that's what it takes to remind you that other men find me attractive... "No," she said. "Not nearly as long and stiff as one of Jim Grillo's celery stalks."

The kids' faces dipped over their troughs and the distinct jingle of tittering could be heard above the cacophony of gnashing, slurping, guzzling and gobbling, especially from the direction of Bridget and Megan.

Charlie was nonplussed. "I can't believe you said that!"

I was considered beautiful in high school, made sixth regional runner up in the Miss Teen Pennsylvania contest, I could have had any number of other guys plus a successful singing career if I didn't get pregnant and have to marry you, yeah we had to get married, that's what I thought, that's what my mother told me and you went along with it, even though I had a great singing voice and a cute figure and could've gone on American Idol or whatever they had back then but I thought you'd do okay... "Sorry," Penny laughed. "I just get sick of hearing you knock Jim all the time."

"More French toast!" cried Brian.

"More oatmeal!" demanded Sean.

"More eggs!" shouted Bridget.

"More sausage!" yelled Megan.

"You see, they don't want that organic crap!" Charlie said. "They want real, red-blooded American food! That's because they're healthy kids! Not emaciated swamp rats from some refugee camp like Jim Grillo's kids!"

You said the factory job was just a stopgap to save some money so you could go back to school, I don't know if I believed you but at least I didn't think you'd work there fifteen years stamping out jigsaw puzzles while we stayed trapped in this pit with your parents, all six of us, me, you and the kids squeezed into two rooms until we finally got your parents into a nursing home, thank God, and not a minute too soon or it would've been me changing their diapers for the rest of my life... "It's time to stop eating and get ready for school," Penny said. "The bus'll be out there in five minutes."

"Just one more bowl of Frosted Flakes?"

"Just one more muffin?"

"Can't I have another glass of milk?"

"I didn't get any eggs benedict!"

Charlie beamed with pride. "I wish my parents were still here to see this."

You're like an old man already, you expect me to humor you, cater to your whims because suddenly you're a big shot selling Tummy Tweezers to fat doctors, though you still haven't sold any, they laugh at you because you look like one of their patients, you drive up in a clunker and probably take them to lunch at Denny's and ask for a doggie bag, oh if they only knew what a loser you are! "OK, but hurry up," Penny told the kids. "I don't want to have to drive you."

The kids lumbered off to brush their teeth as Charlie slipped his arm around Penny's waist and tried to pull her toward him. "Honey, we have a lot to look forward to. Things are turning around, they really are. I know I haven't always lived up to your dreams, I haven't always been Mr. Perfect—"

You throw our salad into the garbage disposal, you bully the kids, burst into tears at the drop of a hat—this is what I'm saddled with, or under, though I'm still young, still in my thirties, I could've married one of those doctors, I still could, if I could just get my real estate license and lose a few pounds... "Let me go!" she squirmed away.

"—but trust me, I've been thinking, we're almost out of the woods. We just need to work together, see things through. Things can change, things can improve..."

Penny stood by the front door, squeezing the kids into their hats and coats, making sure they weren't forgetting their homework or their instruments or their sports clothes or their lunches, kissing them goodbye, and when they were all out the door she turned around and went upstairs without a backward glance or any response to what Charlie had said.

And now you say you're waiting for things to change around here. Just what kind of change are you thinking of? Is it sex? Dream on, Charlie! Jim isn't even paying me and he's way closer to scoring that bull's eye than you've been for a long time. If you think that's what's going to change around here, you've got a lot more thinking to do!

19. From the Journal of Erik Anselmus

November 8: Still struggling with the puzzle. Only five pieces connected so far. Cathy says give it time. Drinking too much wine with dinner. Hold off on report to Administration.

November 9: Up to 9 pieces and can't seem to get any farther. Did I start with the wrong piece?

November 12: Still only 11 pieces connected. Consider starting over. Realize now that the first piece chosen (1 out of 1000) determines the next choice (1 out of 999) and so on, in a branching pattern. Will I ever find my way out of this labyrinth? Harder and harder to concentrate with recurring migraine attacks.

20. Desperate Housewives

Jeff Pangborn wondered if it was his fate to be tortured by women. First Roberta—how had he stayed married to that lunatic for twenty years?—with her incessant demands for money and her slimy divorce lawyer Morton C. McMonigle, Jr., Esq. The two of them had concocted a petition, based on Jeff's alleged bad character, asking the Orphan's Court to place Lindsay and Zachary in their mother's custody as soon as she got out of rehab. They'd bring in psychiatrists, social workers, jilted ex-girlfriends, cranky neighbors, vindictive former employees, all to vouch for his bad character and general unfitness for life on this planet, and everything—"I mean everything," Jeff's lawyer said—would be viewed from the woman's point of view, as if it were not a court hearing but some female sobfest on afternoon TV. All right, he was a jackass: selfish and passive-aggressive like his father, ill-tempered and paranoid like his mother, not exactly the caring, sensitive guy you're supposed to be today if you expect to get laid. But so what? He meant well, he did what he could, he supported his family; he even went out of his way to help people sometimes. Roberta knew he was a self-centered lout when she married him. She must have seen it as insurance, like a man who marries an ugly woman so he can be sure of having her to himself. Well, it didn't work. He'd had plenty of other women, secretaries at his office, nymphos he'd picked up in bars, even bug-eyed Audrey, his father's bookkeeper, who he'd once had sex with on the couch in the old man's office. She'd turned out to be a wack job, claiming he raped her and threatening to castrate him with an X-acto knife, so after that he was more careful. When he met Kellie at the Pickwick Club in Center City, he let the situation gel slowly, instead of just dragging her into bed. Dinners at nice restaurants, expensive gifts, Saturdays at the beach when he was supposed to be golfing with clients. By the time they slept together he realized he'd blundered into a relationship. Not that it was a bad relationship. Kellie saw through his weaknesses and accepted him for what he was, the good with the bad and the ugly. But when Roberta found one of his pornographic videos of Kellie on his cell phone and chased him out of the house with a French chef's knife at three in the morning, siccing Cupcake on him as he fled toward his Mercedes, he knew he'd made a serious mistake. The next day she took Lindsay on that fatal shoplifting spree and ended up in jail—and now she was scheming with McMonigle to take the house, the kids, the dog (thank God) and every last dime of his savings. All he'd been looking for was a little fun and some fresh footage for his fantasy life.

That was why he'd been so excited about Alex, the 25-year-old exotic dancer he'd met on Craigslist. The great thing about the internet is that you can flirt with a woman to your heart's content without having to take her out to dinner. You can be whatever you want to be—suave, strong, sexy—just by imagining it and writing it down. But conducting an affair over the web carries some risks that were only now becoming apparent. In the past week Kellie had been quiet, brooding, uninterested in sex. Since he hadn't told her about the foreclosure or his other financial problems—she still thought he was rich—he could imagine just one explanation: she'd found the messages between him and Alex on his phone. That would also explain why Alex had stopped sending new messages. He made a mental note to change his password.

Slipping upstairs after a dinner of microwaved leftovers—how was it possible to serve leftovers six nights a week?—he peeked at his phone and his worst fears were confirmed. Kellie had not only found the messages, she'd erased them all.

Kellie had been moody and distant in the past few days, but for a reason Jeff never suspected. One evening after class she'd stopped for a drink at one of her old haunts, the Pickwick Club on South 16th Street, which ironically was where she'd met Jeff. It was a somewhat seedy retreat for jaded office workers and neighborhood cranks, where many a makeshift love affair had been cobbled together in the twilight hours before the salesmen and lawyers and secretaries who gathered there went home to their families. Sipping a vodka martini at the piano bar, she became aware of an unwelcome presence beside her—a man of about sixty, with sharp eyes and a slack jaw, eyes hooded and insinuating. He looked cold, shiny, like a lizard in a suit and tie. He introduced himself as Morton C. McMonigle, Jr., Esquire, attorney at law.

"I have a proposition for you," he smiled. And he went on to propose that Kellie provide needed assistance to Roberta in her custody battle with Jeff. "If you were to testify for Mrs. Pangborn, you could corroborate her testimony about the source of the marital problems that led to the divorce—i.e., Mr. Pangborn's illicit affairs, one of which happens to be with you—as well as any other observations you have made about his conduct and character. We recognize that for you to do this would entail significant financial sacrifice, for which in all fairness you should be compensated."

"You're offering to pay me to switch sides?"

McMonigle shook his head. "That would be unethical. And of course we realize you wouldn't consider doing such a thing if you were committed to Mr. Pangborn for the long haul. But if the relationship isn't all you hoped it would be, then why not make your exit now? Especially if he's not going to marry you."

"Maybe he is."

"Well, this may be a total fabrication—you know, just the kind of thing the jilted wife would say—but my client asserts that her daughter reported that Mr. Pangborn told her not to worry, there's no way he'd ever marry you."

"Jeff wouldn't say that to Lindsay."

"*Not in a million years.* I believe those were his exact words."

Kellie could feel her insides turning over. She wanted to knock Morton C. McMonigle, Jr., Esq., off his barstool and kick him in the teeth. Instead she asked him calmly, "How much are we talking about?"

"Low six figures," he said in a barely audible voice. "Very low. In fact the lowest six figure number you can imagine."

"A hundred thousand?"

"Your words, not mine."

Kellie left the bar without giving McMonigle an answer, but she spent the next week stewing over Jeff's declaration that he wouldn't marry her in a million years. The more she brooded, the closer she came to accepting McMonigle's offer. Jeff had been acting strangely, sheepish and belligerent at the same time, as if he was mustering the courage to tell her their relationship must end. She dreaded those words, at the same time welcoming them with a secret hope. But when the confrontation came it was about something she hadn't even begun to suspect.

One night as she lounged on the sofa watching "Desperate Housewives," Jeff muted the TV and said: "Kellie, I swear: I've never met that woman and I never intended to. It was just a little internet flirtation, that's all. Nothing but a bunch of harmless text messages!"

In his desperation he confessed to everything—meeting Alex on Craigslist under the name "Steve," exchanging pictures with her, sending erotic messages back and forth—and Kellie, amazed at her own presence of mind, pretended to know what he was talking about. One of the kids, probably Lindsay, must have found the messages on his phone and erased them.

For dramatic effect, Kellie grabbed a vase off the end table and hurled it into the fireplace. She burst into tears. "How could you do this to me?"

21. From the Journal of Erik Anselmus

November 13: No progress. Cathy advises me to take a couple nights off, but I can't stop. Insomnia three nights in a row.

November 16: Another night's work added only one piece—now 12 pieces connected. Back to hotel for another sleepless night. How long is this going to take? Laptop can't handle the calculation. Do it by hand:

> Assume 1,000 pieces and that each piece offers four choices for the next move.
>
> Total number of possible pathways through the puzzle: 1,000! × 41,000, or roughly 4.62 × 103169.
>
> Time required to calculate each one of those pathways, using the most powerful computer known to man:
> Trillions of years (far longer than our universe will exist).
>
> Eternity, in other words.

How could a depiction of infinite chaos be made within a two-dimensional rectangle no larger than a table top?

22. Doggie Bags

Tuesday was a big day for Charlie—his first business lunch with a potential customer. Bill Symonds had suggested that he cold-call Dr. Wilmer Kaspar, a bariatric surgeon who advertised on daytime TV, and to his surprise the doctor had taken his call and even accepted the invitation. As to venue, Charlie considered Wendy's and the Burger King, but in the end he decided to go all out and take the doctor to lunch at the Denny's on Roosevelt Boulevard. He knew he'd have good luck there because that was where he proposed to Penny.

"I don't usually eat at places like this," Dr. Kaspar sniffed as they stepped inside. He was about fifty, bespectacled, and surprisingly pear-shaped for a man in his field.

"Well, this is a special occasion," Charlie said. "And it's my treat. You can order whatever you want."

A perky waitress who introduced herself as Megan handed them a pair of unwieldy plastic menus and asked them every thirty seconds if they were ready to order. Dr. Kaspar studied his menu for a long time and finally ordered a bowl of New England clam chowder, a grilled chicken salad, and a BLT on whole wheat toast with a double helping of fries.

"Can I get a drink here?" he asked the waitress, explaining to Charlie: "I usually have a couple of martinis before going into surgery. You know, to steady my nerves."

"Sorry, sir," said Megan. "We don't serve alcohol. Can I get you a Coke or a Sprite?"

They talked about sports for a while—the Eagles were having a good season—but Dr. Kaspar quickly changed the subject to himself and his role as chief bariatric surgeon at a local hospital, where the equipment was outdated and the doctors poorly trained, overworked and underpaid. By the time they ordered dessert—Charlie had a bowl of vanilla ice cream and Dr. Kaspar the German chocolate cake—his face was florid and he was stammering with indignation as he denounced the pernicious effects of government healthcare policy. It surprised Charlie to learn that most physicians today, contrary to their reputation as rich, country-club-belonging, Mercedes-driving, Caribbean-vacationing, shore-house-owning, upper-class tax cheats, can hardly make ends meet.

"They won't pay us the value of what we do," Dr. Kaspar growled, shoveling the last forkful of German chocolate cake into his mouth, "but they expect us to keep on doing it. How long do you think that can go on?"

"Not very long," Charlie said.

"You're damn straight." Dr. Kaspar flung his fork down on the table. "The government's got to learn: there's no such thing as a free lunch."

He drained the rest of his coffee and motioned for a refill. "Mind if I order another dessert?" he asked Charlie.

"No problem," Charlie smiled, fending off Megan's attempt to clear the table. "In fact, why don't you get two more? Just to see which one you like best?"

He ordered apple pie and the New York cheese cake, and Charlie asked for a piece of strawberry shortcake as well. "I like you, Charlie," Dr. Kaspar said. "Why don't you come by the hospital next week and show me that new stapling device of yours?"

"I'll check my calendar and see if I can squeeze you in."

Dr. Kaspar's eyes, as it turned out, had been bigger than his considerable stomach. He'd finished his soup and the chocolate cake but left half of his grilled chicken salad and half of his fries, sparing room for the cheese cake, which disappeared without a trace. But his apple pie and strawberry shortcake had been scarcely touched, and in the end he looked a little green, as if he might not be able to perform any bariatric surgery that afternoon.

"If you'll excuse me, I need to use the facilities," he said.

"No problem."

With the doctor safely out of sight, Charlie called Megan back to the table. "I can't bear to see this food go to waste," he told her. "You know, with all those people starving in Africa. Could you put it in a doggie bag?"

"One for you and one for the other gentleman?"

"Just one."

When Charlie went home that night, his kids stood waiting for him at the kitchen door. They must have sensed that he had food in the plastic bag and it was meant for them. Without a word they snatched it out of his hands and carried it to the table, where they divvied it up and began to scarf it down.

"Where'd you get this strawberry shortcake?" Bridget gagged. "It sucks!"

"Jim took us to Applebee's," Brian explained. "Their apple pie's a lot better than this."

Charlie glared at his wife. "What this? He's taking them out for dessert now? Is he going to come over next week with our Thanksgiving dinner?"

Penny braced herself for another all-night whine-fest. But luckily the phone rang and she answered it, handing the cordless receiver to Charlie. "You have a phone call."

Charlie took the phone into the living room and sat down. It was Jeff Pangborn calling from a traffic jam on the Schuylkill Expressway, his voice fading in and out with the road noise. He was in a nasty mood. "Has that insurance guy been in touch with you?" he asked.

Charlie tried to keep his voice down. "Naw, I haven't heard from him."

"He's been pestering me and I keep telling him I don't know you. But it's only a matter of time before he tracks you down and asks you about those puzzles."

"You think so?"

"What are you going to say when he finds you?"

"Nothing. What would I know?"

"That's right," Jeff said. "You're a moron."

"Right."

"What would you know?"

"Nothing."

"You got it."

Jeff shouted an obscenity at another driver—at least Charlie hoped it was at another driver and not at him. He decided to ignore it.

"I could snap my fingers," Jeff said, "and you'd be out of a job."

Charlie didn't like the way the conversation was going, and he was glad Penny couldn't hear it. It was time to use the Free Food Principle. "Jeff, listen," he said, "I just want to say, you know, thanks for everything. I don't know what I would've done—"

"You would have starved."

"Right. So when this is all over, I want to take you out for a nice dinner, to show my appreciation. You and your family. At a really nice restaurant, with linen tablecloths, mixed drinks, appetizers, steaks, seafood, a salad bar—"

"Forget about it."

Sometimes, Charlie had learned, people resist free food. Sometimes you practically have to shove it down their throats. "I insist!" he said—that wasn't a word he used often: it flew off his tongue before he knew where it was going—"I mean..."

"What'd you say?" Jeff asked. "You're breaking up."

"I insist," he muttered, wishing he could stop himself.

There was a long silence.   "OK, we'll see," Jeff said. "What about your friend Spencer?"

"He can come too. We'll go to a nice—"

"No, I mean are you keeping your eye on him?   Is he sticking to the program?"

"I think so."

"You think so? I hope you can do better than that."

"Sure," Charlie said. "Sure I can."

"I stuck my neck pretty far out to get you that job."

"Yeah, and I owe you."

"Yes, you do. So don't make me regret it."

Dr. Kaspar complained to Bill Symonds about Charlie's choice of restaurants.   "Frankly, I'm incredulous," Bill said, pulling Charlie into his office. "You took him to Denny's?"

"They had a special on the grilled chicken salad," Charlie explained.

"It was made with iceberg lettuce," Bill frowned, checking his notes of the conversation with Dr. Kaspar.   "The clam chowder tasted like the can it came out of. The fries were soggy. And he couldn't even get a martini, even though he was scheduled for surgery that afternoon."

To make amends, Charlie took Dr. Kaspar to Applebee's, which had been touted by his kids for its superior desserts. Dr. Kaspar didn't seem to like Applebee's any better than Denny's, though he was able to down two martinis before Charlie finished his Sprite. When it was time for dessert he ordered apple pie, rice pudding and a piece of carrot cake with ice cream. The lunch had been a success, Charlie thought, with the doctor edging closer to letting him demonstrate the Tummy Tweezer at the hospital.

Then, just as the waitress left the check, a sudden drama erupted that would change Charlie's life forever. Dr. Kaspar emitted a dry cough and started pawing at his necktie. His eyes bugged out, sweat poured off his forehead and he turned beet red. Conversation at nearby tables dropped to a whisper, waitresses and busboys stopped in their tracks, the hardhats at the bar swiveled on their barstools, as a time-warped moment of paralysis gripped the restaurant.

Charlie leaped up (heroically, he told Penny that night) and whacked Dr. Kaspar between the shoulder blades, discharging what appeared to be a petrified raisin onto the table. It could have been something much worse—a chunk of rat poison, for example, or a mouse turd—but before Charlie could see what it was, an athletic-looking manager wearing a short-sleeve shirt and a bright red tie swooped in and snatched the offending item off the table.

"I'm so sorry!" the manager said. "Are you all right, sir?"

Dr. Kaspar gawked at him, gasping, his color still high.

"Nothing like this has ever happened before!" The manager slid the check off the table and held it up for all to see. "I've got this covered," he said. "The whole meal is on the house."

Dr. Kaspar struggled to his feet and made his way to the men's room.

"Say, miss!" Charlie called to the waitress. "Could you put all this stuff in a doggie bag?"

She stared at him goggle-eyed. "But the manager said you don't have to pay for it."

"Yeah, but I'm still going to need that doggie bag."

23. My Dad's Girlfriend, by Lindsay Pangborn

I just can't get Spencer out of my mind. I call and text him all the time but he never answers or texts back, it's like I don't even exist. And what would my Dad say if he caught us talking to each other, even through a little hole in a wall like Paramus and Frisbee? Star-crossed lovers, that's what Mr. Siegal would call us, like Romeo and Juliet, which is what we're reading now. Kellie would be so jealous if she found out!

Last night Kellie came to my room after dinner and closed the door. I was lying on my bed watching TV for my Islamic Civilization class. "I know you found those messages between your Dad and Alex," she said in a soft voice. "I know you deleted them, and I know you've got them on your phone or your computer. Now let me see them."

I felt sick to my stomach. "Does my Dad know?"

"He knows they were deleted, but he thinks I did it."

"You're not going to tell him it was me, are you?"

"Not if you let me see them."

Then I sort of lost it. I started rolling around on the bed, pulling out fistfuls of my hair. "I was just trying to protect him," I sobbed. "They're not going to send him to jail, are they? I tried to keep Alex from getting the wrong idea about Dad, or blaming him, or being too upset with him. I pretended to be him and even told her I'm a girl her own age, but that didn't—"

"Her own age?" Kellie interrupted. "What do you mean, her own age?"

"Alex is fourteen, just like me."

Kellie sat down on the bed beside me and for a second she looked like she might start crying too. Then all of a sudden it was like a light bulb flashed over her head. She smiled like a saint in one of those pictures in the Art Museum.

She reached out and wiped away my tears and stroked my hair. "Nobody needs to know about this, Lindsay," she whispered. "It can be our little secret, just you and me. You haven't told anyone else about this, have you?"

"No."

"Promise me you won't say anything to anyone. Whatever happens."

"I won't. I promise."

"You'd better keep texting to Alex or she might blame your Dad. Keep texting until I tell you to stop."

"OK."

"I'll handle this, Lindsay. Trust me. Now let me see those messages."

One night Charlie, the fat guy who worked with Spencer at the puzzle factory, showed up at the front door and asked for my Dad, who wasn't home. Kellie invited him in but he just stood in the doorway (which might have been because of Cupcake, who was trying to get his teeth around his ankle, or it might have been because Kellie was blocking his way and trying to peer around him to see if Spencer was out in the car). Charlie said he needed to talk to Dad, but Kellie was determined to find out why he'd come. She peppered him with questions until he finally sputtered out something I couldn't understand and pulled an envelope out of his pocket and handed it to Kellie. It was an invitation to dinner at Le Papillon Libre, which Kellie says is the fanciest restaurant in Philadelphia, on December 21st, to celebrate his wife's birthday. There was a picture of Charlie's smiling wife and kids, all stuffed into Eagles jerseys, on the front of the invitation. *"The honor of your presence is requested,"* Kellie read out loud—it was one of those engraved cards that cost about ten dollars apiece—and then she laughed as if she thought Charlie was a rude mechanical who had no business eating in such fancy restaurants or sending such fancy invitations, which is what she told me later. Charlie blushed a little and said, "I just want to show my appreciation for everything Jeff has done for me."

"That's very nice," Kellie said, smiling like an evil queen. "I'll talk to Jeff about it."

"I'll call him myself too," Charlie said. "Tell him I'll call him—"

"Is Spencer going to be there?" she interrupted.

"He's invited. He's definitely invited."

Kellie started laughing again as soon as Charlie left, but she marked December 21st on the calendar because, she told me, my Dad has never taken her to Le Papillon Libre or any place half as nice and she's determined to go, even if it means eating dinner with a supersized Tummy Tweezer salesman and his corn-fed wife. I winced when she said that. If Kellie'd ever taken Honors English with Mr. Siegal and read *A Midsummer Night's Dream,* she'd know that you shouldn't make fun of rude mechanicals, even if you're a queen, or you might fall in love with one of them, or wake up with the head of an ass, or an ass for a head, or something like that.

24. From the Journal of Erik Anselmus

November 17: Cathy says I'm crazy. There's only one solution to the puzzle, she says. All the forking paths lead to the same place: a reproduction of Chaos Scape 19 that could be assembled by the average 12-year-old in a couple of rainy afternoons. What am I doing wrong?

November 19: TV special on Stephen Hawking. Hawking is completely paralyzed except for a single muscle in one of his cheeks, which he twitches in order to communicate through a voice-generating computer. He sits in a wheelchair ruminating about the fate of Schrödinger's cat, who, under the laws of quantum mechanics, is both dead and alive, and about the constant bifurcation of the universe into an endless labyrinth of parallel worlds.

I burst out in tears when I hear Hawking say that.

November 22: Up to 14 pieces but increasing desperation. Cathy very sweet, trying to make me feel better. Says there isn't any right way to do the puzzle. Just put it together, she says. If you keep thinking about all the possibilities, you'll never finish it.

Never finishing it—is that even a possibility?

25. Giant Locusts Eat Swath Across Three Counties

The day after Thanksgiving, on the appropriately named Black Friday, Charlie treated his family to dinner at Buonanno's Pizza on Roosevelt Boulevard. He was locked in an escalating arms race with Jim Grillo, who had appeared at their door three days before with an entire Thanksgiving feast: a turkey which, Jim emphasized, had never set foot in a cage (for some reason that seemed to be important) and had been killed by lethal injection, stuffing made from whole-grain bread baked in a brick oven, sweet potatoes, green beans and cranberry sauce boasting an organic pedigree so pure that they made Charlie hanker for a whiff of DDT. Naturally he'd wished he could provide a Thanksgiving dinner with all the trimmings, but he was yet to receive a paycheck larger than the deductions. He'd made reservations for Penny's birthday at Le Papillon Libre—that would be the day of judgment, when Jim Grillo's pretensions and ambitions would bite the dust. In the meantime he'd match Jim tit for tat, raising his bid as high as necessary to stay on top of the game. Of course he needed luck—he was counting on it. He'd always been a lucky person. And Buonanno's Pizza was as good a place to try his luck as any.

As the hostess led them to their booth—it was actually more like a corral, a roped-off area near the kitchen used for corporate functions—Charlie kept his eye peeled for the opportunity he hoped for. He found it on the window ledge beside the booths, where several generations of flies had breathed their last. Scooping a handful of the dead flies into his pocket, he followed the family to their table, where he entertained them with amusing anecdotes about his life as a Tummy Tweezer salesman. After a modest repast of personal-size 14-inch deluxe pizzas for all (except Penny, who ordered a chicken caesar salad), the waitress left the check, which he studied carefully until Penny excused herself to visit the ladies' room. Without delay he waved to the waitress, and as she circled back toward the table he reached in his pocket and covered the kids' plates with a generous sprinkling of dead flies.

"Oh my God!" Bridget gasped. A chorus of "Yuk!"'s followed as the kids gagged and clutched their throats. The waitress stood speechless beside the table, signaling to the manager.

"Will you look at this!" Charlie demanded in a voice that could be heard all over the restaurant. "You're feeding dead flies to my kids!"

The manager loomed over the table. "Is there a problem, sir?"

Charlie beckoned him closer and lowered his voice. "Just tear that check up and no one will get hurt."

The manager plucked the check off the table and tore it in half, stuffing the pieces into his jacket pocket. Then he turned and walked away, and by the time Penny returned from the ladies' room Charlie was on his feet, wiping the fingerprints off his silverware before tossing his napkin on the table. "OK, kids, we're out of here," he said.

"Did you pay?" Penny asked.

"Yeah, it's all taken care of."

This scenario replayed itself—with minor variations (thumb tacks, fish hooks or mouse turds instead of flies, etc.)—on a daily basis along a 30-mile strip of U.S. 1 from Bensalem to Bala

Cynwyd, as the Quills ate a swath across three counties and struck terror into the hearts of restaurant managers everywhere. The managers knew it was a scam, of course, but with all the other customers looking on, what choice did they have but to let themselves be robbed? Disturbing questions were raised in restaurant industry chatrooms: Was this really a "family," as the news media reported, or an accomplished gang of thieves? Surely those enormous "children" could only be hardened criminals in cunning disguise. And the woman—purportedly the "Mom" of the family—always seemed to be off powdering her nose when "Dad" (dubbed the "White Whale" by the media) pulled the trigger. Was she innocent?—or (as the media speculated, based on the White Whale's idiotic appearance) the mastermind of the operation? Fortunately the Philadelphia Police, dedicated to protecting the city from evildoers of every description, rose to the occasion and put two of their best men on the case, Detective Bob "Mean" Kampf and Officer Dennis Gilboy of the 41st District.

At GastroPlonix, Charlie found himself under growing pressure to close the deal with Dr. Kaspar. "Remember what I told you about the three-date rule?" Bill Symonds asked him at a meeting with Dr. Patel. "Well, for Dr. Kaspar it's time for the third date. You took him to Appleby's, you took him to Denny's—it's amazing he'd even consider going to lunch with you after that—but now you're going to take him someplace with linen tablecloths and a full bar and fresh salmon and tuna on the menu. Don't worry, it can all go on your expense account."

"It's like taking a woman out on a date," Dr. Patel explained.

"That's right," Bill Symonds agreed, "and when you do that, what's your goal? To get into her pants—in the case of Dr. Kaspar, into his operating room."

"It's not a perfect analogy," Dr. Patel observed.

"Of course not. But you get the idea, right, Charlie?"

"Sure."

Bill Symonds leaned forward as he brought his point home. "Soften her up with a free lunch, and then"—he dropped into his lewd ventriloquist voice—"take out your magic twanger and show her how it works!"

"Him, in this case," said Dr. Patel. "Show him how it works."

"Right," Bill Symonds agreed.

"And show him the Tummy Tweezer, not your magic twanger."

"I think I get it," Charlie said.

"See, here's the thing," Bill Symonds said, suddenly serious. "You might have to assist at a few operations to get Dr. Kaspar started. Dr. Patel will give you some pointers."

"After you study the owner's manual," Dr. Patel added.

"Me?" Charlie laughed. "Seriously"—he raised his hands, wiggling the five bulbous protuberances on each—"I'm a klutz."

"It couldn't be all that different from the equipment you operated at the puzzle factory," Dr. Patel said.

"Yeah, but look what I did with that." He turned his left hand over to display the self-inflicted reproduction of the Mona Lisa.

Bill Symonds and Dr. Patel gawked at Charlie's hand and then at each other as if they'd just discovered the Shroud of Turin.

"Are you thinking what I'm thinking?" Bill Symonds asked Dr. Patel.

Dr. Patel nodded eagerly.

"This might be just what we needed. Branding."

At lunch, Dr. Kaspar seemed anxious about the operation scheduled for later that afternoon. He downed three vodka martinis in the first fifteen minutes and ordered a bottle of chianti to drink with his meal. Charlie had chosen Toro's, one of the top lunch venues in Northeast Philadelphia, which boasted linen tablecloths, red velvet upholstery and waiters dressed like matadors. Dr. Kaspar seemed satisfied with the menu selections—he ordered one of each and a box to carry them home. He complained about the government, insurance companies and the high cost of living, and Charlie agreed with everything he said. By the time Charlie paid the check with his corporate American Express card, the doctor's speech was slurred and belligerent and he was unsteady on his feet. Charlie had to drive him to the hospital in his van, which burned a quart of oil every ten miles. It was a company car, he lied.

At the hospital, Charlie struggled to get Dr. Kaspar out of the van and through the revolving door. A security guard rolled up a wheelchair but the doctor shoved it aside, threatening to have him fired. They headed straight to the operating room, where they both scrubbed and dressed for the operation.

Wrapping himself in a pair of enormous surgical gowns, Charlie donned a mask and goggles and pulled gauze slippers over his shoes. *If Penny could see me now!* he thought. *I look just like a doctor. Only it's better than that—I'm here to tell the doctor what to do!* He'd studied the Tummy Tweezer owner's manual and the FAQs. He'd even consulted the SAQs (Seldom Asked Questions) which weren't on the website, such as "Why doesn't my Tummy Tweezer™ turn on when I push the Power button?" (Answer: "Batteries not included. Please insert four AA batteries before operating") and the NAQs (Never Asked Questions), such as "What should I do if the patient's heart stops beating?" and "What should I do if I can't find the patient's stomach?" With this preparation he felt comfortable demonstrating the Tummy Tweezer under "real life" conditions. The only question was whether Dr. Kaspar would be able to stay on his feet long enough to perform the operation.

In the operating room they were met by an anesthesiologist and a nurse, also in gowns, goggles and gloves, who looked like they'd just arrived from outer space. The unconscious patient, draped on both ends, filled an oversized operating table. All Charlie could see was an enormous shaved stomach that might have belonged to a man or a woman.

"Look at that stomach!" Dr. Kaspar growled, reaching for a scalpel. "They're all fat! Every last one of them is fat!"

Obese, Charlie thought, his mind spinning. *Overweight. Of course they are, that's the whole—*

Dr. Kaspar shook the scalpel at Charlie as if reading his thoughts. "And don't call me a fat doctor!"

Swaying across the table, Dr. Kaspar carved into the stomach and reached most of his left arm inside as blood spurted out over his scrubs. Then with his right hand he picked up the Tummy Tweezer and groped at the controls. "How do you do this? Dammit, I can't get this thing to work!"

Charlie steadied his hand and showed him how to push the buttons. "See," he said in a soothing voice, "it's just like one of those Black and Deckers you get at Lowe's."

It was the wrong thing to say. Dr. Kaspar shoved the Tummy Tweezer back at Charlie and staggered away. "Dammit! I didn't go to medical school to be a carpet layer!"

He stumbled into a corner and slid to the floor in a sitting position. Charlie felt wobbly on his feet, light-headed, explosively hot under all the gear. The table looked more like the scene of an autopsy than an operation, except for the blood, which was still gushing out. The beep of the EKG monitor seemed to be slowing down.

Charlie shot his eyes at the anesthesiologist, who was texting on her cell phone.

"Aren't you going to finish?" she asked him, glancing up.

"Finish? What are you talking about?"

"The patient is bleeding out. Aren't you going to staple her back together?"

Back at GastroPlonix, Charlie burst into the Medical Director's office, where Dr. Patel and Bill Symonds were tinkering with a new model of Tummy Tweezer™ on Dr. Patel's desk. He'd saved the patient by wheeling her down to the ER, but he wanted to tell them in no uncertain terms that he would never set foot in an operating room again. Still in his scrubs, he carried his mask and goggles in one hand and his Tummy Tweezer in the other.

"Dr. Kaspar just called from the hospital," Bill Symonds said severely. "He's furious about the way you made him look."

"Made him look? He was slumped against the wall in a stupor while the patient bled out."

"Exactly," Dr. Patel said. "Not the best image for a surgeon to project, is it?"

"Or the best image for us," Bill Symonds added. "Bottom line, we won't be needing your services anymore."

"What?"

"You're fired."

Charlie threw his Tummy Tweezer down on Dr. Patel's desk and stamped toward the door.

"By the way, Charlie," Bill Symonds said, "here's something you might be interested in. We're putting the finishing touches on our new 'Mona Lisa' line of Tummy Tweezers. They leave an imprint on the patient's stomach just like the one on your hand."

He drove around in his van for a hour, two hours, three hours, until he lost track of time, stopping every ten miles to add a quart of oil. Then he lumbered into a bar along the Boulevard and drank shots for the next six hours. He'd done the right thing, he thought, saving the patient's life, but no one seemed to care. All they cared about was how they looked. How he made them look, as if he had the power to make anybody look like anything they didn't already look like. He was done with being a salesman, done with medical devices, done with free food. He didn't know what he was going to do. He didn't know what he was going to tell Penny.

At closing time he excused himself to use the bathroom while the bartender ran the tab, then exited through the kitchen to avoid paying it. Though outrageously, impossibly, and hopelessly drunk, he had enough presence of mind not to go home. An idea entered his head, which struck him as the best one he'd had all night. He would drive to the lab where Spencer worked and see what his friend thought he should do. Cruising down Cottman Avenue in a cloud of exhaust fumes, he spotted an all-night convenience store where, he reasoned, he could pick up some tasty item for his kids so they wouldn't look to Jim Grillo for their sustenance. Once inside the store he realized to his chagrin that he'd left his wallet in the van. Undaunted, he found a large cherry pie in the refrigerator and cleverly concealed it under his T-shirt. As he lurched toward the door, the clerk, who'd been spying on him since he walked in, accused him of shoplifting and blocked his exit. Charlie then made a serious error of judgment. He reached into his pocket and pretended that his phone was a gun. He ordered the clerk to lie on the floor and threatened to kill him if he called the police. Then, chuckling with satisfaction, he carried his pie out to the van and climbed inside.

Charlie knew he had plenty of time to escape. The police, as he'd recently seen on the Ten O'Clock News, respond to a typical 911 call in twenty minutes. But no sooner had he started his engine than a police car squealed into the parking lot, lights blazing. How could they have arrived so quickly? His first impulse was to eat the pie, so he could deny that it ever existed—but how could he justify that, when he'd stolen it for his kids? He slumped in his seat until the officer had run inside, then slipped the van in gear and glided away without turning on his lights. Within seconds, in his side mirror, he could see the police car speeding in his direction. Fortunately Spencer's lab was only two blocks away and he was driving about seventy miles an hour. When he saw the lab he sped around a corner and down a side street, where, miraculously, he found a parking space between two similar vans that belonged to a bakery.

He leaped from the van and raced toward Frankford Labs, gobbling what was left of the pie as he ran, sweating and gasping, his heart pounding out of his chest. Red pie juice poured down his chin and over his T-shirt. When the lab's back door came into view, he burst into tears. Just as he reached it, the police car cut into the parking lot behind him and slammed on its brakes, waving a spotlight through the darkness.

He banged on the door, bellowing for Spencer to open it, shoving the last bites of evidence into his mouth.

PART II

26. My Life Sucks,
by Lindsay Pangborn

I don't want to sound like I go around feeling sorry for myself, but deep down I'm a very caring and sympathetic person, and besides myself who else do I have to feel sorry for? My Mom's a criminal, my Dad's a pervert and Zachary is the biggest loser on the planet. If I had any friends they'd probably be more pathetic than me. I can't even pet my dog without getting bitten. So if I seem to be wallowing in self-pity (that's what my Dad accused me of last night when I told him I'd slash my wrists if he didn't let me go to the mall), it's because I'm the only person I know who deserves any sympathy.

My Dad almost had a heart attack when he caught me texting Spencer (I didn't tell him Spencer never texts back). He told me I could never see Spencer again or call him or text him or have anything to do with him, and if I did he would send me to boarding school in North Korea. At least it's good to know he's not doing this because he's a racist. "I want you to understand something, Lindsay," he told me. "The reason I disapprove of Spencer isn't because he's black. It's just that the cultural divide is just too big. How could you be happy with someone who lives in a run-down crack house in the ghetto, without water or heat, fending off rats and drug lords and barely surviving from one welfare check to the next?"

It made me wonder: Does my Dad know Spencer better than I thought? Does he have detectives following him around or something?

"How do you know so much about Spencer?" I asked him.

"Well," he said, "aren't they all like that?"

It's a lot like *Romeo and Juliet*. Mr. Siegal says the two stars, Romeo and Juliet, are our age, fourteen or fifteen at the most. Some of the girls started crying when he said it was a play about teenage suicide. I wasn't upset because I've already made my decision. Without Spencer in my life I don't plan to hang around much longer, even if it means missing the Lady Gaga concert I have tickets for in January.

All I need now is a special friend. The kind of friend you only have once in your entire life because she's your destiny. She understands you and cares about you. Your lives are both leading up to what you're going to share together, like those girls in Jenkintown who jumped in front of the train: it's not pain or sadness or emptiness or unhappiness, though those are all there, but escaping together, like two kids in a story racing through a spooky forest with gnarly roots and dangly vines and spider webs trying to snag them and wrestle them into the ground but instead they—you—run faster and faster toward the light until you finally come out on the other side. There's a brilliant, beautiful flash and then it's over.

That's what I was thinking about when I sent my latest message to Alex. I've started thinking of her as special, the friend who shares my destiny though she may not know it yet. I'm very careful how I put it in my messages. I sent her a link about the two girls from Jenkintown and she said she'd never read such a beautiful story. I try to write with style and eloquence, in language Mr. Siegal would approve of. I never use the "s" word or anything like that but always express it in terms of love, which is really what it's all about.

"Dear Alex," I texted her one day:

I want to share with you the greatest joy and happiness that two people can give to each other: absolute, selfless love. But you have to be sure. There's no room for second thoughts.

Immediately she wrote back:

Lindsay, I think about you all the time. But I'm a little afraid. Will it be painful?

That was a question I'd given a lot of thought to:

Alex, love: Any pain will be over before you even feel it.

Surprisingly, it took her almost a whole day to respond. I stayed up half the night waiting but no messages came in except some penis-enlargement offers from Nigeria. Then, when I came home from school the next afternoon, there it was:

OK, I'm ready. But where?

My hand shook as I thumbed in my reply:

I know a place by the Mall where we can do it. Can you meet me there? Remember: If you say yes, there's no turning back.

I guess I was being a little unfair to Alex in that last message—I should have said, unless Spencer starts texting me back.

27. From the Journal of Erik Anselmus

November 29: Are there pieces missing? Something even more disturbing: duplicate, identical pieces. And some that apparently belong to different puzzles altogether—one of Dali's limp watches, Van Gogh's ear as shown in an early self-portrait, the left breast of Venus from Botticelli's "The Birth of Venus." Innocent packaging errors—or other worlds intruding into this one?

Another sleepless night, thinking about Cathy. Migraines continuing. Increase dosage of painkillers. Ringing in my ears.

December 1: Is there a "butterfly" who set the events of the past few months in motion? Mentioned this hypothesis to Cathy—she suggested that I see a doctor. Two pieces added tonight. Total = 16.

December 3: Cathy always very sweet, but customers loud and inconsiderate, especially on Monday nights when football games monopolize the TV screens. Can't they see that I need to concentrate? Can't they see I'm doing important work?

Work on controlling temper. Don't mention to Administration, would infer recurrence of "anger management" issues reported last year.

28. The Fugitive

Spencer Casey

Sometimes, when Naked Dave goes out to his awgies, I just sit
in the control room and think. You're not supposed to do that
anymore, that's why there's TV's wherever you go and no way to
shut them off. That's why I'm supposed to spend the night
walking around punching codes into security pads, just to show I
didn't waste my time thinking. And all the while I'm asking
myself what am I doing here? I'm guarding something but
nobody ever explains what it is, or why, or who from. If a gang
of terrorists breaks the door down, what exactly am I supposed
to do? Why shouldn't I just turn around and run the other way?

One night—it must've been about one in the morning—I'm
leaning back in my chair, lost in thought, maybe even nodding
off a little, when suddenly there comes a pounding and hollering
at the back door like the Bloods and the Crips are battling it out
with the Junior Black Mafia. I'm out of my chair in a flash,
wishing I still had on my gangsta gear, but something tells me all
the bling in the world won't stop what's about to come through
that door. All I see in the surveillance monitor is a gigantic
white blur, but wait a minute—that's only one guy and he looks
an awful lot like Charlie Quill.

"Charlie?" I crack open the door. "What you doing here?"

"Let me in and lock the door behind me!"

It's Charlie, sure enough, and I've never seen him looking
like this. He's drowning in sweat, face as red as the cherry pie

he's stuffing down his throat, coughing out the most god-awful noises and sucking them back in along with the cherry pie, and soon as he's inside I realize it's not sweat that's pouring off him, it's tears—the man's howling and choking and gasping like a baby. "I got this for my kids," he says, spewing up chunks of the cherry pie on his sleeve. "I wasn't supposed to eat it. I got it for my kids."

"Take it easy, man."

"I gotta get out of sight. They cops are right behind me. They'll be here in about thirty seconds."

"There's no place to hide in here." Then I get an idea. It's not such a great idea but it's better than nothing. I grab Charlie's arm and drag him into Naked Dave's room. You can see the imprint on the mattress where Naked Dave's been spending his time for the last three weeks. I shut the drawer on the night table where Naked Dave stashes his illegal pills. "Take off all your clothes and lay down here," I tell Charlie.

"What?"

"Just do as I say. Take your clothes off and lay down right here." With a towel I wipe what's left of the cherry pie off his face. "Now put this blindfold on."

When Charlie takes his clothes off and stretches out on the bed I sort of wished I was the one wearing the blindfold. He's even whiter and fatter and uglier than he looks with his clothes on, with enough warts to sink a toad.

"Now just hold perfectly still," I tell him. "Don't move, whatever you do."

"Don't move?"

"Lay perfectly still no matter what happens. Pretend you're dead."

"What you gonna tell the cops?"

"Never mind, I know what to tell them. Your name is Naked Dave. Can you remember that?"

Suddenly there's a loud banging on the door and Charlie stiffens like a corpse. "Now what?"

"Just stay that way," I tell him. "Don't move."

"Philadelphia Police! You've got ten seconds to open this door!"

I open the door and a skinny white cop takes one look at me and shoves his way inside. He has an acne face and a nose that looks like he should be leading a pack of reindeer. His badge says his name is Dennis Gilboy.

"Good evening, officer," I tell him, polite as can be. "How can I help you tonight?"

He eyes me suspiciously. "Where is he? Where's the White Whale? I know he ran in here."

For a few minutes he struts around yanking out desk drawers like he thinks the perpetrator might be hiding inside. When he finally spots Charlie on the mattress, he crouches down and holds his gun out in front of him with both hands like they do on TV when they sneak into a crime scene.

"Freeze!"

Charlie lays perfectly still. He looks like he's been dead a week.

Gilboy creeps forward. "Police! Freeze!"

"He's freezing all right," I tell the officer. "You don't need to tell him that."

Gilboy lowers his gun and shines his flashlight on Charlie's face. Then he runs it down all over his fat white body, all puffy and speckled—come to think of it, he looks like a beached whale with a seafood allergy. The officer's right about that. You can't even see if he's breathing or not.

"I've got a naked, blindfolded white male on a mattress at Cottman and Castor," the officer growls into his radio. "Suspect in a convenience store robbery. Could be the White Whale. Unconscious, possible 419."

"What's that mean?" I ask him. "419?"

"Dead. He could already be dead."

"He ain't dead. He's just doing his job."

Gilboy stares at me like I'm crazy.

"That's no whale," I tell him. "That's Naked Dave. He gets paid to lay there perfectly still—all night, every night, weekends and holidays included. He can't sit up, he can't talk, he can't move a muscle or it might spoil the clinical trial."

Gilboy aims his flashlight into my eyes. "What the hell are you talking about?"

"This here's a certified mattress testing facility," I explain, calm as can be. "We conduct clinical trials for hospitals and nursing homes. Naked Dave gets paid to lay there perfectly still, like he's in a coma, to see if the mattress's gonna give him bedsores."

He points back at Charlie. "How long's he been laying there like that?"

"Oh, about two weeks. Or maybe three weeks. Yeah, I think it's three weeks now."

"He's already got bedsores. You can see them."

"Wait'll you turn him over. Looks like a pepperoni pizza."

"I called for backup."

"You're gonna want to call for a chopper when you turn him over."

Gilboy pokes Charlie in the shoulder with his radio but Charlie don't budge. "Sir!" he tells him, polite all of a sudden— and I know what that means. When the cops act polite they already made up their mind to put you in the slammer. "Sir, can you sit up?"

"He ain't going to sit up," I tell the officer.

"Could you give me your name, please?"

"He ain't going to talk. This's a clinical trial."

"You shut up!"

"Don't he have the right to remain silent? Cause that's what he's doing, ain't it? Remaining silent."

Gilboy shoves me into the wall with his radio. "I said shut the hell up!"

Outside I can hear sirens blaring and police cars screeching into the parking lot. Gilboy runs back to open the door and welcome his reinforcements. Something tells me I've got about ten seconds to get Charlie out of there.

I pull the blindfold off and give him a poke in the ribs. "Charlie," I tell him, "get up and run down that hall till you come to the computer room. Behind the big copying machine there's a piece of the wall that slips off where Naked Dave hides his booze and porno movies. See if you can squeeze your fat ass in there."

Charlie leaps up like the Michelin man on steroids and disappears down the hall. I shut the door to Naked Dave's room and settle down in my chair with the Daily News, catching up on last night's Flyers game. Before I know it here comes Gilboy with a whole SWAT team in black leather outfits stomping into the control room yelling "Freeze!" and "Drop your weapons!" and other stuff they heard on TV. It's all I can do to keep from laughing.

When Gilboy finds the door to Naked Dave's room closed, he stops and peers in through the little window. Then he turns on me. "What'd you do with him?"

"Do with who?"

"The white male that was laying there. The White Whale."

"Did you say white male or White Whale? Or was it a white male whale, or a male white whale?"

"A white male who's suspected of being the White Whale."

"Suspected? You don't even know if what you saw was a whale?"

Gilboy grabs my collar and pushes me down like he's going to choke me until the SWAT team cops pull him off. "Back off, Gilboy!"

"I swear to God," Gilboy tells them, out of breath, "there was a white male, mid to late thirties, approximately 300 pounds, lying naked on that bed with a blindfold on."

"Overweight white male with a blindfold on," one of the SWAT team cops says, taking notes. "Lying there naked?"

"Stark naked, except for his blindfold. And covered with boils."

"You sure he wasn't wearing a bunny suit?"

The SWAT team cops laugh like they're going to die. Gilboy tries to strangle me again and they crowd between me and Gilboy like they're my personal bodyguards.

I stay calm as a cucumber. "He must be talking about Naked Dave," I tell them.

Gilboy darts his eyes at the SWAT team to show them he was right all along. "That's right. It was Naked Dave. Where is he?"

"He must have gone out."

"Didn't you say he had to lay there all night without moving a muscle? Didn't you say he had to lay there every night for weeks on end without moving a muscle?"

"Sometimes when Naked Dave's laying here for weeks on end," I tell the SWAT team cops—and I can tell they're enjoying the way I'm making Gilboy look like a jackass—"he gets up and goes out. He don't tell me where he's going. Maybe he drives down to the all-night diner for some coffee, maybe he's got a drinking problem, maybe he's got a girlfriend on the side who don't like bedsores. I don't know and I don't ask."

Now Gilboy's growling like a mad dog and I don't know how much longer the others can keep him off me. I've been trying to give Charlie some time to get good and hid behind that wall but I can't hold out much longer. Then I get a lucky break. Just when the SWAT team cops start to search the place, the real Naked Dave comes strolling into the control room with a big styrofoam coffee cup in his hand. He's a white male, just like Gilboy said. Only trouble is he's 60 years old and weighs about 150 pounds.

"He's back," I tell the SWAT team.

"That's not Naked Dave!" Gilboy yells.

One of the SWAT team cops tells Gilboy to shut up. "Are you Naked Dave?"

"That's what they call me," Naked Dave laughs. "My real name is Dave Brunner. Can I help you?"

"How long have you been gone?"

"Oh, about ten minutes or so." No way he's going to admit he was gone for three hours. "Is something the matter?"

There are questions and answers, and more questions and answers, and finally Naked Dave convinces the SWAT team cops he's not dead or in a coma or covered with boils or bedsores and he really has this job testing the mattresses just like I said. And all he did was slip out to the Wawa for a cup of coffee.

"Gilboy," one of the SWAT team cops tells Gilboy, "maybe you need to get some rest. Take a vacation, spend some time with the family. The job is getting to you."

Naked Dave opens the door to his room and starts peeling off his clothes. "Now if you'll excuse me, gentlemen," he says, stretching out on the bed with his blindfold on, "I've got to get back to work."

At eight o'clock Lester Blount calls in sick, which he always does on Tuesdays on account of Monday Night Football. Half an hour later Ms. Killebrew calls me into her office, and across from her sits Officer Gilboy, looking just as mean and stupid as he did the night before. I've got no choice but to sit down next to him.

Ms. Killebrew picks up some knitting needles and adds a few stitches to a tiny sweater she's knitting for her baby granddaughter, whose pictures are all over the desk. She looks like a kindly grandma but I know better. The officer starts to tell his story: how he was on the alert for a suspect known as the White Whale when a local convenience store called to report an armed robbery, and arriving on the scene he pursued a white male, approximately 300 pounds, onto the Frankford Labs premises and found him stretched out on one of the beds with blood smeared across his face, stark naked and apparently D.O.A., so he radioed for backup but when the SWAT team arrived the white male was gone—

"Spencer"—Ms. Killebrew glares at me—"Is this what happened?"

"Not exactly, Ms. Killebrew."

"Then tell us exactly what happened."

"Well," I tell Ms. Killebrew, "Naked Dave got up to use the bathroom, which he's allowed to do three times a night, and when Officer Gilboy arrived he was in there. Then when the SWAT team got here, Naked Dave came back from the bathroom and laid down on his bed—"

"I tell you I saw him!" Officer Gilboy yells. "I saw the fat guy on the bed. Don't tell me I didn't!"

Ms. Killebrew lays her knitting needles on the desk and flashes her pit bull smile at me like she wants me to tell the truth, only I know she don't. She don't want me to say anything that might jeopardize the clinical trial. "Who was lying on the bed, Spencer."

"The only one I ever saw on there was Naked Dave."

Officer Gilboy jumps up and hovers over me, face red as a turnip. I probably should have felt sorry for him. You could tell it was all he could do to keep from strangling me. "All right, let's cut the crap," he tells Ms. Killebrew. "I saw the guy who came in here and it wasn't Naked Dave. Let's see the surveillance tapes and you can judge for yourself."

"What surveillance tapes would you be referring to?" I ask him before Ms. Killebrew can say anything. She gives me the evil eye but don't stop me from talking.

"You know what surveillance tapes," he says. "The pictures your system takes of all the doorways, 24/7."

"I think you'll need to get a warrant for those," I tell him. "No way you can look at our surveillance tapes without a warrant. That's confidential information. Isn't it, Ms. Killebrew?"

"And just who the hell are you?"

"Acting Chief of Security," I tell him, with a glance at Ms. Killebrew. "In Mr. Blount's absence."

Ms. Killebrew could fire me right then and there, but by this time she knows I'm looking out for the lab as much as myself. "I'll defer to my Acting Chief of Security," she says with a nod.

I nod back, I even smile, because I know something she don't. I know where I had my finger when Charlie pounded on the door. Remember the button Naked Dave rigged up on the surveillance system? Well, that night when Naked Dave slipped out to his awgies and Charlie charged inside and Officer Gilboy and the SWAT came pounding in, the only ones whose comings and goings got recorded were the cops.

"I want to make one thing clear," Ms. Killebrew tells Officer Gilboy, standing up like she's expecting him to leave. "Whoever this intruder was—if he existed—I can assure you he had nothing to do with our work in this lab. We've had some adverse experiences, of course—some bedsores, a couple of minor infections, but never a major disruption or anything close to one. It's all in our FDA reports."

"I want to see those reports, too," he tells her.

Now she's mad, fingering those knitting needles like she's getting ready to jam them in his eyes. "Then I suggest you come back with a search warrant."

The officer scowls. "If you cooperate, I'll make sure it's taken into account. If you don't..."

She takes a step toward Officer Gilboy and he trips backwards. Then she lurches toward him a second time and he stumbles again. It's like watching a cat slap a German shepherd on the nose. Poor dog don't have a prayer.

29. From the Journal of Erik Anselmus

December 5: Email from Administration requesting immediate return to Geneva. Will continue sending detailed progress reports.

December 6: Worrying about Cathy walking home by herself. Must buy a gun to protect her. All Americans carry guns. Does she have a boyfriend? Increasingly short of breath, sweating at night. Migraines and noise becoming unbearable.

December 7: Reading *The Free Food Principle,* by Austin Ivey III. All human behavior as the manifestation of a primal instinct to obtain food with the least expenditure of energy: Egyptian pyramids, fall of Rome, wars and revolutions. Apply to everyday life: how to meet women?

Walked Cathy home from Pinocchio's.   Narrow, deserted sidewalks lined with Italian bakeries and butchers and tiny hardware stores. On the doorstep of the row house where she lives with elderly parents, she tells the story of her life: Married at eighteen, again at twenty-five, then divorced for the second time ten years ago. No children. Why hasn't she remarried?

This way I'm free to do what I want.

People are deluded about that, I tell her. You might be free to do what you want, but you're not free to *want* what you want. And if what you want is pre-determined, then your freedom to do what you want is an illusion. We're compelled to do everything we do by the chain of causes and effects that came before. There's nothing free about any of our choices.

Good night, she smiles back. Thanks for a wonderful evening.

30. Audrey Returns to the City of Brotherly Love

When Audrey lost her job at the puzzle factory, her little sister Diane, a perky blond manicurist who'd moved to California several years before, said it could be the best thing that ever happened to her. One night on the phone she finally talked Audrey into coming out west for a visit—or maybe to stay, if she could find a job. "Who knows?" Diane asked in her high-pitched telephone voice. "Maybe you'll like it!" As a hardened Philadelphia recidivist, convinced of the futility of searching elsewhere for a happiness she never found at home, Audrey knew the Golden State would be a disappointment—if a glass is three-quarters full, isn't that half way to half-empty? But she bought a ticket anyway, more as a gesture of protest and independence than from any illusion that her destination was worth traveling to. It was either that or stay at home plotting revenge against Jeff Pangborn and fending off the intrigues of a mutant Scandinavian psycho, a slime ball attorney, and an increasingly homicidal Mom.

It was easy for California to live up to Audrey's expectations. Diane spent a month driving her around the Blade Runner wilderness of L.A., a hazy land of vast traffic jams where mountain ranges vanished like mirages and all the buildings looked like Taco Bells. There were a million places to go, all of them two hours away from wherever you happened to be, the intervening distance occupied by an internal combustion millipede inching its way through cement canyons or smoggy plains. Audrey hunted for a job and an apartment, but never found a job worth commuting two hours to or an apartment worth commuting two hours from. Her hopes of losing her virginity as a cougar were dashed by the total absence of younger men half as attractive as Spencer Casey, who followed her to California in her dreams. Diane had married a car salesman from Burbank, who tried to convince Audrey that people actually enjoyed living in L.A. What's not to like about living in Paradise? he'd ask about twice a day. And that's what she hated most about the place, after the traffic and the earthquakes and the Lakers and the Dodgers—that smiley-face mentality that made her wish her brother-in-law would drive his Audi off a cliff along Mulholland Drive. When you're from Philadelphia and you're surrounded by people who act happy all the time, you smell a rat.

She hugged her sister goodbye—which meant nothing: in L.A. you hug your accountant—and flew home the Sunday after Thanksgiving. Diane seemed sorry to see her go, but it was understood that Audrey, as the older, unmarried sister, had primary responsibility for their mother. That proud descendant of Lucretia Borgia was threatening to live another fifty years—bad news for the unlucky segment of the population who'd slighted or ignored her at one time or another. Audrey's first order of business upon returning to Philadelphia was to satisfy herself that all nineteen of the neighbors, relatives and former in-laws who'd enjoyed her mother's hospitality on Thanksgiving were still above ground and breathing three days later. Miraculously they had all survived, even (as her mother ruefully admitted) the former in-laws. With that worry behind her, Audrey could focus on her own diminishing prospects. She spent the afternoon making doctor appointments, dentist appointments, hair appointments, nail appointments, gym appointments, car appointments—all of which, she knew, she'd have to cancel if she didn't find a job soon. In her mail she found a few skimpy unemployment checks, along with less happy tidings from an assortment of lawyers and collection agencies. Evidently her bank balance had skipped town without leaving a forwarding address.

What was she going to do for money until she found a job? She thought about Jeff Pangborn, Erik Anselmus, and Morton C. McMonigle, Jr., Esq., and their clumsy attempts to enlist her in their conspiracies. They'd all wanted something from her and were willing to pay the price. She'd told each of them she'd think about it. Now a month had gone by—she'd been to California and back—and without thinking much about it, she'd thought about it. *It* was the opportunity of a lifetime. What was she waiting for?

At Plato's Cave, Morton C. McMonigle, Jr., Esq., materialized in the mirror over the bar and slithered onto the barstool next to Audrey. He wore the same greenish suit and the same half-open raincoat he'd worn the first time she met him. "I'd like to buy you a drink," he said, leaning forward and favoring her with a close-up view of his blotchy face, which seemed on the verge of peeling off, "provided—for income tax purposes—that I can accurately describe this as a business meeting. The topic, as usual in business meetings, is money."

That got Audrey's attention. "What about money?"

"Large quantities of it have been disappearing from the Pangborns' marital estate with no rhyme nor reason. Naturally we suspect malfeasance by Mr. Pangborn—"

"Malfeasance is his middle name."

"—if not defalcation."

"Defalcation always comes to mind when I think of Jeff."

McMonigle tossed a fifty dollar bill on the bar. "According to the financial records we have access to, everything's on the up and up. But the money keeps disappearing. That's where I was hoping you could help out, capitalizing on your relationship with Mr. Pangborn. You said you'd think about it."

"I think I also said, what's in it for me?"

McMonigle dismissed the bartender, who'd returned with his change. "Would something in the mid-five-figure range be acceptable?"

"Fifty thousand dollars?"

"You're the accountant."

Audrey called Jeff Pangborn the next morning from Starbucks and threw herself on his mercy. She still hadn't found a job, she confessed, and although she didn't really want to talk to the insurance guy—"Don't even consider it!" Jeff blurted—she was so desperate for money that she'd do almost anything. Jeff assured her that working for him would be the best thing that ever happened to her. The new business was almost ready to launch, with Phase I expected to close in two or three weeks. The corporate structure would be complex, a web of affiliates, subsidiaries, limited partnerships and franchises. For now she could work out of his office, helping his secretary open bank accounts, apply for tax-ID numbers, and set up the bookkeeping system. Everything was still top secret, strictly on a "need to know" basis.

"The only thing is," Audrey hesitated, "I won't be able to work full time at first. I've got a few things I need to take care of."

"No problem! Take as much time as you need."

She said goodbye to Jeff and checked her messages as she stood in line for another cup of coffee. She flipped through a few apps on her phone, but she didn't bother to open her calendar. Her dentist appointment, her hair appointment, her nail appointment—she knew exactly when they were, and now she'd have the money to pay for them. And there was one other appointment she knew she wouldn't forget.

The next day she was having lunch with Erik Anselmus.

31. Feeling the Heat

Spencer Casey

I probably don't need to tell you what happened when Officer Gilboy came back to the lab with his search warrant. How he puffed himself up into a frenzy when he played the surveillance tapes over and over again without finding the faintest glimpse of a 300-pound white male or Naked Dave or anybody else except his own red-faced, out of control self pounding on the door and the SWAT team coming and going just like I said. How he shook his fist at Ms. Killebrew and me and accused us of tampering with evidence and harboring fugitives, how he threatened to send us both to jail and shut down the lab if we didn't cooperate—and how when it was all over he went bellowing out of there like a dog who bit into a skunk.

All this happens in the middle of the afternoon when I should be home sleeping in the tropical bird sanctuary I share with Shawn and Dewey and Aunt Lorraine. Ms. Killebrew makes me stay until Officer Gilboy arrives with his warrant, sitting in the control room with my boss, Lester Blount, who tells me, over and over again, about his diseases. He also tells me how they made him retire from the cops in some town in the Pine Barrens. About once every half hour he goes out to his pickup truck and comes back with liquor on his breath. Lester has a nose like Rudolph's but if I was Santa I wouldn't let him guide my sleigh on Christmas Eve or any other night. He'd turn off at the first exit for a drink and probably a trip to the emergency room.

It's all I can do to stay awake. Naked Dave is there of course but he has to lay perfectly still and can't talk to me. My only consolation is that Charlie, who got me into this mess, is sweating it out in his own private hell behind the wall of the computer room. Ms. Killebrew suspects something fishy's going on. She sits me down in front of her desk and tells me to come clean. Then she flashes her scariest smile, which is the closest thing to a ghost I ever seen—it looks like it used to belong to somebody else—and asks, "Where's the White Whale, Spencer?"

That one throws me. "I never seen a white whale in here," I tell her. "Officer Gilboy's the only one who saw that. If you ask me, I think he must've been smoking something."

She points one of her knitting needles at me like it's a harpoon. "I'm concerned about what could happen to the lab if there's bad publicity. We do important work here."

"Yes, we do," I agree, keeping my head down. If she only knew about Naked Dave and his awgies.

"I'm glad you see it that way," Ms. Killebrew says. "Do you know why?"

"Why?"

"Because you're hanging by a thread. I just wanted you to know that, Spencer. You're hanging by a thread."

One night about six o'clock I scarf down a bowl of Count Chocula and Aunt Lorraine comes home from work and sits down at the table to eat some tuna salad. Shawn's laying on the couch in his boxer shorts, burning some new CDs to replace the ones about pimps and ho's he sold to the old ladies at church with ones that really are about Jesus, because some of those old ladies complained to Aunt Lorraine. Old Dewey's in his cage

sweating out his last days as an endangered species (though he
don't know it yet). All of a sudden there's a racket at the front
door that sounds like a home invasion. Aunt Lorraine jumps up
and runs in the kitchen to hide. Shawn don't move a muscle—
maybe he thinks Jesus will save him. I run to the window and
peek through the curtains. There's two white cops pounding on
the door, Officer Gilboy in his uniform and a taller one in a suit
and tie and overcoat. When I open the door Officer Gilboy
shoves his badge in my face and says "Philadelphia Police!" as if
maybe I thought he was from the Salvation Army. The tall one's
about twenty years older and even meaner looking. When he
steps inside he gives his name as Detective Kampf. He don't
offer to shake hands.

"Mind if we have a word with you?" Officer Gilboy asks
me. He's smiling like he thinks he's smart, the way you smile
when you're pretending not to smile and you want somebody to
know it. I guess you'd call it a smirk, like what I must've done
when my teachers were always telling me to wipe that smirk off
my face. I never knew exactly what those smirks looked like, I
was so busy wiping them off my face, but now I get to see one
up close and it's not making me feel all warm and fuzzy inside.
I'm wondering, what's that smirk trying to tell me? I already
know Officer Gilboy's not too smart and he knows I know it, so
that can't be the message. No, it's the opposite, it's that he don't
have to be smart because he's wearing a uniform and carrying a
gun and he's got this big mean-looking detective standing next
to him in case I get any ideas. He can smirk all he wants and I
can't tell him to wipe that smirk off his face. But you know
what? Thanks to good old Dewey and his disease, it's a hundred
degrees in this apartment and in a few minutes that smirk's going
to drip off all by itself.

Aunt Lorraine huddles in the kitchen, Shawn sprawls on the couch, Dewey shivers in his cage. The officers ignore them because I'm the only one they want to have a word with. We sit down at the table, on the end of the living room near the kitchen door. The two cops are already sweating before they start to talk, pulling off their jackets, wiping their foreheads, reaching up to loosen their ties.

"Sort of hot in here, isn't it?" Detective Kampf says, without looking at me.

"Like a friggin steam bath," Officer Gilboy agrees.

The detective pulls out a surveillance photo that shows Charlie running out of a convenience store holding a flat white package that could be a cherry pie. "You know this man?" he asks me.

"Could be a lot of guys," I tell him.

"Could be," the detective nods, "but it's not, is it? In fact it's Charlie Quill. He's a friend of yours."

"Charlie's a friend of mine," I agree. "Could be him all right. I can't say for sure."

"I can say for sure," Gilboy says, wiping the sweat off his forehead with his shirt sleeve, "that this is the perpetrator who stole a cherry pie from the Seven Eleven and ran to the door of the testing lab where you let him in—"

"I didn't let nobody in except you."

"—and when I went inside, he was stretched out naked on one of the beds. How could I forget that? This is the guy."

Gilboy wipes his forehead with both sleeves until they're soaked in sweat, then he tries to roll up his sleeves but that just wrings the sweat back out of them. It drips down his arms onto his pants. He picks up one of Aunt Lorraine's napkins off the table—it's the cloth kind with the napkin ring around it that she only lets us use on special occasions—and starts wiping his arms and his face with it. He's still smirking but it's getting harder by the second, what with all the sweating and wiping that's going on, and I'm thinking maybe he is going to wipe that smirk off his face after all.

Aunt Lorraine jumps out of the kitchen and snatches the sweat-soaked napkin out of his hand.

"This heat's killing me," he tells her. "Turn it down, would you?"

"Can't do that," she says. "Doctor's orders." She nods her head toward Dewey's bird cage but it's covered with towels and the officers have no idea what she means.

"So," I tell Officer Gilboy before he can react, "is that what this is all about? Charlie stole a cherry pie from the Seven Eleven?"

Gilboy's panting like a bird dog. Detective Kampf sees that he can't go on much longer. "No, Spencer," he says in a soothing voice—and I know I'm in trouble if he's calling me by my first name—"this is way bigger than a cherry pie."

The detective leans forward, trying to smile without making it into a smirk but I can tell it ain't easy for him, especially in this heat. "There's something about your friend Charlie that you probably aren't aware of," he tells me. "He's the mastermind of a theft-of-services ring that's been eating a swath through three counties. They go into a restaurant and run up a big tab—you know, bacon cheeseburgers, crab cakes, baby back ribs with double orders of fries, sides of cole slaw, corn on the cob, apple sauce, the whole nine yards—and just as the waitress brings the check, one of them fakes a choking fit or finds a hunk of metal or some putrid rodent part in their food. The manager comes running and picks up the tab just to get them out of there before they make a scene. Charlie and his accomplices—who are dressed up to look like a gang of obese teenagers—have run this scam over and over again. And every one of the restaurant managers has picked this picture out of a photo lineup. Charlie Quill. They'd know him anywhere, they say—and who wouldn't? Moby Dick with a carrot top."

Detective Kampf tries to laugh at his own joke but he can't. Probably his throat's swelling shut from the heat. Gilboy looks like he's ready to pass out.

"Officer Gilboy followed Charlie to your door, Spencer," the detective says. "Saw him go inside. Saw him stretched out on one of the beds where you introduced him as Naked Dave. But by the time the SWAT team arrives he's gone and a 60-year-old ex-con named Dave Brunner's laying there claiming to be Naked Dave."

"That dude is Naked Dave," I tell him.

Detective Kampf slams his fist down on the table. "Don't interrupt me, Spencer! I don't give a damn about Naked Dave. Naked Dave has nothing to do with this."

He's getting testy, probably on account of the temperature. I think maybe Aunt Lorraine turned it up to a hundred and ten. "Now here's what I want you to tell me," he says, trying to sound calm. "Where are you hiding this guy?"

"I can't tell you that because I ain't hiding him."

I can tell the detective wants to take a swipe at me but he's wobbling on his chair like a drunk. "We're not leaving here until we get some answers," he says, but I don't believe him. He sounds like he can barely move his tongue.

"You got a glass of water?" he croaks.

"Fresh out," Aunt Lorraine tells him from the kitchen. "Couldn't pay the water bill."

"You're making a big mistake, Spencer. You cooperate and we can help you. You stand in our way and you're looking at jail time."

"Accessory after the fact," Officer Gilboy mutters. "Aiding and abetting."

"Harboring a fugitive," the detective adds. "Uttering false statements to police officers."

"Destruction of evidence."

"Could be looking at 25 years to life."

"And what if somebody gets killed?" Detective Kampf says, slurring his words. "What if one of those restaurant managers has a heart attack? What if the clerk in the next convenience store pulls out a gun and starts shooting? You ever heard of felony murder, Spencer? You could be looking at Murder One. That means the death penalty."

Aunt Lorraine bursts out of the kitchen and glares at those officers with the whites of her eyes as big as golf balls. She's waving a metal frying pan over her head like a tennis racket. They stop panting and gasping and sloshing the sweat off their faces and the room goes quiet. Even the TV seems to go dead. All you can hear is Dewey scratching around in his cage. "The death penalty?" she yells. "For stealing a cherry pie?"

"As I told your son, ma'am—"

"He's not my son. And don't call me 'ma'am.'"

"—this is way bigger than a cherry pie. Now I'm going to ask you to drop that frying pan on the table."

The detective's eyes narrow to a squint. His voice is smooth but he looks terrified, dangerous, like he might reach for his gun if Aunt Lorraine takes one step closer. Everything seems to be happening in slow motion. It's still deadly quiet except for some scratching in the bird cage. I'm wondering when Dewey's going to speak up—usually when he scratches around like that he's getting ready to join the conversation. It must be 105 degrees in here by now, just what makes him chatty. The officers are almost delirious from the heat. They look like they've been wandering in the desert for a month—eyes red, faces swollen, tongues lolling out. I feel sorry for them even though they deserve it. In fact I wish this interrogation could go on a little longer. A few more minutes and I could get them to confess to stealing the cherry pie.

"You don't have a record, Spencer," Detective Kampf says with what sounds like his dying breath. "Let me help you keep it that way, OK?"

"I'm keeping it that way by myself."

"Don't be stupid."

Dewey decides it's time to speak his mind.

"Be stupid!" he croaks. "Be stupid!"

The officers roll onto their feet and stumble around with their guns out in front of them, eyes crazed, gasping for breath. Me and Aunt Lorraine drop to the floor with our hands behind our heads.

"Who the hell was that?" demands Detective Kampf.

"That's Dewey," I tell him. "He's doing life without the possibility of parole."

"What?"

"In that cage over there with the towels over it."

Out of the corner of my eye I watch the detective creep forward like he's expecting Hannibal Lecter to leap out of that cage. He pulls off the towels and stoops down to peek inside, with his nose about an inch from the top of Dewey's head. He sniffs the cage, then backs away and glares down at me with a disgusted face.

"That bird looks sick," he says.

"Yeah," I tell him. "He's got a deadly flesh-eating virus. Careful you don't catch it."

32. From the Journal of Erik Anselmus.

December 9: Emails from the Administration have stopped. Apparent lack of interest in investigation and progress with puzzle.

December 10: Lunch with Audrey Scalzo at Four Seasons. Free Food Principle not effective. Forced to pay her $1,000 for information about Jeff Pangborn.

33. The Biggest Industry in America

Spencer Casey

We all had a good laugh when those two cops, boiled and barbecued within an inch of their lives and gasping through their shirt sleeves to fend off Dewey's deadly virus, finally grabbed their coats and ran out the door. But to tell the truth, I was a little sorry to see them go. Aunt Lorraine don't have to read me my rights before she beats my brains out.

Soon as they leave she backs me against the wall, waving the frying pan over her head. "Who's this Charlie you're protecting?" she wants to know.

"Just a guy I used to work with," I tell her.

"Is he the white man who picked you up and drove you somewhere a few Sundays ago when you should've been in church?"

"Yeah, that's him."

"Is he a drug dealer?"

"No."

"A fence? A pimp?"

"No."

"What is he then?" She pushes her face closer, almost touching mine. "Why are the police after him?"

"You heard the officer. He stole a cherry pie from the Seven Eleven."

I'd never seen Aunt Lorraine up that close before—all her sags and wrinkles and blotches and the makeup she smears on her face to cover them up, her crooked teeth, her false eyelashes, her cracked lips. It's a scary sight up close, enough to make me want to run for my life even though I know she loves me, she's raised me since my mother died when I was two. And she must be thinking the same thing about me—she flinches away and peers at me like I'm an alien life form, but she's got little tears glistening in the corners of her eyes. "You're going to jail to protect some 40-year-old white man who don't pay his restaurant bills?"

"I ain't going to jail," I tell her.

"Don't say ain't. How much is he paying you?"

"He's my friend. that's all. I'm not going to jail."

Aunt Lorraine leans over the table and sets the frying pan down on one of her hot pads, even though it's empty and as cold as anything could be in that house. Then she plops down on a chair and sits there sighing and mopping her brow. From that distance she looks normal again but I don't want to get any closer. "Nothing much I can do, is there?" she says. "But let me just tell you something"— she raises her voice so Shawn can listen too—"Nobody in this house goes to jail! Do you hear me? I didn't bring anybody up in this house so they can go to jail. You hear me? And there aren't going to be any more house calls from the police, scaring the daylights out of me and putting Dewey's life in danger. You hear?"

I'm supposed to meet Monique at 15th and Market, right across from City Hall. She takes some of her college classes down there and she called and asked me to meet her for coffee on my way to work.

"Don't think of this as a date," she warns me on the phone.

"No way," I tell her.

"It's a business meeting," she says, "about a project I'm working on. I need some objective advice from a layman's perspective."

I don't know where she got the idea I'm a layman—maybe she thinks I took a correspondence course—but I'll play along if it means she's calling me instead of her friend Curtis. He might be a financial wizard but I guess he's missing something when it comes to the layman's perspective. Of course I've got to wear my gangsta clothes and my bling just to get out of the neighborhood without the little kids throwing stones at me. I'll change into my uniform at the lab like I always do.

When I get off the bus I can see Monique standing on the next corner waving to me. But before I'm halfway down the block I walk smack into Audrey, or she walks into me, blocking my way and throwing her arms around me like it's for old time's sake all over again. I try to pull away but she's all excited, telling me about how she's digging up dirt on Jeff on his computer. "Give me a call," I tell her, backing away. "I'm late for a business meeting."

That's something I never said before—"I'm late for a business meeting"—and it pumps me up to think I might be the kind of person who'd go to a business meeting and even be late for one. But Monique soon brings me crashing down to earth. "Why'd you wear those ridiculous clothes?" she asks me first thing. "And who was that woman hugging you on the street?"

"Oh, that was Audrey," I tell her. "The bookkeeper from the puzzle factory. She's about a hundred."

"Looks more like a forty-year-old cougar to me."

That makes me laugh. "Audrey couldn't be a cougar in the zoo."

In the coffee shop, even though it's not a date, Monique makes me buy her a cup of coffee that costs more than what I'd spend on dinner, and before long she gets down to business. "I just wanted to hear your opinion on a hypothetical situation," she says.

"Hypothetical," I nod, letting on like I know what it means. If it's anything like hypoglycemia or hypothyroidism, I've heard all about it from Lester Blount.

"That's right," she says. "Not about anyone you know."

"I'm glad to hear that. It can be pretty bad, can't it?"

She looks at me sort of funny and goes on, "Suppose there's a middle-aged, single woman who's been running a business all her life, with a toehold in a major industry, the biggest industry in America, in fact—"

"Which one's that? Oil wells? Fast food? Movies?"

"Beauty," she says, like I should already know the answer.

Up to then I didn't know beauty was an industry, but if it is, and you include Brenda's Hair Styling Salon in West Philadelphia as part of it, then Monique's Mom must be the hypothetical woman Monique's talking about. I didn't even know she was sick. And it's not easy picturing Brenda being sick—she's a small mountain who looks like she'd survive a nuclear attack if anybody was foolish enough to launch one against her. Now I understand, Monique's so upset she don't even want to mention her Mom or let on that's who she means. I've got to pretend I don't know either. "Go on," I nod.

"And this woman," Monique goes on, "has put her whole life into that business, and some people come along—some people she doesn't know—who offer to buy her out for a higher price than she ever imagined she could get for it, and they promise to keep her on as manager with a nice salary. Her accountant reviews the financials and tells her it's a slam dunk, her lawyer tells her she's got nothing to worry about. Her family, her friends—the whole world tells her it's the opportunity of a lifetime. But her heart is telling her something else. Her heart is telling her not to gamble her whole future on a deal that's too good to be true. Should she risk it or not?"

I take my time answering, trying to figure out what advice to give this unlucky hypothetical woman, who I know is Monique's Mom even though I've got to pretend she's somebody else. "You know me," I tell Monique. "I never gamble, except on the lottery, which isn't gambling because I know I can't win. I try to do what people tell me I'm supposed to do, and believe me, they never stop. But there's times when you've got to turn off the noise and listen to what your heart is telling you. Life is short— and for this poor woman, probably shorter than for the rest of us."

Monique wrinkles her forehead like I'm not making any sense. "Why do you say that?"

"I mean, on account of her being hypothetical and all."

"Well," she smiles, "it's not exactly *her* that's hypothetical. And besides—"

"Sorry, I didn't mean to imply that she was."

"Spencer, this is just an example."

I smile back, but I feel cornered, desperate to escape. I wish I really took that correspondence course so I knew what she was talking about. I almost wish she'd ask Curtis about her problems instead of me. "Sure it's an example," I tell her. "I know that. And I could give you an example of my own, an example of how a person might go their own way in spite of what everybody expects them to do. Suppose you work in a puzzle factory and one night you just can't go on chopping and wrapping up those puzzles anymore. It might be your only chance to leave your mark on the world—"

"What?" She grabbed my arm and started to laugh. "You're not the one who did that, are you?"

"Didn't I say this is just an example?"

"You did," she nods, still laughing.

"Because sometimes," I go on, "you've got to flap your wings like that butterfly in China, even if you don't know how it's all going to turn out in the end. You're who you are and sometimes you got to stop listening to everybody else and just listen to yourself. And that's what I would tell this poor hypothetical lady."

By now Monique's laughing her head off and I'm hoping—not just hoping, I can see it in her eyes—that it's not just because I said something funny (which I didn't) but because I'm different, maybe smarter or bolder than she thought. "You're crazy!" is all she says.

But I remember that when she was asking me about Audrey out on the street, there was a little glint of something in her eyes that just might have been jealousy.

And that's a good sign, I think. You don't get jealous at a business meeting.

34. Take Your Daughter To Work Day,
by Lindsay Pangborn

Our school sent out a letter to the parents reminding them about Take Your Daughter To Work Day, which is their way of getting rid of the girls for a whole day. Mr. Siegal said it would be a great opportunity to write something a little out of the ordinary for our chapbooks. My Dad said he'd never heard of it.

"It's a Quaker holiday," Zachary explained. "Like Take A Dweeb To Dinner Day." He sat at the kitchen table dissecting a frog, which he claimed was a Biology project but I think he was just doing it for fun. "The boys ought to get the day off too."

"Too bad they don't have Lock Your Son In A Padded Cell Day," I said. "Then you could participate."

Dad took our bickering in stride. "Sounds like a great learning experience, Lindsay," he told me. "It's about time you learned something about the real world."

Zachary stuck a pin into the frog and made its leg twitch, even though it was supposed to be dead. "You think school is bad," he said, "wait'll you find out what the real world is like."

You learn all sorts of things on Take Your Daughter To Work Day. For instance, you learn that your Dad doesn't actually go to work when he leaves the house but stops at two or three different coffee places where he flirts with the waitresses and expects you to be polite when he introduces you as his daughter, even though you're about to throw up at the sight of all that food so early in the morning, and that he talks on his phone and sends text messages while he's driving, which you wouldn't be allowed to do when you're sixteen if you were still going to be alive then (which you won't be), and passes school buses when the kids are getting on and gives the driver the finger if she honks at him. And then when you finally get to your Dad's office which is a glass building that looks like the monkey house at the zoo and meet his secretary Tammy, who's already worked for him longer than you're going to be alive, you learn what it's like to be compared to the pictures on his desk of yourself and your psychotic brother when you were about eight posing at the beach with a big smile like you were happy even though you were only faking, and later, for about the next three hours, you learn what it's like to sit in a cubicle pretending to do your Navajo Sign Language homework while your Dad goes to the gym.

It turns out my Dad's secretary, Tammy, who he thinks is devoted to him, hates him with a passion. She came up to my cubicle and offered me a Diet Coke, which I took, out of politeness, though I planned to pour it down the sink. She has huge breasts (my Dad says they're fake) and a twangy voice like a country singer. She asked me a lot of questions, and it wasn't long before we were talking about my Dad. At first she tried to defend him, but the more we talked the more she seemed to hate him, especially after I told her some of the things he's told me about her. Most of that stuff wasn't even true. Her hair doesn't come out of a bottle, her fingernails aren't two inches long, she doesn't live in a trailer with her brother who's also her uncle, and she was chewing gum while we were talking so I know my Dad was lying when he said she couldn't do both at the same time. When he didn't come back after three hours, I went into his office and put on a little act, crying and throwing things around.

Tammy hugged me and said she could only imagine what it must be like to be his daughter.

There's another lady here named Audrey who says she's working on a special project for my Dad. She has black hair and eyes that sort of bug out like antennas. When Audrey saw Tammy hugging me in my Dad's office, surrounded by all the junk I'd strewn on the floor, she rushed in and asked if everything was OK. That made me start crying all over again, just knowing there are people who care about me. What was I doing there? Audrey asked. I explained that it was Take Your Daughter To Work Day and I was there to learn about the real world. She and Tammy both laughed at that. Audrey said the only kind of world you could learn about from my Dad isn't one you'd want to live in, or even visit if you had a choice—it's a world of greed and corruption (and sin, Tammy added) that will soon be consumed in a blaze of suffering and retribution (divine retribution, according to Tammy) in which my Dad will either end up in Hell (Tammy) or under an exit ramp on the Schuylkill Expressway (Audrey). It turns out Audrey doesn't like my Dad very much either.

After I stopped crying, Tammy went down to the cafeteria and brought up some Italian hoagies, which I couldn't even stand to look at. The three of us sat in the conference room with the door shut while Tammy and Audrey gobbled their hoagies and downloaded everything that was on their minds. I found out my Dad was even worse than I thought. He terminated the employees' pension plan, cut back on their sick days and made them perform demeaning tasks like typing and filing. He canceled the veterinary health insurance even though Tammy's dog needs an operation for brain cancer. He welched on his United Way pledge and spent the money on a waitress he met at Hooters. Worst of all (according to Audrey), he raided my college trust fund (which came as a relief to me, since now I won't have to go to college, even if I lived that long) and used the money for a secret project he's working on with some guy named Armand Brigantine.

"Do you know who Armand Brigantine is?" Audrey asked me.

The name rang a bell. "Is he on the Phillies?"

She laughed. "I don't think so."

"What about Alex?" Tammy jumped in. "Do you know who Alex is?"

I must have turned as pale as a zombie when she asked that. I could almost feel my brains leaking out. How did she know about Alex? "Alex," I stammered, shaking my head, "Alex..."

"Is that the girl from Hooters?" Audrey wondered.

"Yes," I said. "That's her. Alex from Hooters."

"He talks about her to you?"

"Well, he's mentioned her. She's about twenty-five, I think. Maybe closer to thirty or thirty-five. They're just friends, just really good friends. And I think she has cancer."

"Could be," Tammy smiled. "All I know is, he's always asking me if she called or left a message. Seems like they've sort of lost touch."

"I know what you think about my Dad," I told them, "but it isn't true. He loves Kellie and he's going to marry her as soon as the divorce is final."

Tammy raised her eyebrows so high I could hear the makeup cracking. "Did your Daddy tell you that?"

I nodded. "Even though I told my Mom the opposite, to make her feel better. I told her my Dad said he wouldn't marry Kellie in a million years, but I was just making that up."

"What about the gal from Hooters?" Tammy asked. "Isn't she the one—"

I had to do something to change the subject. "Luckily," I interrupted, "I think we can fix most of the problems my Dad's caused. I've got all his passwords memorized."

Time seemed to stop when I said that. Tammy flickered her fake eyelashes at Audrey, whose eyes bugged out even farther than usual. Without moving her head, she seemed to be taking in everything at once—Tammy, me, her Italian hoagie and the door to the conference room, where my Dad might walk in at any time, freezing it like a screen shot so she could store it in her memory and consider all the possibilities before deciding what to do. "Did I hear you right?" Audrey asked. "Did you say you know all your Dad's passwords?"

"That's right."

She let out a little laugh that sounded like she had something stuck in her throat. "Jeff's world is about to get a little more real," she said.

They led me into my Dad's office and sat me down in front of his computer. "Can you log in to his personal files?" Audrey asked.

"Sure," I said. "I do it all the time." I wasn't worried about them seeing anything about Alex because as far as I knew, that was all on his phone and I'd deleted it long ago.

The three of us sat there together until almost three o'clock. Audrey seemed nervous at first, but Tammy told her that when my Dad goes to the gym he never comes back until late in the afternoon. "It's not like he's really at the gym," she said. "He's probably with that girl he met at Hooters." Tammy was starting to sound a lot like my Mom. I wondered if she and my Dad might have been more than just friends—why else would she hate him so much? When she sat next to me at the computer I understood why my Dad doesn't like her hair. It has a crust on it like it's been stuck together with Super Glue, and it smells like an ash tray. She carries a spray can of air freshener wherever she goes.

With Audrey's help, I was able to undo most of the mean stuff my Dad has been doing lately. His software allows all employee benefits to be managed on a single, user-friendly platform. Under "Health Insurance," for example, I could restore and actually improve Tammy's health coverage without charging her a premium by simply checking "Employer Self-Insured Plan," so now my Dad's company will pay the full cost of her dog's brain cancer surgery and any other treatments she and her family will ever need. I was able to reinstate the pension plan and, with a little help from Audrey, to fund it with transfers from one of my Dad's bank accounts, the one he uses for paying his online gambling debts (he was about to send $73,000 to some guy named Carlos in Las Vegas but it was easy to route that payment to the pension account). I made good on his United Way pledge and sent generous donations to Greenpeace, PETA and the Victims of Circumstance Reparations Fund. I paid some disputed taxes and some long overdue bills from suppliers, and had plenty of time left over to copy all the "Brigantine" files on a flash drive for Audrey. All in all I felt really good about what I'd accomplished that afternoon. As I told my Dad on the way home in the Mercedes, it was a valuable learning experience. I had no idea how complicated it is to run a business.

"You're one of the fortunate few," he said. "A lot of young people never get an opportunity to learn how the real world works." We stopped at a stop sign, which my Dad doesn't usually do, and across the street there were a bunch of girls a few years older than me waiting for a bus. They looked black or Hispanic or maybe Asian. I thought I recognized one of them from when she came to clean our house. "For instance," my

Dad said, "look at that bunch over there. I'd like to take them to the office some day so they can find out what it's like to work for a living."

35. End Times

Spencer Casey

At work I've got a 300-pound ex-Tummy Tweezer salesman slurping my whole paycheck into his supersize paunch. I've got to sneak in about fifty pounds of food a day—pizza, French fries, Tastykakes, Italian subs, cheese steaks, cases of diet Pepsi—all without being seen by Lester Blount or Ms. Killebrew or anybody else. After everybody leaves for the night, Charlie crawls out of his hiding place (there's no cell reception in there) so he can call his wife from the control room. When he's talking to her he acts like he's on a business trip to China, which is supposed to explain why he never comes home and can only call her in the middle of the night. Personally I doubt if she believes it because the cops went looking for him at his house and they probably told her he lost his job at GastroPlonix. But she plays along, pretending he's selling those Tummy Tweezers to the Chinese so she can keep fooling around with the real estate dude while he's gone.

After he's done talking to his wife he hangs out with me and Naked Dave in the control room, drinking vodka tonics and watching porno movies. Naked Dave charges him rent on his living quarters, he charges him for the vodka tonics and the ice cubes, he even charges him to watch the porno movies—and now he confiscated the keys to his van as collateral for what he owes.

"The dude's killing me," Charlie tells me after Naked Dave slips out to his awgies. "This dump's costing me more than my house. But you, Spencer—I don't know how I can ever thank you for bringing in all this free food."

"It ain't exactly free," I tell him.

"No, of course not. Nothing's free, is it? Especially food. I owe you one."

"Or two."

He looks at me funny. "Whatever. I'll pay you back. Soon as I get back on my feet."

Might take a forklift, I'm thinking, or maybe a crane to get Charlie back on his feet. But not to worry, he's a man with a plan. "Next Thursday's Penny's birthday," he tells me. "I made reservations at Le Papillon Libre. You heard of that place? It's gonna be the meal of a lifetime and you're invited, Spencer. You and your girlfriend, Monique or whatever her name is."

"I don't want to be horning in on your wife's birthday."

"No, I insist! My kids'll be there, and I invited Jeff Pangborn and his family."

That throws me a little. "How you going to lure that shark away from his pool?"

"Free food."

"Jeff's a millionaire, maybe a billionaire. He don't need free food."

"Like he'd pass up a free meal at the best restaurant in Philadelphia? Are you kidding? Anyway his girlfriend—Kellie? Is that her name?—and his daughter really want to come. He never takes them anywhere."

I hate to rain on Charlie's parade but this one looks like it could use a Category 5. "How you going to pay for this?" I ask him.

"I've got a plan," he says with a sly look. "And you're a big part of it."

That look tells me everything I need to know—more free food. "No," I tell him, reaching into the popcorn bowl. "No way I'm going to be a big part of that kind of plan. Not even a little one."

He clamps his huge hand around my wrist. "Spencer, don't let me down!"

My arm's numb, beyond pain, from the way he's squeezing it—it'll be falling off in the popcorn bowl any minute. "I've got an idea. Why don't you plan to get your ass out of here and park it someplace else?"

"I've got no place to go."

"What are you going to do, then?"

"You don't want to know, Spencer." He gives me the biggest, stupidest grin I've ever seen on his big, stupid face. "That way you can plead ignorance."

At home, the heat's finally getting to Shawn. He stopped going to school, he stopped making up hip hop lyrics, he even stopped watching TV except for church shows where all they talk about is Jesus and the Bible. He talks back to the TV when they say something he don't agree with. I just try to stay out of his way. One day when Aunt Lorraine's at work he jumps up off the couch and throws his clothes on and runs out the door, then he comes back about two hours later. "Big changes coming," he tells me. "We're living in end times."

"End of what?" I ask him.

His eyes are bloodshot and blazing. "The end of living in this sweat box."

"You been smoking something?"

He crouches down and glances around like he's afraid there might be somebody listening, but who could it be? Dewey's the only one home except me. You can hear him over there scratching and coughing in his cage.

"You know that pet shop down on Baltimore Avenue?" Shawn whispers. "For $39.99 they'll sell you a bird that looks exactly like Dewey used to look before he got sick."

"Is that right?"

"Spencer, you chip in half the money and we can buy that new bird in time for Christmas."

"Bring another bird in here? Won't it catch what Dewey's got?"

Shawn looks surprised and a little sly. "You don't understand, Spencer. The new bird's going to *be* Dewey. Just the way he was before he got sick."

What's he talking about? Some kind of magic? "Your mama don't want some other bird," I tell him. "She wants Dewey."

"She won't know the difference."

"Sure she will. Dewey looks like he just came out of the freezer."

Shawn steps over to Dewey's cage and stares down at him with a pitying look. "That's what he looks like now. But you and I, Spencer, we're going to pray over this bird day and night until he's cured. The Lord will hear our prayers and answer them with a miracle."

This talk of prayers and miracles makes me nervous. "What if he don't?"

Shawn's voice sounds kind of oily, like one of those preachers on TV. "What kind of Lord you think we're talking about here? You think He wants us to keep on living in a sweatbox?"—I can tell by the gleam in his eyes that he's putting a capital *H* on *He* like they do in church—"You think that's what He put us on the earth for?"

Now every night when we hear Aunt Lorraine coming in the door we fall on our knees next to Dewey's cage and pray that one day we'll wake up and find the poor bird restored to the way he used to be. We both kneel but Shawn does most of the actual praying. I feel a little guilty but Shawn says we're doing the right thing—the new bird he's going to buy for $39.99 at the pet store is going to make her happy, which is all that matters. Sometimes he even argues that the Lord, knowing everything and being all powerful, must agree with what we're doing. I can't agree with that because then everything that anybody does, no matter how good or bad, would always be the right thing. Shawn laughs at that and says it shows how ignorant I am. You've got to look at the results, he says—substituting that new bird for Dewey is the right thing to do because Dewey'll die in a few months anyway and how would that make Aunt Lorraine feel? Aunt Lorraine thinks we're crazy. She took Dewey to the doctor, she says, and gave him all the medicines, and no amount of praying's going to save him. She trusts in the Lord, she says, but the Lord made nature and nature has to take its course, even if a poor bird's got to die. To me that's even worse than Shawn's idea that the Lord controls every good or bad thing that ever happens. Aunt Lorraine's Lord can't control a thing—he just sits there and watches everybody die. I'd just as soon not believe in any Lord as believe in that one. That's why I consider myself a Zen Baptist. Luckily, Dewey the Second is waiting for us at the pet shop, all paid for and looking forward to Christmas in a new home. The Lord helps those who help themselves, Shawn says.

That girl Lindsay's been calling and texting me just about every day. She's Jeff Pangborn's daughter and crazy as they come, always dropping hints that if I don't take her out she might jump off a bridge with her friend Alex. I feel like blocking her calls but then I picture her jumping off that bridge and cursing me on the way down.

"That girl needs something to live for," Shawn says. "Something besides painting her nails and sending text messages."

We're in our usual places, Shawn on the couch, me in my chair, both half naked and sweating like pigs with the heater set at 95. I'm fanning myself with the menu from the Korean place on the corner. "I'll give her your number," I tell Shawn, "so she can call you instead."

Shawn don't crack a smile. "She's the daughter of that millionaire you used to work for, right? And she still lives in that mansion with him?"

"Sure she does. She's only fifteen."

"Then she ought to adopt Dewey. Give him a good home. That would give her something to live for."

I remember Jeff's house with its sacrificing block and shelves of Eagles bobbleheads and an entire room devoted to the Three Stooges and a psycho dog chewing on my pants leg and Lindsay dressed up like a hooker and Jeff's girlfriend Kellie, who's also dressed like a hooker and probably is one, threatening me with a butcher knife when I'm trying to find the bathroom, and I've got to laugh—is this what Shawn means by a good home? Is this the kind of place you'd send a defenseless bird who's probably got only a few months to live?

"Some day soon," Shawn says, mopping the sweat off his forehead with his sleeve, "when our prayers are answered, poor Dewey's going to need a new home. You don't want to just toss him out in the cold, do you?"

"That was your idea," I remind him.

"A mansion in the suburbs with a heated pool and a hot tub is just the place for Dewey. Lindsay'll take good care of him, won't she?"

I picture Jeff Pangborn sweltering shirtless in his kitchen, Kellie stripped to bra and panties, steam swirling around the sacrificing block as Lindsay stokes the wood stove and cranks up the hot tub to the boiling point, and I've got to laugh. "I know she'll make sure it's a hundred degrees in there."

"If Jeff Pangborn's half as evil as you say he is," Shawn says, "he's going to roast in Hell. Might as well get used to it."

Every time I close my eyes I can see what's on my mind—Charlie inside that wall, smelling more like a dead man every day. He knows he's doomed but he won't give up the fight. He's got to make it to Penny's birthday, he says, or he'll die trying. Everybody's against him—Ms. Killebrew, Naked Dave, Lester Blount, the cops, even Monique and Aunt Lorraine, all of them pointing at me, pressuring me to turn him in. I know I should but I just can't do it. And now Shawn hounds me all day long about Dewey. Daytime's when I'm supposed to be sleeping but it's 100 degrees in here and Shawn's church shows blast out of the TV all day long. If I open my eyes he notices it somehow even though he's in the other room. He runs in here and wants to know when I'm going to get rid of Dewey. "That girl said she'd take him, didn't she?" he asks me. "Send her a text message. I need to know when you're going to hand him over so I can pick up the new bird at the pet store."

I've got problems I can't tell Shawn about. Lindsay says she wants Dewey but I'm afraid what she wants is me. On the phone she says she'll come over and pick Dewey up some time when nobody's home, but I tell her no, there's no time when nobody's home in this house, we've got about fifty people living here, mothers and uncles and cousins and aunts and a whole crew of drug addicts and murderers like you'd expect in this sort of neighborhood. Naturally she believes me. She says OK, then bring him out to my house in the afternoon when my Dad and Kellie are at work and Zachary's still at lacrosse practice. I can't do that, I tell her, I don't have a car, and besides, why does it have to be when nobody's home?

"You know," she says, "so we can hook up." She says it just like that, casual as can be, as if it don't mean a thing.

"Well," I tell her, playing dumb, "it's true we've got to hook the heating coil up to the bird cage, but why can't we do that when your Dad's home? Maybe he can help."

She laughs, a little too loud, and I laugh along with her. I've got to be careful with this girl or I'm going to end up in a cage of my own.

"OK," she says. "I was just testing you. Can you meet me at the mall?"

"What mall?"

"Whatever one's closest to your house," she laughs, like I'm fooling with her.

"We don't even have a drug store in this neighborhood," I tell her. "And anyway I can't go lugging Dewey's bird cage around or he'll get too cold and probably die."

OK," she finally says, "I'll come down to your house in a taxi and pick him up. How big is the cage?"

36. From the Journal of Erik Anselmus.

December 14: Headaches, cold sweats, insomnia, now unbearable. Sometimes in the night I hear voices I'm not sure are there.

Note to the Administration:

> God—if there is a God—must love the insurance industry, to have created a universe containing just the right proportions of order and uncertainty. In a completely determined universe, no one would buy insurance; in a random one, no one would sell it. Astonishingly, the ideal conditions for the insurance industry have arisen in our universe, like certain physical constants that seem to be fine-tuned to enable intelligent life. Is this proof that God exists? Or merely that in an infinite number of possible universes arising in an infinite amount of time, one universe—ours—has arisen in which the insurance industry is not only possible but necessary?

December 15: At closing time Cathy sits down across from me in my booth, noting my lack of progress on the puzzle. It's time to go, she says. You can work on it more tomorrow.

I tell her: We can't allow ourselves to live at the mercy of butterflies flapping their wings any time they get the notion.

Of course not, she agrees. Butterflies? Of course not. Who said anything about butterflies?

And yet there are times, I explain, usually late at night when I can't sleep, after I've counted to infinity and back, when I think that God (not that there is one) does play at dice with the universe. When I think this is not the best of all possible worlds, or the worst, or even one that's likely to last longer than another thirty seconds. And when I'm lying awake in that darkness, I sense that the worm of chaos has crawled into the world and begun to devour it. I think nothing is determined, that anything can happen—that people really are free. But do you know what? At those times, I don't feel free. I feel more trapped than ever.

37. Take Your Dad's Live-In Girlfriend to Work Day, by Lindsay Pangborn

When I got back from Take Your Daughter To Work Day, Kellie backed me into a corner and pumped me for information until I could hardly stand up. Now I know what it's like to be waterboarded or paraded around naked on a leash until you confess. *Was his secretary Tammy there?* Yes. *Is he sleeping with her?* I don't think so. She has Super Glue hair and Cracker Jack teeth and she hates his guts. *(Bitter laughter) That never stopped him before. Who else was there?* Audrey. *Who's Audrey?* Some lady that used to work at the puzzle factory. *The bookkeeper?* I think so. *(More bitter laughter) What was she doing there?* She's working on my Dad's new project. *What new project?* Project Brigantine. *Project Brigantine?* That's what Audrey called it. *Does Tammy know about Alex?* She thinks Alex is some waitress he met at Hooters. *(Even more bitter laughter) Why would she think that?* I don't know. *Where is he getting the money for his new project?* He's embezzling it from our college funds. *Where else?* You'd have to ask Audrey. *Why Audrey?* She made copies of all my Dad's computer files. *How could she do that?* I gave her all his passwords.

Kellie backed away with her eyes wide. "You did what?"

"I gave Audrey all my Dad's passwords so she could copy his files."

"Why did you do that?"

"She and Tammy were starting to ask about Alex and I wanted to change the subject."

Kellie glared at me with murder in her eyes. For a minute I wished I was wearing a suicide belt instead of the suede kind you get at the Gap.

In the morning I went with Kellie to my Dad's office. I pretended to be getting ready for school until my Dad left in his Mercedes. Then I pretended to be sick until Kellie drove Zachary to the bus stop in the Land Cruiser and came back to pick me and Cupcake up. It wasn't hard pretending to be sick. All I had to do was watch Zachary eat breakfast. Cupcake was upset when he realized we weren't going directly to Wagsmore Manor. He started barking insanely and hurling himself snarling and drooling against the bars of his cage behind the back seat. White foamy globs of drool flew into the back seat and some of them even landed on my lap in the front passenger seat and splatted on the rear view mirror. He calmed down when I talked to him in the dog voice and explained that he'd only miss his first couple of classes.

When we arrived at my Dad's office park, Kellie parked the Land Cruiser between two other SUVs so you couldn't see who was in it. I felt sort of guilty lying in wait for Audrey. Since Kellie didn't know her, couldn't I just pretend not to recognize her and everything would be OK? But Kellie must have read my mind. "Don't even think about it," she said. "If you don't want your life to be a living hell, you'd better pray that Audrey shows up for work this morning."

I almost felt like crying when Audrey parked her car and headed toward the door. What did I care if my miserable life was a living hell for a few more days? Isn't that what it was already? Wasn't I getting ready to jump off a bridge? But then I remembered—I needed Kellie to drive me to the mall ahead of time so I could see how far the bridge was from the Gap so I'd know which shoes to wear.

"There she is," I said. "That's Audrey."

Kellie stuck her head out the window and called Audrey's name. Audrey walked toward the Land Cruiser, peering at us through the windshield. She smiled when she saw me. "Hi, Lindsay." She looked sort of puzzled. "Is everything OK?"

By this time Kellie was out of the car, holding the back door open. "My name is Kellie," she said. "I'm Jeff Pangborn's girlfriend. You and I need to have a little talk." She shoved Audrey into the back seat, even though it was all white and slimy with dog drool, and climbed in after her. Cupcake tried to leap through the bars and take Audrey's head off.

"He's friendly," Kellie assured her.

"Is something the matter?" Audrey asked. She was holding her ears and she looked scared.

Kellie's face looked red and mean in the rear view mirror. "Something's the matter, all right," she told Audrey, shouting to be heard. "You took advantage of this fourteen-year-old girl and got her to give you all her father's passwords so you could use them to hack into his computer and copy his files. Lock the doors, Lindsay!"

"I'm working with Jeff on his new project," Audrey shouted. "I had every right to access those files."

"Why didn't you get them from him?"

Audrey reached for the door handle. "Let me out of here."

"I think I have a pretty good idea of what's going on," Kellie said. "There's a nasty custody battle going on and Lindsay and Zachary are caught in the middle. Their mother is a very sick woman and you're working for her and her slimeball lawyer. How much are they paying you?"

By this time Audrey was swearing at the top of her lungs, yanking frantically at the door handle and threatening to have Kellie buried in cement up to her neck and dumped in the Schuylkill River if she didn't let her out of the car.

"I'm not going to let you get away with it!" Kellie shouted. "Do you understand?"

Audrey had her cell phone out. "If you don't open that door, I'm dialing 9-1-1 and you can tell the police why you locked me in here against my will to be attacked and spat on by this dog."

"Nobody's holding you against your will," Kellie said. "And if this dog—who has a name, by the way: his name is Cupcake—is upset with you, it's because your fear is provoking him. But you haven't heard the end of this, believe me. Lindsay, would you reach over and unlock the doors, please?"

"You're such a hypocrite," Audrey said as she climbed out. "Pretending to care so much about the kids when it's only yourself you care about. You're marrying Jeff for his money and you don't want to share any of it with his wife. It's as simple as that." She turned around and headed toward the entrance to the building.

"You don't know what you're talking about," Kellie called after her. "He's not even going to marry me. He said he wouldn't marry me in a million years."

Audrey stopped and turned around, peering back at Kellie with a funny look on her face. At first it was like she was trying to understand what Kellie'd just said, and then like she was mocking her, scrunching up her nose and squinting through her bug eyes (that's what my Dad calls them). "He told you that?" Audrey asked. "He said he wouldn't marry you in a million years?"

It was all Kellie could do to keep from crying. "Not to my face," she said, "but he told it to someone else and I found out about it. And believe me, it hurts." By now the tears were streaming down her cheeks. "I've had to let go of my own dreams for the sake of the kids. I'm just trying to do the right thing."

Audrey stood watching Kellie for a minute as if maybe she felt a little sympathy, but then she shook her head and smiled like it was all a joke. Then she turned around and went inside.

I know it sounds hokey and sentimental, but I was so proud of Kellie for sticking up for me and Zachary that I started crying too. It broke my heart to think that my Dad wouldn't marry her in a million years, even though I'd just made that up when I told it to my Mom. I knew Kellie was a good person who loved me and I could trust. Audrey, on the other hand, had turned out to be evil. I prayed that I would never see her again.

Which, a little voice told me, wouldn't be all that hard, since I was only going to be on the planet for another three days.

38. Not In A Million Years

When Audrey turned her back on Kellie and Lindsay in their Land Cruiser and stepped toward Jeff's shiny all-glass office building, her ears were buzzing with the astonishing revelation Kellie had just made without realizing its significance. She remembered exactly what Lindsay said on Take Your Daughter To Work Day: that she (Lindsay) had told her Mom that Jeff said he wouldn't marry Kellie in a million years, but this was not true—Jeff hadn't really said that. Lindsay just told it to her Mom (who hated Kellie) to make her feel better. So if Kellie had found out about it from "someone else," who could that have been? She didn't hear it from Lindsay, certainly not from Jeff, or from Roberta herself. She could only have heard it from Roberta's scheming attorney, Morton C. McMonigle, Jr., Esq. Which meant that Kellie had been negotiating with McMonigle to give him what he wanted—Jeff's head on a silver platter—in exchange for a sum of money that was probably comparable to what McMonigle had offered Audrey for a similar trophy.

What was in Jeff's computer files that could be so dangerous? Not just a few messages to some waitress at Hooters—who would care about that, other than Kellie herself? No, it must be something far more valuable, something much more incriminating than the information Audrey had turned over to Erik Anselmus a few days before. Maybe Kellie already had it, or could easily put her hands on it; she had to be stopped before she talked to McMonigle. Unfortunately Jeff could only be destroyed once.

Inside the lobby, Audrey stopped at the coffee kiosk to pick up some breakfast. Before she took the elevator up to the sixth floor, she dialed McMonigle's office and left a voice message. "If you want information from me," she told him, "don't talk to Kellie again. What I have is far more valuable than anything she can give you. I just need a couple of days to pull it together. In the meantime, if I hear that you've been talking to Kellie, you'll never hear from me again."

39. Romeo and Juliet, Part Deux,
by Lindsay Pangborn

Spencer's aunt has this parrot named Dewey he wants to give me
to take care of. It's not a present exactly, more like an animal
rescue, like the time I bought all the goldfish in the pet store to
keep them from being fed to the snakes. At least parrots are
vegetarians—I looked that up in Wikipedia—though I don't
know if they're vegans or not, or if they eat gluten. I hate the
idea of eating but I realize you have to make allowances for
animals, especially birds. Considering the way they've been
brought up, with their parents literally stuffing insects and
worms down their throats—at least my Mom never did that!—
you can't blame them for trying to devour all those grasshoppers
and mosquitos. At least they eat the mosquitos and don't spray
them with poisons or try to lure them into a bug zapper. And
even predatory birds deserve credit for hunting locally instead of
shipping in genetically modified roadkill made by Monsanto.
But Spencer says the trouble with his bird isn't that he eats—it's
that he has some fatal disease that made all his feathers fall out,
except a little tuft on the top of his head. The virus isn't
catching to humans, or I'd take the bird for sure and stick it in
Zachary's room. What Dewey needs, Spencer says, is a good
home (doesn't he realize my Dad's a pervert who couldn't even
be trusted with a bird?) where he'll be kept warm, unlike
Spencer's house where it's ice cold, like all crack houses, because
his aunt can't afford to pay the heating bill until she gets her
welfare check.

At first I went along with this because I was so excited that Spencer was calling and texting me back. I thought maybe he'd bring the bird to our house, in a taxi or something, some day when I was here by myself. I had a lot of fantasies about what would happen when we were alone together. But he kept making excuses until I realized he wouldn't come to the house unless my Dad was here—he wouldn't even meet me at the mall! There must be a couple of malls in his neighborhood so I suggested we meet there, but he says all they have is liquor stores and crack houses and shoot-outs between drug gangs. He offered to meet me at the McDonald's downtown for a cheeseburger and I almost threw up. Why does he want my Dad around? Does he think Dad would stand for us going out, even for a minute?

Our relationship is doomed, just like the one in *Romeo and Juliet*, which (according to Mr. Siegal) is a tragedy, unlike *A Midsummer Night's Dream*, which is a comedy. If my life was a play (which is what it seems like more and more), I'd rather be in a tragedy, even if I had to die in the end, than in a comedy, where the plot takes over your life like a stupid dream and when you wake up you don't even know if you were dreaming or not. At least in a tragedy you can be noble—you have to be noble— even if you kill yourself, which is what you usually do. And in the meantime you can deliver soliloquies—those are when a character talks and nobody listens, which sums up my whole pathetic life. I used to think I could undo the plan with Alex if Spencer started texting me back, but now I realize that you can't escape your Fate, even if you set it up yourself. I feel pretty committed to Alex at this point. Unless Spencer starts showing some serious interest—I mean serious, like being willing to do some of the stuff Alex wanted to do with my Dad—then I might as well get used to my Fate. Alex is the only friend I'll ever have.

40. Time To Turn The Page

Detective Bob "Mean" Kampf had grown increasingly alarmed at Officer Gilboy's furtive, obsessive behavior. The constant emails, the surreptitious downloads, the prying questions, all spelled disaster for Police District 41. Kampf was convinced that Gilboy was a spy sent by Headquarters, a whistleblower, a snitch. Probably a pervert himself, if not something worse. His hot and heavy internet romance with the 45-year-old man named "Steve" who claimed to be a girl named Lindsay had taken a morbid turn, adding a suicide pact into the mix. What if this Lindsay was really a 14-year-old girl? What did that make Gilboy?

"Gilboy," Kampf said as they sipped coffee in the lunch room, "I want to see this pervert in the can by Christmas. In fact I want him in the can by the Friday before Christmas, which is when I leave to go fishing in the Keys."

"I'm doing my best to nail him, Detective."

"Is that a yes? I need a yes."

Gilboy's eyes flared. "Don't you think I want to get this scum off the streets?"

"You ever do any fishing, Gilboy?" Kampf's red face glowed a little brighter than usual. "You know, sometimes dangling the bait isn't enough. Sometimes, when you feel a nibble, you've got to give the line a little twitch so you can snag the fish and reel it in."

Gilboy stared down at his coffee. "I play it by the book, Detective."

"What book is that? The book that says sit around playing with yourself while the perverts go home for the holidays?"

"The book that says I can't make the first move."

"Maybe it's time to turn the page."

Kampf stood up and threw the rest of his coffee into the trash can. "Just to be clear, Gilboy," he said, "I want an arrest in this case and I want one before Christmas."

"You will, Detective."

"This guy's beyond being a pervert. He could be a serial killer. Trying to lure this little girl into suicide."

Gilboy blinked in confusion. "What little girl?"

"You, Gilboy. You're Alex, aren't you? Or are you somebody else?"

41. From the Journal of Erik Anselmus

December 16: Moved out of hotel, now living incognito with homeless men in Love Park, near City Hall. Sleeping on a grate. Headaches and other symptoms have stopped. Have never felt better—relieved to know I'm not going crazy. Handgun obtained from drug dealer for $100.

December 17: Paid Audrey $2,000 for information about Jeff Pangborn's new business venture: Buying up depressed real estate occupied by small businesses in need of cash—hundreds of hair salons and beauty spas—then leasing property back to former owners at exorbitant rents. Millions of dollars of real estate. Closing scheduled for Thursday.

Found Spencer Casey at last. The hour of reckoning is at hand.

December 18: Follow up call to Audrey: What is the name of Jeff Pangborn's new business partner? She says: "Armand Brigantine." My head is exploding! How can this be?

42. Only Five Shopping Days Left 'Til Christmas!
by Lindsay Pangborn

Sometimes I have a strange sensation, only it's not physical like being cold or nauseated, it's more like a sudden feeling that I know something, I absolutely know it, though I'm not sure what it is, and I'm afraid to find out. Ms. Stebbins says I'm only fooling myself when I feel that way. You can fall in love with your own fantasies, she says, so you start to act as if they're real even though you know they're not. This happens with lies that you tell or other people tell you and it happens with movies and TV shows and stuff you see on the internet—you can get caught up in them as if you believed them, and then your life is ruined. Ms. Stebbins doesn't like the internet. She says it's like a spider web that sends out millions of tiny strands all over the world— "Why do you think they call it the world wide web?"—that ensnare you and capture your mind the way a spider catches a fly. She looked a little scary when she said that.

One night about a week ago we went down to the family room after dinner. Zachary and I clicked on the TV while my Dad read a big book about NASCAR racing. He tried to make us watch an old movie called *It's A Wonderful Life,* which we've seen about a hundred times. When Zachary wanted to change the channel, my Dad wouldn't let him. "You should watch *It's A Wonderful Life,"* he said. "You might learn something from it."

"It's totally boring," Zachary said, and I agreed. "What's the point?"

"The point is that your life matters and you should make the most of it." He gave us this bullying look he uses when he doesn't really believe what he's saying. "Everyone can find inspiration in this movie."

"Everyone?" Zachary asked. "Even you?"

"Sure. Why not?"

Zachary winked at me and I knew why. It was because of my Dad's idea that the movie might apply to him. "Let's face it, Dad," he said, smiling. "You're no George Bailey. The world wouldn't have been any different without you."

My Dad sort of gulped. "You've seen it, then?"

"In fact," Zachary added, "it might have been a whole lot better off."

I didn't chime in—I didn't want my Dad to take it personally. And it was a good thing I didn't. He threw his book down like he wished he could aim it at Zachary's head. "What are you talking about?"

Zachary shrugged like he was just innocently saying whatever popped into his head. "Maybe the puzzle factory wouldn't have gone under—"

"That wasn't my fault!"

"—and all those people wouldn't have been thrown out of work."

"I found them all good jobs!"

"And look at me!"—Zachary grinned like a chimpanzee and pushed one of his scary Goth tattoos right in front of my Dad's face—"Your only son."

"I try not to," Dad said, gritting his teeth.

"That's the point. If I'm half as bad as you think I am, you ought to jump in front of a train."

"It wouldn't work," my Dad muttered. "They're never on time."

After that we got to watch what we wanted, which was a cartoon version of *A Christmas Carol* about the old miser Scrooge who stays home counting his money on Christmas Eve and won't even let his clerk Bob Cratchit take the day off. Naturally that got Zachary raging against the machine and the ruling class and quoting from Kurt Cobain and Che Guevara. My Dad and I both ignored him and that only seemed to fire him up. I could hardly hear what Bob Cratchit was saying.

"So," Dad asked during one of the commercials, "what do you guys want for Christmas this year?"

I rolled my eyes. "Nothing for me, thanks."

Dad looked up from his book in amazement. "You've got something against Christmas?"

"Christmas is just another occasion for conspicuous consumption," Zachary said. "It's like sending your kids to Guatemala to build hovels for the natives."

"Huh?"

"Or turning them into galley slaves so they can get into some stupid college," I chimed in.

Zachary stood up and hovered in front of Dad's chair as he spoke. "Let's face it, Dad. You want our lives to be totally pointless and meaningless."

"I do?"

"Sure. It's all in a book called *The Theory of the Leisure Class*. The more useless your kids are, the more your friends will be impressed with how rich you must be."

"If you had any friends," I couldn't help adding.

Zachary danced around the room like a ghost, waving his hands together over his head to a silent beat. "Listen to me, mon!" he croaked in a fake West Indian accent. "I am the ghost of Bob Marley!"

He stopped dancing and stared Dad straight in the eye, growling in a low voice: "You will be haunted by three spirits, mon! Expect the first in two days, when the bell tolls three."

Dad tried to turn it into a joke but I think he was a little annoyed. "Bah! Humbug!" was all he could say before Zachary skittered back to his room.

I don't really feel that way about Christmas but I know that buying me any presents would be a big waste. Alex and I considered waiting until after Christmas, but it didn't seem fair to our parents, who would have spent all that money on presents we'd never be able to exchange. Besides, getting out to the mall at this time of year is a nightmare and I know I'll have to take the bus—I can't exactly ask my Dad to drive me, can I?—and the crowds only get worse after Christmas. Kellie's been really nice lately, ever since we talked about my Dad's text messages. He doesn't even suspect I was the one who read them. No one but Kellie and I know he's ever had anything to do with Alex.

Yesterday I asked Kellie to take me out to the mall, supposedly for Christmas shopping, though my real purpose was to scope out the plan. The bridge—or overpass, I guess you'd call it—goes across an expressway that's always full of trucks roaring by at about eighty miles an hour. The guard rail is pretty low, with a ledge you can stand on, and it's an easy walk from the Gap, where I'm going to meet Alex at 4:00 o'clock. I'll have to skip crew practice and come home early from school so I can get out there in time.

Sometimes I have second thoughts but at this point I feel sort of committed. Alex seems really anxious, she texts every day. She wants to make sure she's still included. Of course she is, I reassure her. That's the whole point, to share my sacrifice with a special friend—though sometimes I wonder, what if she isn't a virgin? Zachary says you have to be a virgin to be sacrificed, and sometimes I tell myself I'd still have time to be disqualified if I could get Spencer to cooperate. But then there's that other girl, Bridget Morrison, at school, who smirked when she saw what kind of shoes I was wearing. I feel committed to her too, in a funny way. I want her to remember me.

Spencer wants me to come down to his house in a taxi and pick up his sick bird so I can keep it warm until it dies. It's a featherless parrot, he says, who talks in rhymes and can only survive under rain forest conditions. Is that all I mean to Spencer? Does he think I'm so desperate for friends that I need to hang out with a character from a Dr. Seuss book? Anyway I have crew practice this afternoon and I'm only going to be on the planet a couple more days. If I brought the bird home, what would happen to it after Alex and I keep our appointment at the mall? Would Mr. and Ms. Selfish (i.e., my Dad and Kellie) give it the kind of care and attention it needs? If I left it to Zachary he'd probably just feed it to Cupcake, if he didn't bite its head off to see what it's like to be a real geek. So there's nothing I can do, is there? I'm sorry, Spencer. I'm afraid I can't help you.

43. The Bird Who Loved Me

Spencer Casey

It's 4:30 and almost dark and I'm out on the stoop watching for Lindsay's taxi that was supposed to come a half hour ago. I left Dewey's cage just inside the door to keep him warm. Shawn's in the living room with the new bird waiting for me to get rid of Dewey so we can show Aunt Lorraine the miracle cure soon as she comes home from work. With Lindsay being so late we're cutting it a little too close. I can hear Shawn hollering to hurry up like I can just make that taxi appear out of thin air like another miracle. I've got enough on my mind without worrying about that. Mostly I'm thinking about Charlie, who won't last more than a couple more days in his cave. Ms. Killebrew thinks there's something dead behind that wall, maybe a raccoon or a possum, or maybe even Charlie himself—that's what it smells like—and the stink's so bad it's going to put her out of business if the FDA makes a surprise inspection. She already called an exterminator and if Charlie gets caught and they find out I've been feeding him, Ms. Killebrew will nail my ears to the wall and use me for target practice. I spend a lot of time wondering why I'm doing this for Charlie. Maybe I ought to look out for myself. Maybe I ought to let Charlie look out for himself. Maybe I ought to give him to Lindsay to take care of instead of that bird.

It's quarter to five and I can see my breath fogging up on the stoop. Still no sign of a taxi. Aunt Lorraine'll be home in a half hour. Five o'clock, I hear a little beep and there's a message from Lindsay. Like all her messages it's just a jumble of letters—*Srry cdnt mke it had crew prac mayB nxt wk*—but I know what it means. She's not coming tonight and *MayB nxt wk* means never. I can't say why but I feel almost sick when I read that message, weak in the knees like I'm going to fall off the stoop. I'm standing there wobbling and staring at my phone when Shawn comes over to the door.

"Where's your girlfriend?" he asks me, squinting out through the screen.

"Not coming," I tell him. "She has crew prac. Whatever that is."

"Rich people are different," he says.

"I don't know what to do with Dewey."

Shawn opens the door and hands me the cage. "Just let him fly away."

"What do you mean?"

"He's a bird."

"But he'll die. It's cold out here."

Shawn slams the door in my face and locks it from inside. "Let him go!"

"Hey!" I yell. "What you doing? Open that door!"

"Let him fly away!"

"Open that door! I'm not letting him loose and I'm not going nowhere. You want me to be out here with this cage when your mama comes home?"

He stands there a minute, then he cracks open the door. I can tell from the look in his eyes that he's almost ready to cry. His whole plan's going down the drain and Aunt Lorraine'll be home in about five minutes.

"You want to let Dewey out of his cage," I tell him, "why don't you do it yourself?"

"I couldn't do that to my mama," Shawn says.

"What about me?"

"She's not your mama." He opens the door and sticks his head outside, rolling his eyes like he's having a fit. "Please, Spencer. Do it for my sake. I can't stand this heat anymore."

"OK, Shawn. I'll do this for you."

"I love you, man."

It's wrong—I know that. Dewey's an orphan just like I was. I know it's wrong. But sometimes you've got to do something bad to stop something worse. I believe Shawn when he says he can't take it anymore. We had a plan, Shawn and me, and unless we want to spend the rest of our lives broiling like a couple of steaks on a grill, we've got about two minutes to put that plan into action.

I open the cage and reach inside for Dewey. He shudders when I touch him, my hand is so cold. He's croaking and coughing and clearing his throat like he knows what I'm doing and he's going to try to talk me out of it. Lifting him out of the cage, I hold him up over the railing so when I let him go he can fly out over the sidewalk and maybe make it across the street and die over there.

"Good-bye, Dewey," I tell him.

He tilts his head and looks at me sideways with his beady yellow eyes. "I love you, man," he says in his smart-alecky voice. "I love you."

Shawn jiggles the door and waves his arm. "Go ahead, Spencer. Let him go!"

Dewey tilts his head the other way and looks at me again with his sad eyes. "I love you, man."

Suddenly I feel weak in the knees like I felt before Shawn came to the door. I'm out of breath and my heart's pounding a mile a minute. I step back from the railing with Dewey who's staring at me with his dumb, trusting eyes. I can't kid myself—letting him go in the cold is a death sentence. It's like I'm strapping him into the electric chair, and what did he do to deserve it?

I shove him back through the cage door and slide it shut.

Shawn hollers, "Hey, what you doing?"

"I can't do it."

I never saw Shawn so upset. "That bird don't give a damn about you!" he yells. "He says he loves you but you think he gives a damn? He's just repeating what he heard me say to you. Don't you remember? I said, 'I love you, man.' That was just a joke, I didn't even mean it. He don't mean it either!"

"You do it, then." I swing the cage toward Shawn and he stumbles backwards. "You let him out."

Shawn hangs his head like he's been beaten. And he has been, though he'll never admit it—beaten by a parrot. He can't let Dewey die either.

We've got to hurry or it'll be us on death row, soon as Aunt Lorraine gets home. We put the cage back in the dining room with Dewey in it and hide the new bird down the basement in a cozy spot behind the furnace. By the time Aunt Lorraine steps through the door we're huddled over Dewey's cage, according to plan, praying for a miracle cure. I don't know what's going to happen next. I'm thinking maybe we should start praying for a new plan. That new bird cost us $39.99 plus tax and now it's going to take a miracle to keep us from losing our money.

44. From the Journal of Erik Anselmus

December 19: Everything different now. Migraines again, unable to sleep on this grate. Boom boxes and skateboards unbearable. Pigeons: remote-control toys? William Penn spying down from the top of City Hall. If Armand Brigantine is Jeff Pangborn's business partner—nowhere to hide.

Lunch at soup kitchen next to Philadelphia Free Library. In art collection found monograph, *Armand Brigantine: Visionary of Chaos,* by Nancy P. Zhang, Ph.D. Reference Copy Not To Be Taken From This Room.

Notes from book:

Page 1: "Armand Brigantine studied painting at Cooper Union for two years and dropped out. Culturally, he was a child of the Sixties. He assumed, as everyone did in those heady times, that the purpose of life was to find freedom in an absurd, mechanistic universe."

Freedom? Absurd.

Page 3: "Brigantine became obsessed with the idea of freedom, which he equated with resistance to the unjust order of the cosmos. 'People expect an artist to create order out of chaos,' he wrote, 'but my ambition is just the opposite.' He started with order—the deterministic order of the universe—and against that he tried to create chaos. Why? As a cry of protest, a declaration of freedom for the human race."

Page 4: "He found himself making deliberate mistakes, inserting random elements, vandalizing his own work with explosions of indeterminacy. The more his technical skill increased, the more he rebelled against it. Finally he realized that he wanted to paint chaos itself: pure, metaphysical chaos—art, as he put it, that was *without form and void.*"

Page 8: "From an early age he had showed signs of mental instability: fits of depression, flights of fantasy, angry outbursts. In his early thirties, he began to drift into paranoia and delusions of grandeur."

Page 18: "Brigantine wanted to paint chaos itself—no order, no pattern, no boundaries, no beauty. He began to feel that something in the nature of things was conspiring against him. How would he know if he created a picture of chaos? How could he be sure it was not part of some larger pattern spread across time or space on a scale no human being could perceive? For all he knew there were similar images in a recurring pattern throughout the universe, or in other universes that mirror ours, forming a matrix which set his paintings into an orderly, repetitive pattern."

Page 30: "One of the critics wrote in *Art Forum* that in painting Chaos Scape 19, Brigantine had created a picture of chaos so perfect that it could not be described, or even conceived, by any human being. Brigantine called it 'the chaos before creation.'"

He thought he was God!

Page 38: "A few weeks after he had sold Chaos Scape 19 to the Museum of Modern Art for $2,000,000, Brigantine learned that MOMA was offering a $25 color reproduction of the painting in its gift shop. He blocked the museum entrance and shouted:

'Two copies of chaos is a reflection! Three is a pattern! Ten thousand is an abomination!'"

Page 39: "Two weeks later he learned that MOMA had licensed the print to a jigsaw puzzle company in Philadelphia. The thought that his masterpiece—his picture of perfect chaos that made him God—would be stamped into a repetitive pattern, chopped in a thousand pieces and poured into cardboard boxes for reassembly by weak-minded senior citizens and bored 10-year-olds tipped him over the edge."

He had gone mad.

Page 40: "Following the violent MOMA protest, at which dozens of tourists were injured, Brigantine was committed to a nursing home in Philadelphia, where he remains to this day."

45. You Can't Pray a Lie

Spencer Casey

One of the problems with this place is there's no shower. Naked Dave gets swabbed down every afternoon by the nurses to make his life as close as possible to being in a coma, but Charlie just festers in his hole in the wall like a dead fish. The smell's so bad now that Ms. Killebrew brought in an exterminator who had to put on a moon suit before he went in the computer room. Luckily this won't go on much longer. Charlie's got to be out of here tomorrow if he's going to keep his date at Le Papillon Libre.

Tonight everybody's staying much later than usual, Ms. Killebrew whispering to Lester Blount in her office with the door closed—Lester's never stayed this late before—while I listen to Naked Dave, stretched out on his bed naked (except for his blindfold) bragging about his days as a hit man in New Yawwwk. I'm not sure if that was before or after he was a professor, in fact I'm starting to wonder if the whole professor thing and even the Ph.D. might just be something he told Ms. Killebrew to get the job. He stops talking soon as Ms. Killebrew and Lester Blount come out of her office, like he's been in a coma all night, and for a minute all I hear is Lester whistling some stupid country song until Ms. Killebrew says good night and the outside door slams shut. Lester walks over and gives Naked Dave a poke in the ribs to make sure he's awake and then looks straight at me. "I guess you boys heard the exterminator was here today about that stench in the computer room," he says in his folksy voice, the one he uses when he's trying to be sly. "Well, he's coming back in the morning to take down the wall behind the copying machine. That's where the smell's coming from. It's a dead animal, he says—and not a small one, neither."

"It's a big animal then?" I play along. "Like what? A dog?"

"Bigger'n a dog."

That's a tough one. "A deer? A horse?"

Lester squints at me like he thinks I'm a idiot, which is just about right. Always let your boss think he's just a little smarter than you. "How d'you think a horse'd get in there, Spencer?" he asks, wheezing out a fake laugh that sounds like one of his asthma attacks. "You ride him in?"

"Maybe some homeless guy crawled in there and starved to death," Naked Dave says from under his blindfold.

"You want to know what I'm thinking?" Lester asks. "I'm thinking"—he looks sly and stupid and proud of himself, like he just won a hatful of quarters from a slot machine—"maybe it's that 300-pound white male the police chased in here that neither of you boys seemed to notice, and he's as alive as you or me."

"That guy'd be dead by now," I tell Lester.

"Could be, Spencer," he says. "But if that fat boy's in there and he ain't dead, what does that tell you, if you're Officer Gilboy? Somebody's been keeping him alive."

You can tell Lester's an ex-cop. He's got a belly that hangs two feet below his belt and a smirk on his face you couldn't wipe off with a Brillo pad. The whites of his eyes are the color of Miller Light. "And by the way," he says, "the only reason I mention Officer Gilboy is that the exterminator gave him a call when he was here. Officer Gilboy jumped to the conclusion—I know this, because he called me to the phone—that Charlie Quill is hiding in there. That name ring a bell?"

"A bell? Can't say that it does." I glance at Naked Dave. "That name ring a bell for you?"

"Not even a little chime," Naked Dave says.

"Bottom line," Lester says, like he's getting annoyed, "Officer Gilboy'll be here tomorrow morning and he's expecting to find Charlie Quill behind that wall. And he's holding me personally responsible, as Chief of Security, for making sure that happens."

"That's harsh," I tell him.

"Not fair, really," Naked Dave says.

Lester's got a nervous tick, probably something he picked up in the Pine Barrens or got from one of his diseases. When he's talking to me his yellow eyes keep darting toward Naked Dave—even though Naked Dave's wearing his blindfold—like he's really talking to him. "I want you boys to know I've got your backs," he says. "I got Officer Gilboy to agree that if we deliver Charlie Quill, there will be no questions asked."

I don't like the sound of that. "What kind of no questions is he going to ask?"

"No questions, period. Not about how the guy got in here, or who's been feeding him, or anything. You boys and myself and Ms. Killebrew will not be questioned or charged with any crimes, and the police won't notify the FDA about the unsanitary conditions in the lab."

Naked Dave pulls off his blindfold and sits up on the bed. "What do you mean 'deliver' him? What do you want us to do?"

"Dave," Lester says, dropping into his good cop voice, "you work with me on this and I guarantee there'll be something in it for you. You can think of it as hazardous duty pay."

He switches to his bad cop voice and glares at me. "As for you, Spencer, I think Ms. Killebrew already made it crystal clear, you're hanging by a thread. That status is still in effect."

"OK," I tell him, trying to look on the bright side. "At least nothing's changed."

"Don't be so sure. The thread's getting thinner every minute. Could snap any time." He flashes a stupid smile and disappears out the door. "See you boys at eight A.M. sharp."

Thirty seconds after Lester leaves, Naked Dave's towering over me in his bathrobe and slippers, his blindfold in one hand, my wrist in the other. He's smiling but his face isn't friendly, more like a dog getting ready to bite. When he talks it reminds me of one of the hit men in Goodfellas.

"OK, Spencer," he says through his teeth, "let me tell you what's going down here tonight."

I try to stand up but he shoves me back into my seat. "I talk, you listen. Tonight you've got some work to do for a change. You're gonna clear all my stuff out of that stink-hole and carry it out to my car. The refrigerator, the booze, the movies, everything. I don't want Lester to find it and ruin my gig."

"What about Charlie?" I ask him.

He squeezes my arm like he's thinking about breaking it in half. "You heard Lester. Charlie better still be in there in the morning."

"I promised to get him out of here."

He lets out a little dry laugh, like he's gagging on a chicken bone. "Listen to me," he says. "Charlie can come out here like he always does but don't tell him what's going on. You give him so much as a hint about the cops coming in the morning and I'll call them right away and tell them you hid him in there and fed him the whole time."

I still can't understand what's happening. "You can't just let him—"

He squeezes my arm again and pulls it halfway out of the socket. "I'll say this once, Spencer, and I'm not gonna say it again. I'm being handsomely paid to lie around in bed all day and night wearing only a blindfold while pretty young nurses swab me down and check my vital signs. If I lose this job—well, let me just say this: My life will become a lot less pleasant and so will yours. End of discussion."

"But, man—"

"End of discussion."

He lets go of my arm and I feel like crying, though I don't. "What am I going to do?" I ask him.

"You're not gonna do anything, Spencer. Except keep your mouth shut."

I spend the night doing what Naked Dave tells me to do, hauling his refrigerator and his awgie clothes and the rest of the stuff in the hiding place out to his car, all the while letting on to Charlie that our escape plan is still in effect. Poor Charlie's clueless and happy as a clam, if you can picture a 300 pound clam. It's Penny's birthday and he can't talk about anything but the big party he's throwing at Le Papillon Libre. He don't know anything about the exterminator and the cops coming back, he thinks we're sneaking him out before Ms. Killebrew arrives and then we're going to drive his van (which he left parked a couple blocks away) to Aunt Lorraine's, where he can take a shower and hide in the basement with Dewey the Second until it's time to leave for the party. He just laughs when Naked Dave reminds him about the rent and all the extra charges he still owes, even after Naked Dave jangles the keys to his van and threatens to run him over if he don't pay them. Something tells me I'll be picking up the tab for Charlie's stay at this hotel, probably with the money I just took out of the ATM on my way to work.

Now I'm sitting in a stall in the men's room trying to decide what to do. I've been here so long the motion detector forgot all about me and switched off the lights and left me sitting in the dark. Most nights this is where I do my best thinking, but tonight my mind's just running in circles. Everything I've been worrying myself sick about lately's flashing by like a horror movie I can't turn off. What are the cops going to do to Charlie when they find him hiding in that wall? What's Aunt Lorraine going to say when she finds out I've been hiding him? Charlie might look and smell like a beached white whale or something worse, but on the inside he's just like everybody else. I hope Aunt Lorraine can accept that. I want to do the right thing— that's what she always told me, just do the right thing—but sometimes that's not so simple. The cops say it's a crime to harbor a fugitive even if he's your best friend, but in your heart you know you shouldn't turn him in. I try praying, hoping I can save Charlie that way, but you can't pray a lie. We already tried that with Dewey. You can't let on to the Lord like Charlie didn't steal that pie and a lot of other stuff—whole feasts in fancy restaurants if you can believe his tales—and you can't ask the Lord to forgive him, Aunt Lorraine says, unless he's really sorry in his heart for what he done and don't plan to ever do it again. Charlie's never repented and he never will, he thinks he's right to steal all that food for his kids—though if I remember right, the last I saw of the cherry pie it was disappearing into his own mouth—and I haven't either, I haven't repented for hiding him in that wall and feeding him and protecting him all this time, which probably makes me worse than him. I know I'm breaking the law but when I think about Charlie and what'll happen if they catch him, his wife leaving him and his kids starving and all, I don't know what else I could do. Even Dewey would do the same, small-brained and pathetic as he is—I knew that when he looked at me with those sad eyes and said "I love you" just as I was putting him out in the cold to die. So I'm going to do what I know I've got to do, even if Naked Dave don't like it. I'm going to save Charlie and I better do it fast, before Lester and the cops get here. It's like when I jumbled up those puzzles in the puzzle factory. Sometimes you've got to turn off the machine and mix up the pieces a little, flap your wings like that butterfly in China, even if you don't know how it's all going to turn out in the end. You're who you are and sometimes you've got to stop listening to everybody else and just listen to yourself.

This bathroom's a good place to listen, it's so dark and so quiet, all I can hear is my own voice echoing inside my head. I could lose myself in that echo, forget where I am and even who I am if I'm not careful. I've lost track of the time and I can't see a thing but I know Lester will be here at eight o'clock sharp. I've got to get out of here but it's pitch dark so when I stand up I just sort of stumble to my feet and lurch out of the stall, pants tangled around my ankles, hoping the motion sensor will notice me and switch on the lights before I trip and break my neck.

Ten seconds, twenty seconds, thirty seconds, hopping madly with my feet looped together, trying to keep from falling over. But it's like I'm the invisible man, the motion sensor still can't see me—then all of a sudden the door flies open and somebody bursts in and the lights flash on like they've been waiting all night for this chance to put me in the high beams.

I'm praying it's Charlie coming in the door, I'm praying it's Naked Dave, but no, it's Lester Blount and his eyes are popping like firecrackers at the sight of me jumping around the bathroom with my pants down around my ankles.

"Spencer," Lester says, covering his eyes and staggering back into the wall, "I'm not even going to ask what kind of weird, sick, disgusting perversion you're acting out in here—no, don't try to explain or I might throw up—but from now on you'll be doing it on your own time, because you're fired! You got that? You're fired!" His whole face is as red as his nose usually is and he's gasping and wheezing like he's having one of his asthma attacks. "And you're going to Hell!"

He bolts out the door and runs for his life. He's right to be worried—I am going to Hell, though he don't know the real reason. It's for hiding Charlie, and now I've got to do something even worse—I've got to bust Charlie out. And I better think fast. If Lester came in this early—it couldn't be much after 6:30—the cops can't be far behind. I can't just drag Charlie out of his hole and walk him out the way I planned.

I find Naked Dave lounging on his bed reading a Hustler magazine. He looks annoyed but satisfied with himself, like Aunt Lorraine when I do something stupid she warned me not to do.

"No questions asked," I tell him, keeping my voice down. "You believe that?"

"What do you mean?"

"What Lester said. There'd be no questions asked. That just means they already got their minds made up."

"Spencer—"

"He's got our back, he says. So he can stab us in it."

Naked Dave stares back like it just dawned on him I might have a brain. "I can't afford to get mixed up with the cops," he says. "That's the last thing I need."

"Then we better get rid of Charlie before they get here."

He peers over my shoulder to make sure Lester's not listening at the door. "Lester's already here."

"I know that."

"You know what Gilboy told him—Charlie better be here in the morning."

"Not if he's dead."

Naked Dave sits up and smiles at me with new respect. "You going to kill him?"

I smile back. "Just enough to make Lester think he's dead. Then he'll want him out of here as much as we do."

Before Naked Dave can answer I hear Lester growling in the doorway behind me. He looks sort of wild-eyed, like he's been drinking. "What part of 'You're fired' don't you understand, Spencer?" he says. "I told you to get out! You don't work here anymore!"

"Shut up, Lester," Naked Dave says.

"Who's telling me to shut up?"

"I am," Naked Dave says, calm as can be. "Now listen to me, Lester, or you're going to get fired as soon as Ms. Killebrew gets here. We did a little investigating of that smell in the back. And you know what?"

"What?"

"There's a dead body in there."

Lester loses his balance, like he's about to die of one of his diseases. He shoots his desperate eyes at me. "It's that fat guy you let in here, isn't it?"

"Nobody I know," I tell him, shaking my head.

"Me neither," says Naked Dave.

"Probably some homeless guy," I add.

"Never saw him before," Naked Dave agrees.

"Must have crawled in when nobody was looking. You know, sometimes—"

"Shut up!" Lester yells. "I'm trying to think."

Naked Dave reaches in his drawer for Charlie's keys and hands them to me. "Maybe you better go get the van, Spencer," he says. "This could take a while."

I squeeze past Lester and behind me I hear Naked Dave trying to calm him down. "Don't even think about telling the cops about that dead body," he tells Lester. "If they find it, the first thing they'll do is tell the TV news, then they'll call the FDA, and—"

"They'll be here in half an hour," Lester whines.

I sneak back to the computer room and tap on the wall. "Charlie!"

"What?"

"If anybody opens this wall, you just lay there and play dead, you hear? Just like you did when you were pretending to be Naked Dave. Can you do that?"

"I think so."

"You better or it just might come true."

It takes me fifteen minutes to find Charlie's van and drive it back to the lab in a cloud of exhaust. By that time, Naked Dave and Lester are in the computer room hovering over a lifeless mountain of flesh. It takes the three of us ten minutes to lift it onto one of the beds—I almost wished he was dead, a little rigor mortis might have gave us something to hold on to—and five minutes more to roll the bed outside and tumble Charlie into the van. If he wasn't dead you could have fooled me by the smell alone.

Lester didn't need any convincing. He had that terrified to the bones look that you hope if you live to be a hundred nobody's ever going to see in your eyes. He wasn't afraid of wrestling with a corpse. He wasn't afraid of the cops. He was afraid of Ms. Killebrew.

46. Officer Gilboy

Police blotter. Thursday, December 21

Officer Dennis Gilboy arrived at Frankford Testing Labs at 7:45 a.m., having been informed the previous afternoon by U-Dirty Rat Exterminators, Inc. that they would begin their operations at 8:00 o'clock sharp. He was greeted by Lester Blount, the Chief of Security, who appeared to be nervous and intoxicated. Mr. Blount informed him that Spencer Casey, the night guard, had been terminated for unspecified misconduct and escorted off the premises. Officer Gilboy was disappointed by this news, as he had anticipated that the opening of a certain wall by the exterminators would provide probable cause for the arrest of said Spencer Casey, a black male approximately twenty years of age, for aiding and abetting the escape of a suspect in a convenience store robbery, one Charles Quill, a white male approximately forty years of age, and for concealing said suspect, or his dead body, behind said wall for a period of approximately three weeks. Officer Gilboy's investigation of said Spencer Casey was commenced on the night of the convenience store robbery. Responding to a call, he observed the robbery suspect entering the Frankford Testing Labs premises, but when he attempted to follow him inside he was willfully blocked and deceived by said Spencer Casey, who is believed to have concealed the suspect in concert with a white male identified only as Naked Dave. Subsequently Officer Gilboy and his supervisor, Detective Bob "Mean" Kampf, were exposed to serious bodily harm while visiting the home of said Spencer Casey, a two-story row home in West Philadelphia which, on the occasion of their visit, had been heated to a temperature of over 100 degrees F., allegedly for the benefit of a featherless bird with a deadly communicable disease, the presence of which was concealed from the officers until after they had been induced to breathe in close proximity to its cage. In view of such provocations, it should not be surprising that Officer Gilboy reacted with anger when U-Dirty Rat Exterminators, in his presence, opened the wall in question and disclosed an empty space, large enough to accommodate said suspect but in fact empty except for a nauseating odor, indicating to Officer Gilboy that the body of said Charles Quill, either dead or alive, had recently been removed from such space. Under the circumstances, Officer Gilboy's violent assault on Lester Blount (which, according to the hospital report, is not expected to result in death or permanent disability), while arguably excessive, can best be described as a demonstration of laudable self-restraint.

* * *

Officer Gilboy sat in the waiting area sipping coffee from a styrofoam cup while the District secretary typed up his statement about the violence at Frankford Testing Labs that morning. If he seemed anxious and preoccupied, it wasn't due to that little fracas, though he did regret the damage to his flashlight. Frankly he had more important things on his mind than the bellyaching of some redneck security guard about a few bruises and broken teeth. If he'd had his way, that clown would have been locked in the empty stink hole for a few days instead of being taken in the ambulance. Okay, there'd be some extra paperwork to fill out, but both his supervisor and the union shop steward had assured him the incident would be handled as a routine disciplinary matter, like tardiness or excessive sick time. What was worrying him at the moment—and the District secretary later testified that he seemed unusually nervous and evasive—was something altogether more important.

This was the day his most important case would come to its long-anticipated climax. For two months he'd posed as "Alex," the underage girl being stalked by a pervert who originally called himself "Steve" and later tried to pass himself off as a 14-year-old girl named "Lindsay." In their latest exchange of messages, "Alex" and "Lindsay" had agreed to meet at King of Prussia Mall that afternoon, and in a bizarre twist their rendezvous had morphed into a suicide pact. "Probably just a ruse," Detective Kampf had told him. "Happens all the time." But if it was all so simple and commonplace, why had Detective Kampf spent so much time teasing and tormenting him about his conduct of the case (which the detective termed an "obsession"), suggesting that he, Officer Gilboy, by carrying on his investigation—and his impersonation of "Alex"—with such dedication and zeal, had shown himself to be mentally unbalanced, if not a pervert of some kind himself? Detective Kampf had been out to get him ever since he started at the District, even asking him once if he was a spy sent by Headquarters; now he'd taken his hostility to the next level, goading him one minute to make an arrest before Christmas, taunting him the next minute for his so-called obsession, pumping up his moral outrage and then knocking it down with crude jokes and insinuations. For Officer Gilboy the case had become a test of his character and endurance, calling into question his very survival as a police officer. The tension and anxiety were almost unbearable. At least, he told himself, it would all be over by the end of the day.

47. From the Journal of Erik Anselmus

December 21: Success! Located Armand Brigantine in Dwight D. Schopenhauer Memorial Health Center, Northeast Philadelphia. Pleasant, well-lighted facility.

Dr. Heffler (well-dressed woman of about sixty) greets me in visiting area with the patient, Armand Brigantine: Elderly man in wheelchair, wrists and ankles strapped down. Wearing bulky New York Giants sweatshirt, purple sweatpants, white sneakers. Face pale and sagging, badly in need of a shave. Deep-set, suspicious eyes; fierce expression. When I introduce myself, he shouts: "Get out of here!"

Dr. Heffler: "Sorry, we'll have to cut this short. The Administration is very strict."

The Administration? What is she talking about? The administration of the nursing home? The government?

I ask: "Why is Mr. Brigantine strapped into his wheelchair?"

Dr. Heffler: "Stephen Hawking can move only a single muscle in one of his cheeks. Armand can move his limbs so well that he's constantly trying to escape. He's a very lucky man."

Armand: "Get out of here!"

Dr. Heffler: "The Administration exists to enforce the law, which happens automatically, because everyone is part of the Administration and everyone is subject to it, whether they know it or not, and everything anybody does is aimed at carrying out the Administration's purposes. And part of the law, which applies to everyone, is to believe that you're not subject to it. You're required to believe—not just to say you believe, but to really believe, to believe fanatically and be willing to die for your belief—that somehow, in the end, the law won't apply to you and you'll escape its operation. That's a false belief, of course, and a subversive one, and the Administration won't tolerate false or subversive beliefs, especially when fanatically held. But there you are: you have no choice, and you would be punished severely for the violation except for this one saving grace, which we can all be thankful for—that no violation is possible."

Mind spinning, throat dry, can't talk.

Dr. Heffler (sternly): "There are no exceptions. Harsh as that may seem—harsh as the whole system may seem at times—it's still preferable to the alternative, which is anarchy, randomness, arbitrary caprice. Chaos, if you will. Who would want to live under such a regime? The aim of the Administration, for all its faults, is to guarantee your freedom—no, your inalienable right—to remain true to your own nature, which is the only sure path to happiness. There's no freedom in chaos—except for..."

I ask: "Except for what?"

Dr. Heffler: "God. Only God can be free. Unfortunately there isn't any God, is there, Armand?"

Armand (shouting): "Get the hell out of here!"

48. Bounded in a Nutshell

The nurse glided back into the visiting area with a sweet smile and wheeled Armand Brigantine down the hall toward the dining room. Dr. Heffler scribbled something on a piece of paper and folded it neatly in half. "Here," she said, handing the paper to Erik. "Please give this to the receptionist on your way out." Then she turned and followed Brigantine's wheelchair down the hall.

Erik sat by himself in the visiting area for a few minutes, trying to grasp what had just happened. His pulse was racing and he felt light-headed, as if an enormous weight had been lifted off his shoulders. Dr. Heffler was responsible for that: she had shown him the way to the kind of enlightenment he'd been craving all his life. Thanks to her, he now understood how the universe worked. The Administration, she'd called it. It was something vast and powerful, an occult bureaucracy of causes and effects reaching back into the mists of time. Everything that happens is determined by what has gone before, but some things have to be willed, chosen by someone, the way a chess player chooses his next move from among the alternatives made available by the rules of the game and all the prior moves. Would the Administration ever allow him to choose something that wasn't one of the available moves? No, of course not, only God could do that—only God (if he existed) could create chaos, as Armand Brigantine had realized before he went mad; and God would never do that, because God (if he existed) had created the Administration and made the entire universe subject to it; and if

God didn't exist (as seemed likely), the Administration itself was all that existed. And yet in spite of all this Erik felt an exhilarating sense of freedom, as if he believed (even while knowing he had no choice but to believe) that having grasped the workings of the Administration, he was somehow beyond its reach.

At the reception desk, Erik handed the folded paper to the receptionist. "Dr. Heffler asked me to give this to you on my way out," he said.

"Dr. Heffler?" The receptionist eyed him skeptically. "We don't have a Dr. Heffler here."

"She's tall, about sixty, long brownish hair. Wearing a beige suit—"

"Oh," the receptionist laughed. "You mean Margaret. She's one of the patients."

49. The Curse of the Leisure Class

It was Thursday, December 21, the day of the closing, and Jeff Pangborn should have been happy. When the papers were signed that afternoon, his financial nightmare triggered by the demise of the puzzle factory would be over. The foreclosure sale scheduled for the following day (which he'd been careful never to mention to Kellie) would remain one of history's scary might-have-beens. After many a sleepless night imagining the Sheriff's deputies seizing his collections of Eagles bobbleheads and Three Stooges memorabilia, catastrophe had been averted through superior business acumen and a little bit of luck: Third Millennium Bank (which was financing his new venture) had been persuaded to apply part of the loan proceeds to the overdue mortgage, and they'd agreed to a full release of his guarantee of the puzzle factory debt. As if by magic, all his liabilities would vanish and he could get on with his so-called wonderful life.

That was the reason for his gnawing unhappiness—getting on with his life. As he spun the Beamer downtown (the closing was scheduled to begin at 2:00, at the Rittenhouse law firm on the 32nd floor of the Third Millennium Center), he felt anything but triumphant. As usual—no, more than as usual—his mood was self-pitying and dyspeptic, tinged by a deep sense of foreboding. Yes, he could see the light at the end of the tunnel, but how did he know it wasn't a freight train speeding toward him at a hundred miles an hour? He couldn't help thinking of Murphy's law: If something can go wrong, it will. Was that really a law? he wondered. Or was it more like the laws of chance—not really a law at all but the opposite, a declaration of anarchy that revealed the true nature of the universe? Life was at best an uphill struggle against entropy, at worst a toboggan ride into the abyss. For months he'd been so focused on the financial meltdown that he'd lost sight of everything else that was wrong with his life. Roberta, of course, and her rapacious lawyer McMonigle, and their attempt to get custody of the kids (he was willing to concede Cupcake). Kellie's moods, which fluctuated with the weather. Lindsay and Zachary, kindly pointing out that the world would have been better off without him. It was true—he was no George Bailey, but so what? Does everybody have to be Everyman? Zachary, who'd been reading a book called *The Theory of the Leisure Class* ("Hey, Dad, you ought to read this—it's about you!"), claimed that even his most selfless acts—*especially* his most selfless acts (though admittedly few in number)—were nothing but conspicuous consumption. Not that he was ever allowed to actually consume anything. The kids buzzed through life like the aptly named 17-year locusts, devouring everything in their path; Kellie's American Express bills (*his* American Express bills) were piling up like the national debt (what was she shopping for—aircraft carriers?); and Roberta expected him to pay for everything she couldn't steal. And what did he get for his superhuman efforts to put food on the table? Fat-free butter, sodium-free salt, meatless meatballs, creamless ice cream. Calorie-free lunches, dinners worthy of a maximum-security prison. Breakfasts prepared under UN supervision, limited to eggs laid by free-ranging, non-corporate, non-carbon-dioxide-exhaling, non-bullying chickens raised in spacious solar-heated spas and fed only organic, gluten-free grain hand-picked by Romanian orphans earning $50 an hour. If this is conspicuous consumption, he wanted to know, why aren't I having more fun? And if this is the leisure class, why don't I ever get a day off?

The black marble lobby of the Third Millennium Center did nothing to lighten his mood. It reminded him of an Egyptian tomb, and as he waited for the elevator he was struck by a sinister coincidence: Le Papillon Libre, the famous French restaurant, occupied the building's pyramid-shaped peak. At breakfast that morning, he'd narrowly escaped a conspiracy to dragoon him into dining there that very night, at the behest of Charlie Quill, a low-life he'd hoped never to see or think about again. Charlie had been fired by GastroPlonix and—according to Bill Symonds, his former boss—was wanted by the police. So Jeff was astonished when Kellie, having apparently received Security Council clearance to serve scrambled eggs, had summoned him to breakfast and informed him, as she scraped the eggs onto his plate, that Charlie had confirmed in a text message that the long-anticipated dinner at Le Papillon Libre would take place as planned that evening.

Jeff made the tactical mistake of laughing. "No way we're going to that," he said, biting into a piece of bacon-free bacon.

"Why not?" Kellie demanded, holding her chef's fork dangerously close to his face.

"The guy's wanted by the police for skipping out on restaurant bills. Is that who you want to have dinner with?"

"Maybe you should pick up the tab," Zachary suggested.

"I'm sure that's what he thinks," Jeff laughed again. "Well, I can tell you, it's not going to happen, because we're not going to be there."

Lindsay burst into tears and started beating her head on the table.

"You've got to take her," Kellie said. "Le Papillon Libre is a once-in-a-lifetime experience."

"Especially for me," Lindsay sobbed.

Zachary pounced on that one. "You planning to die soon?"

"Not if I had something to live for!" She buried her head under her arms and whimpered like a puppy.

That was too much for Jeff. "What are you complaining about? You don't even eat!"

"That's right," Kellie said, opening the latch on Cupcake's cage, "blame the victim. Why don't you make fun of her acne while you're at it?"

"Or her stringy hair," Zachary added.   "Or her buck teeth—"

"Why do you think she has an eating disorder in the first place?"

The closing documents were lined up in piles around the edge of a huge conference table. Jeff's lawyers were there, of course, a couple of dweebs in Dockers and short-sleeve shirts who'd probably just come back from the gym. Is this what he was paying them $500 an hour for? At least the bank's lawyers wore suits: a couple of spindly, wall-eyed women who looked like they'd never been let out of the conference room. The President of the Philadelphia Beauticians and Cosmetologists Association was scheduled to arrive at 4:00 to sign the documents. Then Jeff would sign, hand them their check, and the deal would be done. His partner was late, as usual; Audrey was late, too, with the spreadsheets he'd asked her to prepare. She finally showed up at 3:00, nicely dressed for a change, probably so she could flirt with the lawyers. When she started snooping through the piles of closing documents, Jeff told her to take the rest of the day off. He didn't expect any excitement that afternoon. The closing routine was as predictable and boring as the tides.

Then at 3:15 his phone beeped with a text message and his life changed forever.

Two days earlier, after her last phone conversation with Erik Anselmus, Audrey had decided to intensify her search for information she could sell to McMonigle. Erik's removal to Love Park, his paranoid mutterings, his mad obsession with Jeff Pangborn's new business venture—all this told Audrey that his days as a reliable cash cow were over. He was so far off the deep end that in a few days she'd need diving equipment to find him. He really thought Jeff's partner was Armand Brigantine, the artist whose biography he'd found in the public library; and now, apparently, he was out searching for him. And what had he said about Spencer? *I know where he lives. The hour of reckoning is at hand.* Thank God the man didn't have a gun.

The next day—Wednesday—when Jeff had asked her to prepare some spreadsheets for Thursday's closing, she realized that Erik's paranoid vision wasn't far from the truth. The closing documents outlined the transaction pretty much as Erik had described it, adding a few details which, if Spencer had known about them, would have set the alarm bells blaring.

Thursday, the day of the closing, was a cold, blustery day. Audrey picked out some stylish winter clothes—a red silk blouse, a long woolen skirt, a pair of heels—and drove downtown. When she arrived at the Third Millennium Center, the closing was well under way: lawyers arguing with each other, paralegals scurrying around making last-minute corrections to the documents, bankers gloating in anticipation of the fees they were soon to collect. And there was Jeff, the mastermind, strutting along beside the conference table, self-importantly checking his messages, bored and peevish, as if funding a mechanism to swindle hundreds of people out of their life savings was hardly worth his time. Oh, how she hated that man!

Then a strange thing happened: At about 3:15 Jeff sat in a leather armchair reading messages on his phone. The blood seemed to drain out of him and he swayed on his feet, reaching down to support himself on the table. He threw on his coat and ran out of the conference room without a word to anyone. The bankers stopped gloating for a moment as they pondered what might have just happened. The lawyers shrugged and returned to their work.

Audrey grabbed her phone from her purse and dialed Spencer. "I've got to talk to you," she told him. "Are you at home? I'll be over in a half hour."

50. La Cage Aux Folles

Spencer Casey

Escaping from the lab could've been exciting, like a car chase in a movie, if Charlie's van went more than ten miles an hour. Soon as I start the engine, the exterminator truck cruises into the parking lot with a cop car right behind it, and I can see Officer Gilboy through the windshield, smirking and gloating because he knows that in a few minutes Charlie and me will be on our way to the slammer. Luckily the van's surrounded by a cloud of burning oil and Charlie's huddling on the floor out of sight. "Take side streets so they can't follow us," Charlie says.

"You could follow this van from outer space," I tell him.

Cars are swerving and screeching all around us as they dive through the smoke. I feel like a fighter pilot going down in flames.

Charlie's giant rabbit face pops up in the rearview mirror. "Listen," he says. "We need to go to my house but I can't be seen there. I can't let the cops grab me before the party."

"You planning a party?"

"The dinner at Le Papillon Libre, remember? It's tonight. You bringing Monique?"

I don't say anything until he asks, "What's the matter?"

"No way you're planning to pay for that dinner," I tell him.

We're still only going about ten miles an hour, belching out smoke on all sides. When I stop at a light, the whole sky seems to darken like the world's coming to an end. Charlie leans over the back of the front seat and looks me straight in the eye. "I understand why you'd think that, Spencer," he says. "I'm not offended—honestly—because we're such good friends. But I want you to know that since I've been stuck inside that wall I've been doing some deep thinking. You know what I mean? Deep. About free food and all that."

"Free food, yeah. What'd you decide?"

"There's no such thing."

The light's turned green. Cars are racing around me but I keep my eyes on Charlie. "Le Papillon Libre. I hear that's an expensive place."

A sly little smile flits across his Mr. Potato Head face for about the time it takes me to blink. "Why do you think I invited Jeff Pangborn?"

On the way to his house, Charlie brings me up to date on some of his other deep thinking. "Spencer," he says, "what do you think made that butterfly in China flap its wings?"

"Nothing," I tell him. "He just got a notion to start flapping."

In the rearview mirror I can see him shaking his head. "Something must've made him do it."

"No, he did it of his own free will."

Soon as I say that, I'm not sure it answers the question, and Charlie's not so sure either. "Maybe it was the last hurricane that came around from the other side of the earth," he says. "Did you ever think of that?"

In front of the house, he hides in the van while I slip inside. Upstairs in what he calls the master bedroom I find him a clean shirt and a suit, a necktie, some dress shoes and a pair of underwear the size of a parachute. I'm hoping he's planning to jump out of a plane or maybe just spend the day in his van forgetting I ever existed. But Charlie's got other plans. "Let's go to your house," he says. "I've got to get ready for the party."

Luckily Aunt Lorraine's at work, Shawn's at school, and none of the neighbors is out on their stoops. First thing I do is take Charlie around back and hose him down like a dog—he don't seem to mind—and then I lead him inside and shove him into the shower. When he's dressed in his clean clothes, I bring him down the basement and sit him in a nice comfortable chair next to the furnace, where he can spend the day comparing notes with Dewey the Second about what it's like to have a brain the size of a pea. "Don't worry, Spencer," he tells me as I'm climbing the stairs. "Everything's going to turn out fine."

Upstairs as usual it's about a hundred degrees—I don't even notice the heat anymore—and Old Dewey's scratching and cursing in his cage. He still claims he loves me but I don't believe him. I know he's just buttering me up because Shawn told him if he don't sprout his feathers back by Christmas Eve, Dewey the Second will be coming in off the bench.

I stretch out on the couch in my boxer shorts, hoping to get some sleep. But after a half hour I'm still tossing and turning, thinking maybe I ought to go to Charlie's party at the French restaurant after all. It's the only place I ever heard of, except a bait store, where you can get snails and frog legs and barnacles, which is what Charlie says they serve there. Not that I'd want to eat any of that stuff, even if it's free, but just *watching* people eat it might count as getting out and seeing the world, which is what Monique says I need to do more of. Expanding my horizons, is how she put it, though if it was up to me I wouldn't bother. I feel like I've seen a little too much of the world lately, and to tell the truth I'd just as soon stay home and watch Shawn play video games as see a whole lot more of it just now. But I can't help thinking about Monique and what she's looking for in a man, and it occurs to me that maybe she'd really love to go to that French restaurant with me, just like Charlie says. Maybe I should call her up and invite her.

So before I go to sleep, I call Monique's number and leave a message. *Monique*, I tell her, *I'm going to a gourmet restaurant tonight, Le Papillon Libre, all expenses paid. Can you come along? Trying to get out and see the world. Give me a call.*

In a heartbeat I'm dead to the world, and when the phone rings—I don't know how long I've been asleep—naturally I'm sure it's Monique. But no, it's not Monique, it's Audrey and she's all worked into a lather about something. "I've got to talk to you," she says. "Are you at home? Can I come over?"

"Yeah," I tell her, not thinking very hard about what I'm saying. "But I've got to get some sleep."

"I'll be over in a half hour."

I'm still asleep when Audrey bangs on the door and walks in, dressed to kill. I guess Shawn forgot to lock the door when he went to school.

"I had to come right over," she says, slipping off her coat. She's out of breath, a little unsteady in her long skirt and high heels. "What I've got to tell you can't wait."

"OK," I tell her, still a little groggy. "Want to sit down?"

There's only two chairs in the living room, both of them piled high with video games, so she stumbles around a little before parking herself next to me on the couch. She's wearing red lipstick and some kind of perfume that almost makes me sick. "You know I've been doing some work for Jeff Pangborn," she says. "Helping set up his new business, though until yesterday I didn't know much about it. Mostly I've been digging in his files for dirt I could use against him." She reaches up to flip a strand of hair off her forehead but it's already plastered down with sweat. "God, it's hot in here! You growing a rain forest or something?"

"We've got to keep it that way for Dewey," I tell her.

She grabs the Daily News off the coffee table and wags it in front of her like a fan. "Can't we open a window or something? It's about ninety in here."

"More like a hundred," I tell her.

"I need to bring you up to date on that weird insurance guy Erik Anselmus. He found out where you live."

By now she's bright red, fanning herself like crazy, and the next thing I know she's unbuttoning her blouse. I'm starting to panic. This is a little too much like déja vu, which was bad enough the first time around. "You're not here for old time's sake, are you? Because if you are—"

"I understand perfectly, Spencer. And I'm completely OK with it. Who you love is nobody's business but your own."

That touches a chord for Dewey. "I love you, man," he croaks. "I love you."

Audrey tries not to look surprised. "Is that... Naked Dave?"

"That's Dewey," I tell her. "He says he loves me, but Shawn says he don't give a damn."

"He sounds sort of... sick."

"He's one sick bird, all right. Might have to pull the plug on him if he don't sprout some feathers by Christmas."

"God, I'm sweating like a pig!" She peels off her blouse and drops it on the couch between us. "You don't mind, do you?"

Underneath she's wearing a bra that probably came from Victoria's Secret, but that's the only attraction. When I try to look somewhere else, all I see is her shiny red face and her black eyes bugging out like a lobster's. "Don't be taking your clothes off like that!"

"Why should *you* care?" she laughs.

I reach down to pull her blouse over my lap. "Dewey cares, don't you, Dewey?"

"I love you, man," he says. "I love you."

She's still fanning herself with the newspaper, sweating hard. "I finally figured out what they're doing with this business deal," she says. "There's a closing going on right now in the Third Millennium Center downtown. Jeff and his partner, who goes by the name of Armand Brigantine, are taking out a huge bank loan and using the money to buy up all the hair salons and nail parlors in Philadelphia. They're keeping the owners on as employees blah blah blah...."

Her voice buzzes on but I can hardly listen. I feel like Dewey, trapped in a cage and praying for a miracle. I want to run out the door but I can't just leave her sitting there. I didn't tell her Charlie's in the basement. Shawn could be coming home from school any minute, Aunt Lorraine might have left work early. And things are going from very bad to much, much worse. Audrey's not just sitting there anymore, she's squirming around, panting like a dog, fluttering her eyelashes. She kicks off her high heels and the next thing I know she's wriggling out of her skirt.

"Whew!" she says, tossing the skirt on the floor. "It's unbearable in here!"

If you ask me, that's the last play of the game, no way I'm sticking around for the extra point. I try to stand up but she grabs my arm and pulls me back down. "They're working with a trade organization, the Philadelphia Beauticians and Cosmetologists Association, and the first business they're taking over is right in this neighborhood. Maybe you know the address—"

There's a loud thump and the front door swings open. In walks Shawn and right behind him Monique, who must have got to the door just as Shawn came home. A cold wind blows in behind them and the four of us freeze like we're caught in a spell: Shawn hanging his head, suddenly not a boy anymore. Monique astonished, icy, her eyes burning black fire. Me in my boxer shorts, a red silk blouse over my lap. Audrey beside me in bra and panties, sweat streaming down her face like tears.

I want to say: *I can explain everything!* But my mouth's glued shut and I know I'll never open it again.

Audrey's the first to flinch. She's embarrassed now that there's another woman staring at her. She grabs her clothes and tries to cover herself up.

"You must be Audrey," Monique says. "The hundred-year-old bookkeeper who couldn't be a cougar in the zoo." Then she aims her blazing eyes at me: "Does that pretty well sum it up, Spencer?"

I can explain, I want to say. But I don't.

Audrey scoops up her shoes and runs out the door, throwing her coat around her as she goes. Monique glares at me just long enough to give Audrey a head start, then turns around and stomps outside. Shawn is still on Pause like a movie that stopped in the middle. Maybe he thinks if he don't move a muscle nobody'll know he was there.

And as for me, I'm rocking back and forth with my head in my hands, but it's getting too heavy to hold onto much longer. In another minute I'll be sinking into the floor. I'm hoping Dewey will say I love you, but he don't.

Instead Charlie comes up the basement steps in his suit and tie, whistling the theme from Mission Impossible, and pokes his jolly giant's head around the corner. "You almost ready to go, man? It's after five o'clock."

51. Entrapment

Jeff stood in the conference room chatting with one of the lawyers when his phone pinged with a text message. He glanced at the screen just long enough to see that the message was from his daughter. The lawyer asked him something and he almost skipped the message. I'll read it later, he thought. Then the lawyer walked away and Jeff looked back at the screen:

hi dad this is goodbye i'm sorry for all the trouble i caused u. love always lindsay.

He snorted, almost laughed, but caught himself. It was a joke but not a funny one. Did Zachary write this? What did she mean, *this is goodbye?* Was she going someplace? He tapped out a reply:

I'm in the middle of a closing or I'd call. Where are you going? Remember you have to be home by 6.

Three minutes later his phone beeped again, and he read:

i'm not coming home read my messages if u want to know y - password xxycupcake.

When he dialed her number there was no answer. He sat in a leather armchair in the corner of the conference room and dialed in for Lindsay's messages. They had a family plan so all he needed was her password. The last message she'd sent was at 3:09 pm:

hi alex i'm on my way - meet in front of the gap at 4 - i'm wearing my jeans and tommy hilfiger sweatshirt - y don't u wear the same outfit so we'll look like twins?

OK, so she's going to the mall, Jeff thought. What's the big deal? But as he worked his way back through the earlier messages, the sickening enormity of the truth overwhelmed the phone's tiny screen. His hand shook as he learned about Lindsay's special friend Alex, the overpass near the mall, the two girls in Jenkintown.

My God, he thought, his stomach turning over. They're going to jump off an overpass.

He glanced back at his phone. It was 3:15 PM. If he left now, he could get to the mall in time.

3:21 PM. Soaked with sweat from head to toe, Jeff jumped into his silver Mercedes and squealed out of the parking garage, blasting his way through traffic lights and stop signs to the Schuylkill Expressway. Once on the expressway, which was jammed as usual, he raced along on the shoulder as far as Manayunk, flashing his lights like an unmarked police car, then jumped off the highway in favor of the narrow back roads that wind their way toward the mall.

3:39 PM. Speeding through the hilly suburbs, he passed within a mile of his house. His phone rang and he answered when he saw that it was Kellie. Before he could get a word in, she rattled off a list of complaints and reiterated her demand that he take her to the dinner at Le Papillon Libre.

"Kellie, listen," he interrupted. "We'll have to talk it about it later. Lindsay sent me a suicide note. She's meeting up with some other girl at the mall and they're going to jump off an overpass."

Kellie sounded more angry than alarmed. "It's Alex, isn't it? The girl you picked up on Craigslist."

"Alex? No, that was a different Alex. This is some teenage girl—"

"You idiot! The Alex you met on Craigslist *is* a teenage girl. She's fourteen. Lindsay found your messages and she's been texting back and forth with her."

"I can't believe this!"

3:46 PM. A top-heavy landscaping truck loomed in front on him as he sped toward a blind curve. He stepped down on the accelerator and nipped around the truck just in time to avoid colliding with a school bus as it lurched around the bend.

"Jeff," Kellie said, her voice strangely calm, "there's something you need to know. McMonigle called me—"

"I can't talk about that now."

"Yes, you can. He offered me a hundred thousand dollars to rat you out."

"Rat me out? About what? You haven't told him about Alex, have you?"

"Not yet. But if I tell him, you're not only going to lose custody of the kids, you'll be going to jail."

"I didn't know she was fourteen!"

"That's not a defense."

"You wouldn't do that to me!"

"Not if you make a better offer."

3:52 PM. Jeff veered to the right, narrowly missing an elderly man retrieving his mail from a mailbox near the road. "What are you saying?"

"If we were married I'd have no reason to cooperate with McMonigle. They couldn't even force me to testify."

"I told you we can get married as soon as the divorce is final."

"You've got to mean it."

"I mean it! I mean it! Will you marry me? OK, fine. Now I've got to get off the phone. I'm almost there."

3:53 PM. On the main road now, Jeff raced along the shoulder, flashed his lights and flew through a red light, leaving a gridlock of fender-benders in his wake.

Kellie heard the commotion and screamed into the phone: "Jeff, turn around and come home right now! You can't go in there! The whole thing sounds like a trap."

"What are you talking about? You think Lindsay—?"

"No, not Lindsay. The police. They're probably waiting to grab you the minute you set foot in the mall."

"A minute ago you were threatening to send me to jail."

"That was before you agreed to marry me."

"The only thing that matters right now is Lindsay. I've got to find Lindsay before she hurts herself."

"Listen to me, Jeff! You've got to listen to me!"

3:54 PM. Jeff couldn't listen. He couldn't think of anything but Lindsay. He knew Kellie was saying something important—he'd heard about sting operations that lured innocent men like himself into compromising situations with young girls—but he couldn't imagine anything so elaborate, so improbable, so insidious as what she was suggesting, with his own daughter being used as bait. And he didn't care about himself, he only cared about Lindsay.

3:55 PM. He clicked off the phone, leaving Kellie yelling hysterically on the other end. A vast expanse of mall parking lot stretched before him, congested and seemingly impassable.

3:57 PM. The Mercedes screeched into the covered parking area and bullied its way into a space ahead of a little old lady. Jeff sprang out of the car, dodging past minivans and SUVs and shoals of holiday shoppers, into the teeming mall. The usual Santas and Salvation Army bell ringers and other assorted Christmas freaks blocked his way as he barged past swarms of shoppers and millions of teenage girls frowning down at their phones like monks into prayer books.

3:58 PM. He struggled for breath, his heart pounding almost out of his chest, but he kept running, feeling a power he didn't know he had, an elemental power that took its shape on the primeval savannas of Africa. Two million years of evolution had found its goal in his desperate race to save his daughter.

3:59 PM. An army of plainclothes cops loitered in front of the open shops, burly ex-Navy Seals and ex-juvenile delinquents disguised as elves and nutcrackers or wearing Santa suits and Dickensian top hats, eyeing Jeff and muttering into hidden microphones as he rushed past. He didn't care, all he cared about was finding Lindsay. And there she was, bobbing through the crowd about fifty feet ahead of him in her Tommy Hilfiger sweatshirt, just what she told Alex she'd be wearing.

4:00 PM. The Gap was straight ahead, Lindsay rushing toward it, with at least ten other girls in sight wearing jeans and Tommy Hilfiger sweatshirts. Jeff stepped up his pace, running now, oblivious to the elves and Scrooge impersonators closing in around him.

None of the girls in the Tommy Hilfiger sweatshirts paused in front of the store. Instead a man in a blue jacket—short, dark, intense—stepped forward. As Lindsay came closer, the man's eyes darted toward her and then glanced at Jeff. Jeff stopped running and stood motionless as he watched the scene unfold.

"Alex!" Lindsay called out. "Alex!"

The man in the blue jacket touched her arm. "I'm Alex," he said.

"I'm Lindsay." She looked confused.

"You're really Lindsay?" The man squinted suspiciously over at Jeff. "You're not Steve?"

"No, I'm Lindsay. Who are you?"

The man touched her elbow and started to lead her away. "Lindsay, I need to talk to you. You've got to trust me."

A sudden clamor of shouts and stamping feet shook the mall like an explosion.

"Freeze! Police! Put your hands up!"

Jeff froze, threw his hands over his head, stood waiting to be tossed down on the floor. But the cops hurtled past him and clamped their arms around the man in the blue jacket, knocking him violently against the wall. "I've got you, Gilboy!" one of them shouted—he was a large, red-faced man, evidently the leader, disguised as Santa Claus. He yanked off his fake beard and glared at the man in the blue jacket. "I've been onto you all along!"

Jeff Pangborn and Dennis Gilboy locked eyes for one long moment and suddenly both of them knew who the other one was and what he was doing there. The trap was sprung and one of them had to be caught. If Jeff had arrived thirty seconds sooner it would have been him—a dirty old man preying on an underage girl who turned out to be a cop—but his daughter, in her innocence, had saved him, enticing Gilboy with her heartfelt messages, her undying love, her mad suicide scheme, into becoming the predator. Because she arrived first, because Gilboy recognized her and touched her, possibly because

Gilboy, knowing she was a young girl, had wanted to save her—for all these reasons destiny, until then in suspense, tipped in Jeff's favor at the critical moment when Santa Claus a/k/a Detective Bob "Mean" Kampf, waiting to see if a man or a girl would appear in front of the Gap, spotted Lindsay and heard her calling out for Alex. Kampf held his breath as Gilboy spoke her name and reached out to touch her and then with a thrill of satisfaction he gave the signal and moved in for the arrest. Gilboy was defenseless, as defenseless as a snitch deserves to be. Hadn't she told him she was a girl? There she was, the girl who'd brought all of them together in this drama, crying and yanking at her hair as a female officer led her away through the crowd. Gilboy writhed, yelled, struggled to pull his arms free as he fended off the mob of cops in holiday garb. Jeff lowered his eyes and blended into the tide of Tommy Hilfiger sweatshirts and Aéropostale hoodies and DKNY jeans that surged toward the exit. He felt a little sorry for Gilboy, but one of them had to be the bad guy, one of them had to be beaten and dragged handcuffed to a police car, kicking and shouting curses at the top of his lungs. And the other one had to escape, had to steal through the parking lot like a thief and climb, shaking, into his Mercedes and disappear into the traffic, eyes clouding up, unworthy of his daughter's innocence but praying that it would buy him another chance. In a few minutes his phone would ring and it would be Detective Kampf, reassuring him that his daughter was safe. The predator, Detective Kampf was ashamed to admit, had been a police officer.

Jeff thanked him and burst into tears. As he drove toward the children's shelter he wiped away his tears and started laughing, giddy with love and good fortune. He'd never felt this way before. He thought about calling Kellie, even Roberta, but dialed Lindsay instead to tell her he loved her and was coming to pick her up. Almost as an afterthought he told her that he and Kellie had decided to get married. Cruising through the wooded hills and ravines that usually led him home, he drove right past his house but didn't stop, even though Kellie's car was in the driveway. He wanted this moment for himself, for Lindsay and himself. He seemed to be floating, his mind spinning with joy at the thought of the child who was his most precious gift. It was Lindsay who saved him, not the other way around. On that desperate drive to the mall he'd been baptized in his own fear and now he was a new man, not the one who drove out there, not afraid any more, not ashamed. All was forgiven, though he didn't deserve it—he was as much of a jackass as ever but somehow the way he'd felt at the mall, the way he felt now, made everything right. Loving a child is being a child. It makes the world start all over again.

PART III

52. Le Papillon Libre,
by Lindsay Pangborn

They took me to the same children's shelter as when my Mom got arrested, and after awhile my Dad called and said he was on his way to pick me up. It was a little hard to understand him on the phone. He sounded wheezy and out of breath, like he was laughing and crying at the same time, and when he hung up he said "I love you" like the Dads on TV. I'm glad he didn't turn out to be a pervert—that was the other guy, the policeman who posed as Alex so he could lure me to the mall. At least that's what Detective Kampf said. Detective Kampf—he was really nice—said I was the victim, but I'm not sure about that. I mean, didn't I just pick up where my Dad left off? Didn't this other policeman start out thinking I was a forty-five-year-old man? And wasn't I the one who suggested meeting in front of the Gap? I explained all that to Detective Kampf but he was busy writing in his notebook and didn't seem all that interested.

To get me out of there, my Dad had to sign a bunch of papers agreeing to bring me back to talk to social workers every day for the rest of my life. That's what I dread most, social workers. They're always asking you why you did what you did, over and over again, like you're a criminal, and they don't believe you when you say you don't know. Does there have to be a reason for everything? They just keep asking *Why?* like you're covering something up and it's always the same thing: somebody's abusing you—"Is it your Dad? An uncle maybe? Do you have an older brother?"—and when you shake your head and pull your hair and shout No! they don't believe you, especially if you're crying (which is naturally what you're doing by this time), and when you refuse to talk to them any more they say they're disappointed but what they really are is mad, even though they pretend not to be. They just smile knowingly and look sad and make you come back the next day and you know they're going to keep at it until you confess.

"I'm taking you home," my Dad said when we got in the car, smiling like a tooth whitener commercial. "I love you. You know that, don't you, Sweetheart? I love you. I'll do anything for you."

"OK," I told him. "Then don't take me home."

"What do you mean? Of course I'm taking you home. Kellie's waiting—"

"No, I want to go to the dinner with Spencer. The dinner at Le Papillon Libre."

"Dinner?" He wasn't smiling anymore. "You can't stand the sight of food!"

"You said you'd do anything for me!"

He put his key in the ignition and started the engine, as if we were having a normal conversation. "I'm afraid I can't do that tonight," he said. "When I got the call about—about your trip to the mall—I was in the middle of an important business transaction, right in the middle of the closing, and—"

I unlocked my door and released my seat belt, determined to jump out of the car before it went any farther. He slammed on the brakes, hurling me into the dashboard, and pushed his button to lock all the doors. I burst into tears. "You said you'd do anything for me!" I screamed, unlocking my door again before he snapped it shut. "That was only two minutes ago! You said you loved me!"

Luckily my Dad isn't a social worker or we might have spent the night in that parking lot, locking and unlocking the doors and yelling at each other. As it was, we stopped at the house just long enough to pick up Kellie and Zachary and change our clothes so we could arrive at Le Papillon Libre by 7:00 o'clock. As he drove, my Dad talked on the phone with his business partner (who was my cousin Curtis) and explained that he would come down to the lawyer's office after dinner to finish signing the papers and in the meantime he had more important things to do—he winked at me when he said that—and he was sorry, the lawyers and the bankers were just going to have to wait. I loved hearing him say I was more important than his lawyers who charge $500 an hour. Kellie seemed happy too, all dolled up in her evening gown, and even Zachary rose to the occasion in his matching set of lip, nose and eyebrow plugs.

Le Papillon Libre was everything I hoped it would be. It was at the very top of one of the tallest buildings in Philadelphia, with giant picture windows all around, the city sparkling in every direction, and even its own helicopter pad—in fact it was the same building where my Dad's closing was taking place, at some law firm about fifty floors below us, when he rushed out to the mall to rescue me, and the lawyers and bankers were still sitting there with the unsigned papers in front of them, all waiting because my Dad promised me he wouldn't go down there again until the dinner was over. There was a maître d' to greet you and escort you to your table and waiters in identical black jackets standing along the walls with napkins draped over their arms, watching to see if anybody needed more rolls or a refill of their wine glass or something, everybody talking in hushed tones and trying not to spill anything or chew with their mouths open or drop any of the silverware, which weighed a ton. It was all so elegant I almost wanted to cry. Yes, there was food, which was disgusting—I think they even served snails—and Charlie and his wife Penny and their four supersize kids (the manager had to pull an extra table over for them), who came in their Eagles jerseys and smuggled in Cokes and bags of Doritos to eat while they were waiting, and of course Zachary, who sat next to me dipping his finger in the olive oil plate and licking it clean (I think he was stoned). But the main thing for me, the only reason I could stand all this, was that Spencer was there. He sat between Charlie and my Dad, dressed in a dark suit and tie like I'd never seen him before, and I kept hoping he would notice me. That's all I wanted, really, I just wanted him to smile and say, "Hi, Lindsay!" but for a long time he and Charlie just sat whispering to each other like a couple of girls. Kellie kept trying to talk to him, leaning across the table with enough cleavage showing to swallow him whole if he glanced in her direction. She made me wear this stupid knit dress that goes up to my ears.

The waiter took our orders—I just asked for gluten-free water—and when they brought our food my Dad raised his wine glass for a toast. "This is a very special occasion," he said.

"Yeah," Zachary growled in my ear. "The Feast of Fools."

Luckily nobody else seemed to hear him. "What?" I whispered to Zachary.

"The Roman festival of the winter solstice. Also known as Saturnalia."

"One of those occasions," my Dad went on, "that must be celebrated as soon as it occurs—"

"It was celebrated with bloody sacrifices."

"Chill out, Zachary! It's almost Christmas!"

"It was Saturnalia before it was Christmas."

My Dad gave Zachary a sharp look—"and then celebrated again and again"—he beamed at Kellie—"for the rest of our lives."

"I thought you were a Goth," I whispered to Zachary. "Didn't the Goths sack Rome?"

"Sure, and one of the things we got was their holidays."

"I want you all to be the first to know that Kellie and I are engaged to be married."

Everyone hollered and clapped, even a few people we didn't know who sat at other tables. "To my bride to be!" my Dad said, and we all drank a toast with whatever drink we had in front of us. I sipped some of my gluten-free water. Charlie and Spencer emptied their wine glasses and my Dad poured more wine into them. Charlie's kids finished their Cokes and crushed the cans on the table.

"Who will be the Lord of Misrule?" Zachary asked, a little too loud. By this time there were a lot of people staring at us from around the room.

For a minute I thought my Dad might leap over and clobber him. Kellie laid her hand on my Dad's arm as if she thought she could hold him back.

Surprisingly, it was Charlie who took control of the situation. He rolled into a standing position, his face red, his eyes twinkling, his smile beaming out to the people at the other tables. "As the host of this dinner," he said, aiming his smile at Zachary, then at my Dad, "which I've been planning for over two months, and as a man who spent fifteen years in a puzzle factory, stamping Masterpieces of Western Art wherever they needed to be stamped"—he leaned forward and shoved his hand in front of my Dad's face—"If this looks like the Mona Lisa, all I can say is it wasn't Leonardo di Caprio who put it there!—I'll gladly accept that honor."

Then a funny thing happened. Two policemen walked in with the maître d' and sat down at the next table. One of them I'd never seen before. The other one was Detective Kampf, who'd been so nice to me at the children's shelter. I smiled and waved to him but he didn't seem to notice. He had a mean look on his face and he was aiming it at Charlie.

53. Chaos Is Come Again

Erik Anselmus sat in the back corner booth at Pinocchio's, staring down at the fragmented puzzle that had baffled him for so many weeks. The remaining pieces, he realized, would never come together. He could still see Armand Brigantine writhing in his wheelchair, incensed at the thought of Chaos Scape 19 being turned into a puzzle: any pattern imposed on it, any illusion that it could be understood, was an abomination. No wonder that woman—Dr. Heffler, she called herself—had turned out to be a mental patient. What she called the Administration was a monstrous delusion, a vast bureaucracy of effects without causes. Chaos is the ground of being. It can never be defeated or destroyed. It's older than God and will exist long after no one is left to forget that God, if he exists, ever existed. Your only choice is to submit to it, and in that submission is freedom, absolute freedom. He realized that now.

After she fled from Spencer's house, Audrey drove around for a couple of hours, fighting the rush hour traffic as if she had someplace to go. Finding herself perilously close to home, she wedged into a parking space on Passyunk and walked the three blocks to Pinocchio's, praying that Cathy would be there. She hurried past the low brick building, now a garage, that had once housed the puzzle factory. To think that she'd spent ten years of her life in that hell-hole almost her nauseated her. What she needed now—what she was determined to have—was a new beginning. Inside Pinocchio's, she headed straight for the bar and sat down without noticing Erik in the back corner booth. Cathy stood listening as she told the story of what had happened at Spencer's house that afternoon.

Erik crouched in his booth, the glint of madness in his eyes. When the two women started talking, he squirmed out of the booth and tiptoed toward the bar. Reaching the point where he could hear their conversation, he leaned in to listen.

"I tried to warn Spencer but I didn't get there in time," he heard Audrey saying. "Then Monique arrived and I tried to warn her, but she was too angry, she wouldn't listen. And now Spencer's at that restaurant with Charlie, waiting for Jeff—"

"Spencer and Charlie!" Erik thought, his hackles rising. "She's been protecting them all along!" He thrust his hand in his pants pocket and wrapped his fingers around his gun. It felt heavy and cold but he knew it would come to life quickly. The relentlessly flashing "Pizza" sign in the window seemed to be pushing him towards violence. Jiminy Cricket, larger than life on the wall, counseled moderation and urged him to accept his fate.

Fate? That made him smile. Only a madman would believe in that. Fate was nothing. He could do whatever he pleased. He could flap his wings and change the course of history forever.

He raised his gun and aimed it at Audrey as he considered his options.

54. Feast of Fools

Spencer Casey

When Detective Kampf and his new partner hunker down at the next table, I know Charlie's in big trouble. By this time most people are done with their dinners. I have the crab legs but the others order a bunch of French stuff I never heard of, which turn out to be fried chicken wrapped in cheese, and filet-o-fish with tartar sauce poured over it, except for Jeff, who gets the calf's liver, and Kellie, who I feel sorry for—she orders tuna and they bring her a slab of raw meat. Lindsay just asks for water, like she's on a hunger strike, and I don't blame her. If this is what gourmets have to eat, I'll take my chances with starvation. Charlie's kids order filet mignons and a cheese plate, then carve it all up into little pieces and pile it on their rolls to make cheese steaks, about a dozen each, which they swallow whole like sharks cleaning out a fish tank. I can feel my crab legs twitching like they want to crawl somewhere else. I have to stop them with my fork—it's got a long handle and it's sharp enough to spear the Devil.

I pour myself another glass of wine so I can keep up with Charlie's toasts. The cops keep him in their sights, hoping to catch him red-handed if he tries to skip out without paying, but he just keeps talking as if they're not there. Nobody's listening except the cops. Jeff's tapping his fingers, checking his watch, brushing crumbs off his navy blue blazer. Kellie's joking with Zachary, Lindsay's texting on her phone. Penny looks a little sick, probably because she can see the disaster coming. The waiters are cruising in with the desserts and coffee and it's only a matter of time before they bring the check.

"Lindsay, please put your phone away," Jeff says. You can tell he's being real careful whenever he talks to Lindsay, like he's talking to a crazy person. "Texting at the table isn't polite."

"Who are you texting?" Zachary asks her, grabbing the phone.

"Curtis," she says. "He's at the closing."

Jeff frowns and leans forward. "Curtis is texting you from the closing?"

"He says, 'Tell your Dad he better get down here.'"

"OK," Jeff tells her. "Tell him OK, I'll be down in a few minutes."

"But you said you wouldn't go down there until after dinner!"

"That's what I mean. As soon as dinner's over."

Her phone keeps beeping with new messages. "Curtis says, 'How are we going to get these idiots to hand over their life savings unless you're here to sign the documents?' What does he mean by that, Dad?"

"He doesn't mean anything. It's just a stupid joke."

"What else did he say?" Zachary wants to know.

"Stop doing that. Stop texting at the table, I told you."

"Come on, Lindsay! What else did he say?"

"He says, 'I've got the President of the Philadelphia Beauticians Association swearing at me and throwing the documents off the table. She says if you're not down here in five minutes she's going to throw me out the window. Her daughter says the same thing.'"

"OK," Jeff stands up and drops his napkin on the table "Tell him I'll be right down."

Lindsay bursts into tears. "But Dad! You *promised!*"

"It's another one of your swindles, isn't it, Dad?" Zachary asks.

"Nobody's getting swindled," Jeff barks. "It's just an arm's length business deal, that's all."

"With Curtis?"

"It's the least he can do to make up my losses from the puzzle factory."

I'm enjoying a nice buzz from the wine. I hear Charlie bubbling along in one ear and all this Pangborn static in the other—the President of the Philadelphia Beauticians Association—her daughter—if Jeff don't get down there to sign the papers—how are we going to get these idiots to hand over their life sayings?—and I'm thinking: Jeff's a sleazeball, all right, his new business's no different from his old ones, but who am I to criticize how a man makes his living? This is America. Then all of a sudden my brain wakes up. Wait a minute! That's Brenda and Monique they're talking about!

I reach out and grab Lindsay's arm. "Who's this Curtis you're texting with?"

"He's my cousin," she tells me. "You must know him. He used to work at the puzzle factory. Everybody calls him Stupid Butchie."

"Stupid Butchie?" What did Stupid Butchie have to do with Brenda and Monique?

Then all of a sudden it hits me: That's how I found out about the job at the puzzle factory in the first place—it was posted on the bulletin board at Brenda's beauty salon. Monique must have put it there for her friend from business school, the one nobody ever saw who drove the black BMW with the tinted glass. Stupid Butchie! Who, even before I started, was robbing the place blind, stealing the puzzles and shrink wrapping them and selling them to his own customers, sending the puzzle factory (with a big assist from a butterfly) into its downward spiral. I was the butterfly, but Stupid Butchie was the reason I'd been there to flap my wings.

Was it fate—or just stupidity?

And even then I'm thinking: There's more to come. Fate (or stupidity) isn't done with us yet, and never will be.

The waiter glides up with a skinny leather folder and lays it down in front of Jeff, who laughs and tosses it over to Charlie. "This one's on you, my friend."

"You bet!" Charlie says, but his hand is shaking. Peeking over at the check, I'm about to tell him they made a mistake, they gave you the bill for somebody's heart transplant, but no, it says Le Papillon Libre at the top and something that looks a lot like $5,000 at the bottom. Charlie pretends to study it, like it's in a foreign language, but I know he's just stalling for time. I can see Detective Kampf perched on the edge of his chair, ready to jump over and wrap the long arm of the law around Charlie's 20-inch neck.

All eyes are on Charlie. Penny steals a glance at the check and turns as white as the tablecloth. Kellie and Jeff exchange smirks and fold up their napkins. The maître-d' huddles by the window wringing his hands, his lips trembling, like he's praying to stop the explosion that's about to blow up his restaurant.

But Charlie, I've got to say, handles the situation like the pro that he is. Charlie is to Free Food what George Foreman is to meat, what Jimmy Dean is to sausage, what Colonel Sanders is to chicken. He's performed this act in every two-bit crab shack on Route 1 and he's not about to lose his nerve when he finally makes it to the big time. What's Le Papillon Libre but an Appleby's with snails?

He lets go of the check, letting it drift down to the table while he fumbles in his pocket, maybe for his wallet, or more likely, I'm thinking, for a cyanide capsule. As he's doing this he leans closer and whispers in my ear, "Plan B."

I shake my head and whisper, "Say what?"

"Just hold your glass as steady and tight as you can. Don't flinch no matter what happens."

He fills my glass with red wine and stands up, looking out over the audience. "Before we go, I just want to propose one more toast," he says. "In honor of this holiday season. Christmas, Hanukkah, Kwanzaa—"

"Saturnalia," Zachary chimes in.

"Yes, even Saturnalia, for those of you who are Pagans and Goths. To all of you"—he turns in a slow circle, tipping his glass toward the audience, even Detective Kampf—"who've been with us here tonight. Especially those at our table: Jeff Pangborn, and his wonderful children Lindsay and Zachary; his beautiful fiancée Kellie; my good friend Spencer Casey, who's helped me so much. And last but not least, my family: My loving wife Penny, and of course my terrific kids"—he points down to his kids, who sit pawing through their half-eaten salads for croutons and tossing them into each other's mouths—"I'm so proud of them. They're not just my kids. I think of them as my offensive line—the Seven Blocks of Granite, I call them. I know I can depend on them to *stand by me* no matter what happens..."

The hot air gurgles on like that for another ten minutes. Maybe Charlie's trying to run out the clock, I'm thinking, or just bore the cops to death along with everybody else. There isn't a shred of truth in anything he says. He's only got four kids and they're more like mounds of flesh than blocks of granite, and his wife would throw him under a bus, if she could find a big enough bus, for a chance to take the real estate exam and shack up with Jim Grillo.

Finally he acts like he needs to stop for breath. He bends down to pour more wine for himself and me. "Stand up, Spencer," he whispers. "And remember what I said before."

What did he say before? *Hold your glass steady and tight as you can.*

I stand up and we both raise our glasses for the toast.

"To everybody here tonight!" Charlie shouts. "Happy Holidays!"

His hand swings forward but instead of clinking the glasses together, like you're supposed to do, he smashes his glass into mine as hard as he can. I hold steady, just like he said: my glass shatters but his hand keeps coming until he slices his wrist on my glass, and now blood's shooting out all over the place along with wine and broken glass, all over Penny's hair-do and Kellie's cleavage and Jeff's half-eaten plate of calf's liver.

Charlie clutches his wrist and sways around gasping for breath. "Oh my God!"

At least it sounds like 'Oh my God!' but I think it might've been "Omaha!" because as soon as he says it the Four Mounds of Flesh rise up like a wall between their Dad and Detective Kampf, who's rushing like a madman screaming that Charlie won't get away with it this time, Charlie's under arrest, the kids are under arrest, the whole restaurant's under arrest! But nobody hears the detective because the crowd's going wild and he can't break through the line, and by now Charlie is slumped in Penny's arms with the maître-d' standing over him waving his arms at the crowd and telling them not to worry, it's just a little mishap, everything's going to be all right.

The waiters crowd around Charlie like EMTs, wrapping his wrist in napkins to block the bleeding. And before Detective

Kampf can stop him, the maître-d' plucks the $5,000 check off the table and tears it into little pieces, tossing them in the air like confetti. "Your dinner's on the house, sir!" He raises his arm and waves again at the crowd. "Now, everyone, please go back to your dinners. And enjoy your evening!"

I wish I could say the excitement was over. But there was more to come.

55. Mt. Brenda Erupts

Brenda Watkins was a short, volcano-shaped woman who, when deceived or disrespected, had been known to erupt with a righteous fury sufficient to destroy entire civilizations. The warning signs were well-known to friends and relatives: seismic rumbles, eyes glowing like molten lava, smoke venting out her ears. Patrons of her beauty salon had learned to flee when an eruption threatened to shake the earth.

At the closing that afternoon, which she attended as President of the Philadelphia Beauticians and Cosmetologists Association as well as in her own right as proprietor of Brenda's Hair Salon, Brenda felt her mood shifting from baffled to frustrated, annoyed, chagrined, incensed and finally infuriated. At the same time her temperature rose from smoldering to fuming, from seething to blazing and at last to igneous and explosive. In fact (as one of the paralegals, trained as a geologist, observed at the time) her state of mind, as the hours clocked by, closely mirrored measurements on the Richter scale. Arriving between 3:00 and 4:00 (Richter scale: "Shaking of indoor objects noticeable") with her daughter Monique, she was informed that Jeff Pangborn, for no apparent reason, had thrown on his coat and run out of the conference room a few minutes earlier—surely, Jeff's attorney assured her, he would return soon. Brenda and Monique sat down to wait after helping themselves to some lukewarm coffee dribbled from an urn into styrofoam cups. Between 4:00 and 5:00 ("Some objects may fall off shelves or be knocked over"), Brenda felt her temperature rising and the

steam beginning to build. As she listened to the lawyers
spinning out lame excuses for why Jeff had not returned, she
reached for her coffee with a noticeable tremor and spilled it
over some documents, which had to be retyped. Monique
escaped to run an errand, leaving her mother alone for over an
hour; this, perhaps, was a mistake. Between 5:00 and 6:00
("Tremors felt by everyone, casualties range from none to a
few"), Brenda's stomach began to rumble and she became aware
of a throbbing in her ears that she assumed was audible to
everyone in the room. When Jeff called and told his lawyer that
he would return to the closing only after dinner, she stood up
and demanded in a thunderous voice that food be brought in for
those stranded in the conference room. The lawyers readily
agreed, and a tray of sandwiches soon appeared on the table.
But between 6:00 and 7:00 ("Strong to violent shaking"), when
she learned that Jeff was dining at Le Papillon Libre, located in
the very same building, she swept what was left of those
sandwiches into the trash and demanded—in tones which, even
for the corporate lawyers present, foreclosed the possibility of
negotiation—that gourmet meals be brought down from the
restaurant not only for herself and Monique (who had returned
from her errand, visibly upset) but for all the paralegals,
secretaries, cleaning people and other unfortunates who'd been
dragooned into staying beyond the expected time so Jeff and his
family could dine on imported delicacies. Between 7:00 and 8:00
("Major damage, structures likely to be destroyed"), she made
the lawyers and the documents jump as she hammered her fists
on the conference table, demanding that the lawyers call Jeff on
his cell phone and summon him to the closing without further
delay. By this time Jeff's partner Curtis, Monique's supposed
friend who'd lured them into this deal, was exchanging text
messages with Jeff's daughter Lindsay at Le Papillon Libre.

When Curtis explained that Jeff had promised his daughter he wouldn't leave the restaurant until dinner was over, the eruption came at last. Brenda hurled piles of documents off the table, overturned chairs and threatened to throw Curtis out the window; and finally, between 8:00 and 9:00 ("Death toll ranges from 1,000 to 1 million"), when there was still no sign of Jeff, she seized Curtis by the ear and dragged him out through the law firm lobby to the elevators, followed by Monique, who pleaded for moderation.

When the elevator doors opened, Monique's mind reeled as she confronted a shocking and unbelievable sight. There stood the woman who, a few hours earlier, she'd surprised half naked on Spencer's couch, now fully dressed and being held at gunpoint by a hulking albino zombie, while a tall blonde in a Pinocchio outfit cowered in the corner. Both women's eyes locked with Monique's in a desperate plea for help, but the gunman's gaze warned them all not to move or make a sound. It was like a glimpse into a parallel world, an impossible world which, Monique told herself, would exist only as long as the elevator doors remained open. When they glided shut, she closed her eyes and said a silent prayer.

Brenda, never one to be cowed by firepower inferior to her own, reached her hand toward the elevator button. "Let's take the next one."

56. Last Chance To Be A Hero

Spencer Casey

Detective Kampf yanks me away from the table. "Spencer Casey!" he says, spitting out my name like it's choking him. "You're under arrest!"

"You're arresting *me?*"

"You have the right to remain silent," he growls, digging his claws into my arm.

"But I don't *have* to remain silent, do I? I mean, if I want to know why you're arresting me—"

"Shut up!"

Me and the detective chat like that for a few minutes while his partner pats me down. They're getting ready to snap me in cuffs when there's a loud commotion and our heads spin around. What we see is a sight I won't forget: Audrey, looking scared half to death, and right behind her, prodding her forward like she's his prisoner, a huge bloodless zombie in a suit who must be the insane insurance man everybody keeps talking about. And whimpering along behind them—I wouldn't believe this if I didn't see it myself—a big blonde dressed like Pinocchio, who looks a little crazed herself.

But that's not all. Ten steps behind the blonde comes the next wave of the invasion: Brenda and Monique marching in like a pair of avenging angels, and behind them, sort of sheepish, Stupid Butchie, looking just as rat-faced and shiftless as ever.

There's an explosion coming, you can feel it in the air. Maybe Zachary's right, civilization is coming to an end. That's what the other gourmets seem to think. They're running for the exits, leaving their half-eaten T-bones and lobster tails and chicken cordon blues on their plates, unpaid for, compliments of Charlie, who showed them how to get free food even in a place like this. The waiters can't stop them, the maître-d' can't stop them, all he can do is wave his arms and yell at the waiters to get Charlie the hell out of here. Before you know it he's sprawled over the pastry cart on his way out to the helicopter pad.

There's not much left of our table but Jeff still sits at the head of it, calling out orders to the waiters, to Lindsay, Zachary, the Four Mounds of Flesh, anyone who'll listen. Kellie's beside him mopping the blood and wine out of her cleavage, with a little too much help from Zachary. She pushes him away and he jumps up and greets his cousin Curtis a/k/a Stupid Butchie with a fist bump. "At last," he laughs, "the Lord of Misrule!"

When the maître-d' sees the new crowd trooping in, he hurries over to Jeff: "Are these people with you?"

"It's OK," Jeff tells him, pointing at Stupid Butchie. "This is my business partner. And these ladies"—he gestures toward Brenda and Monique—"are a couple of our investors."

Audrey pulls away from the insurance man and lurches toward Jeff. "Your partner?" she asks. "Stupid Butchie's your partner? I thought your partner was Armand Brigantine!"

"No, that's just a code name. Armand Brigantine—"

The insurance man grabs Stupid Butchie around the throat and lifts him off the floor.

"You're not Armand Brigantine!" Then he tosses him aside and yanks Jeff out of his chair. "What have you done with Armand Brigantine?"

"Look, dillweed," Jeff says, flicking his fingers like he's shooing a fly. "This is a private party. Why don't you roll up your Swiss cheese and go find some crackers of your own?"

You've got to admire Jeff for staying so cool, but at the same time you've got to ask, is this the way to talk to the Jolly Green Giant? I don't even talk that way to Aunt Lorraine. That insurance man could break Jeff in half with one hand behind his back. But he doesn't do that—all he's got to do is pull a gun out of his pocket and shove it in Jeff's face. "I want to know what you've done with Armand Brigantine!"

You can practically hear the air whistling out of Jeff as he cringes into a tiny heap. "No, please!" His voice is about two octaves higher than usual. "Don't kill me! Please!"

All this time I'm watching from the sidelines with Detective Kampf, who's still doing his best to break my arm. It seems like we're watching a comedy, a bunch of fools making fools of themselves, then all of a sudden things get real when the insurance man pulls the gun on Jeff. The next thing I know, Detective Kampf's got his gun in front of my nose and he's shouting at the top of his lungs: "Police officer! Drop your weapon! Now!" His hand's still clamped on my arm.

I'm not exactly cringing like Jeff but I can feel it coming on. First time I ever get arrested and two minutes later I'm clamped in a face-off with a lunatic. Is this what they teach at the Police Academy? "Hey, man, let me go!" I beg the detective. "What am I, a hostage?"

He shoves me away, and when I turn back around everything looks different. The big blonde in the Pinocchio outfit is wrapped in front of the insurance man like she's daring Detective Kampf to shoot her. She's no hostage—the insurance man seems as surprised to see her as everybody else. He keeps his gun on Jeff, who's whining like a puppy and begging for his life.

"Don't fire!" the Pinocchio lady tells the detective.

"Stand aside!" he shouts, holding his gun up in both hands like the cops on TV. "Step out of the way!"

"I'm staying right here until you back off."

"Stand aside!"

"I'm not moving. Erik, put your gun down."

"I'm going to shoot Jeff Pangborn," he tells her.

"Not today," she says.

"He deserves it."

"Of course he does. It's just not the best time."

"I'm free to do whatever I want."

"Freedom is a delusion," the Pinocchio lady says. "Put your gun down."

The two cops tackle the insurance man as soon as he drops the gun, leaving Jeff drooling and shaking in his chair, Kellie smirking at Jeff and shaking her head, Lindsay crying her eyes out, Zachary high-fiving with Stupid Butchie, Audrey and the big blonde sobbing in each other's arms—and me slinking away, before anybody remembers I'm under arrest.

It's easier than you think. All I've got to do is pick up a tray and pretend to be a busboy, and nobody looks at me anymore. I'm the only brother in the place so naturally they think I'm part of the help. There's the door to the kitchen, probably a back elevator I could escape on; I could disappear and nobody'd be the wiser. But I don't go that route. I've still got important business to take care of. Our table—Jeff Pangborn's table—still needs to be cleared. It's my last chance to be a hero.

Jeff's sitting there, trying to catch his breath, enough terror left in his eyes to keep him quivering for an hour. I bend over the table, loading the dirty plates and glasses onto my tray—it looks like Jeff didn't quite finish his calf's liver—and in my right hand I grab one of those sharp, long-handled forks I used on my crab legs. Crouching down next to Jeff, I reach under his navy blue blazer and jab the fork up against his shirt, just below the ribs.

"What's the idea, Spencer?" he wants to know.

"The idea, Jeff," I tell him in a low voice, "is that unless you want your own liver to go back to the kitchen on this tray, carved up into little bitty pieces, you're going to stand up and come with me, and you're not going to say a word to anybody."

"Where are you taking me?"

"Got to get you down to the closing."

I put my free arm around his shoulder, like I'm helping him to his feet, keeping the fork stuck into him below the ribs, and the two of us tango toward the lobby. Monique stares at me like I'm crazy, which I probably am, but with my eyes I signal to her and Brenda to follow us. Monique's looking a little shell shocked after almost getting caught in a shootout. "Come along," I tell her. "Everything's going to turn out OK."

She takes Brenda's hand and hurries along beside me out to the elevators—awed by the way I've taken control of the situation.

Lindsay catches up just as we're getting on the elevator. "Spencer, are you kidnapping my Dad?" she asks me. "How cool is that?"

"No," I tell her. "Just escorting him down to the closing so he can take care of some unfinished business."

"You want me to sign the documents?" Jeff squeals. "You don't need to threaten me to do that."

"Shut up," I explain, pushing the fork in a little deeper.

"The deal's changed a little," I tell him. "The only thing you're going to be signing is a check."

57. Miracles

Spencer Casey

You know the rest of the story, Monique. How we cruised down that elevator with Jeff, and after one look at the conference room, with the papers all strewn around, he passed out, and Lindsay poured a can of Coke over his head to revive him and we sat him down and made him write your Mom a big check, even though she refused to sign the documents to give him control of her beauty salon or the Beauticians Association. I didn't even need to poke him with the fork—he was a broken man that nobody wanted, like an old TV that don't work anymore. By the time we left he just sat there whimpering. I felt sorry for the dog, almost wanted to forgive him. But for what? You can't forgive somebody for being the way he is, any more than you can blame him.

And you and me since then—I don't need to tell you about that either. It's a beautiful thing to find out the one you loved all along was just waiting for you to grow up and be the hero. Aunt Lorraine says I do everything the hard way, even growing up, which almost anybody can do right the first time. Now that I've got you on my side, I'm working hard at getting where I need to be. I like my new job at the Archaeology Museum, guarding the mummies and Neanderthals in case they try to escape in the middle of the night. It leaves me plenty of time to think, and most of what I think about is you. The rest of what I think about is the train wreck we've all been living through for the past six months.

Like I said at the beginning, you can blame me if you've got to blame somebody. I was the one who started it all, flapping my wings like some butterfly without knowing what I was doing or why. My freedom is somebody else's fate, I know that now. But no matter how much I scrambled things up, I didn't really change anything. All the puzzles are one puzzle, but people don't know that. They go crazy because they can't put the puzzle together with the pieces they've got. They think the other pieces are missing but they're out there. They're just in a different box.

Aunt Lorraine wonders if I'll ever learn to let well enough alone. Isn't it time I made my peace with what's meant to be? Well, I don't know what runs this world—blind chance? some kind of crazy plan?—but I know one thing: whatever it is, it'll blow you away if you don't keep flapping your wings. And when it comes to how the world works, who's to say Aunt Lorraine is such an expert? She thinks Dewey's feathers sprouted back on Christmas Eve because Shawn prayed for him. And Shawn, now that he's got performing miracles under his belt, is letting on like he can walk on the water. Naturally he gets all the credit for saving the bird, but it was me who wrapped old Dewey up and took him out to Lindsay's when we couldn't keep him in the basement any more. What a scene that was, with the sheriff's deputies boarding up the house, the family out on the street—I couldn't leave the poor bird there. So I called Charlie and he said he'd give Dewey a chance. "You've got to keep it a hundred degrees inside," I warned him. "No problem, man," he says. "I owe you one."

"And Charlie," I started to tell him, "about that hundred dollars—"

"Money in the bank, Spencer. Soon as I get this ankle cuff off."

Charlie says house arrest is the best thing that ever happened to him. The D.A. offered probation, but Charlie and the kids held out for prison on account of the food. They had their trial and the judge put them all under house arrest for six months, even Penny. "It's really brought us together as a family," Charlie says. At first they called out for pizza and cheese steaks and Chinese food, whatever they could get delivered, but pretty soon the money ran out, and you can't get free food when you're ordering in. They came so close to starving, Charlie says, they were seriously thinking of eating Jim Grillo the next time he stopped by with his organic vegetables, especially after they found out he tipped off the cops to the dinner at Le Papillon Libre. I knew I was tempting fate taking Dewey over there. And sure enough, half an hour after I left, Charlie had the soup pot boiling, the spices laid out on the stove, and the poor bird thrashing in his hands. Just as he was lowering him into the pot, Dewey tilted his head and peered at Charlie with his sad yellow eyes. "I love you, man," he said in his smart-alecky voice. "I love you." To Charlie that was a miracle, a sign from above, just as surely as Dewey's healing was to Aunt Lorraine. The whole family burst into tears—for them nothing would ever be the same. They couldn't eat Dewey, they couldn't eat Jim Grillo, they couldn't even eat the Domino's pizza they tricked the delivery man into leaving on the steps without paying for. And with the house boiling like a steam bath twenty-four hours a day, they started sweating off the pounds in bucketfuls. Charlie says he's going to run a marathon when his sentence is up. He owes it all to Dewey, he says, because Dewey found it in his heart to love him. I didn't tell Charlie, Dewey says that to everybody who's getting ready to kill him. Why spoil a miracle?

You see, Monique, even a bird brain like Dewey knows you can't just go along with what's meant to be. At the Archaeology Museum you can see the whole history of the human race, and sometimes you've got to wonder, what were those people *thinking?* So one night after everybody went home, I made some changes to one of the exhibits. It was easy enough to get the top off the display case, and by moving some labels around and penciling in a few dates, I left the ancient world a little better than I found it. If I can't change the present, maybe I can at least do something about the past. If it changed enough, maybe we could start all over again.

I know what you're thinking. Won't I ever learn?

58. What Fools These Mortals Be,
by Lindsay Pangborn

I'm almost ready to hand in my chapbook, putting together everything I've written all year. I'd show it to my Dad but he's so hard to reach since he moved into the Greyhound bus station without even a phone. That was the day after Christmas, when the bank threw us out of the house. Kellie was already gone (I think she's a dancer again, or something like that), so it was just me and Dad and Zachary there when the sheriff's deputies came to the door and started reading us our rights (none) and hauling our stuff (all of it) out to the street. They were really nice about it, considering that Cupcake was barking and snapping at their heels the whole time, they carried the Christmas tree outside without knocking off any of the decorations and set it up on the curb in the freezing rain, with all the presents around it just like they found them, and they let Zachary eat some of the food in the refrigerator, even though technically it belonged to the bank. When they finally nailed the foreclosure sign to the door and drove away, we built a little fire (my Dad wanted to burn some of his papers anyway) and arranged some beach chairs around the Christmas tree, and sat in the rain with the food from the refrigerator (this was before my Mom drove up in her Audi and forced me and Zachary to go home with her). We weren't in the mood for a holiday feast, but that's all we had—leftover turkey with dressing, sweet potatoes, cranberry sauce and apple pie (I actually ate a little of it)—and when the food was gone my Dad poured what was left of the eggnog into our Hunger Games mugs. "Don't anyone say Merry Christmas," he grumbled.

Zachary raised his cup as if somebody'd just proposed a toast. "God bless us every one!"

I think he was being ironic, if that's the right word. See what I mean? He really is a fool.

I still think about Spencer a lot. He tried to give me his sick parrot the day they foreclosed on our house, but since then I haven't heard from him at all. He's with Monique now and she doesn't want him hanging out with a 14-year-old girl. I can understand that—look what happened to poor Officer Gilboy. But the one Monique really hates is Audrey. I used to think Audrey was evil but now I think she's a really nice person. For instance, even though she hardly knows my Mom's lawyer, Mr. McMonigle, she gave him all my Dad's files about Alex so my Dad would have to pay my Mom enough money to buy our house back at the foreclosure sale. And even though she only met me a couple of times, she asked me and Zachary if we wanted to go to a nursing home to visit the crazy insurance guy who threatened my Dad with a gun at Le Papillon Libre. I didn't expect my Mom to let us go but she said it was OK. I think my Mom looks at the insurance guy as a hero because he almost shot my Dad.

His name is Erik and he's in the nursing home because a judge decided he's too crazy to go to jail. When we got there we met a friend of Audrey's named Cathy who I remembered from the restaurant. Cathy said she loves Erik and is dedicating her life to nursing him back to health. I think it might take a long time.

He sat in a wheelchair next to a woman named Margaret and an old man named Armand who were also in wheelchairs.

"Get out of here!" Armand said when we walked into the visiting room.

A lady with hamster teeth and a scary look in her eyes came in and started hugging us. I thought she must have escaped from some other part of the hospital but it turned out she was just a social worker. "I'm Irene," she smiled. "We thought it might be helpful to have everyone here at once—Erik, Audrey and the Pangborn family—to bring closure. Unfortunately we don't know how to reach your Dad."

"He lives in the Greyhound bus station," I told her. "With Cupcake. My Dad got custody of Cupcake."

"Cupcake's a dog," Audrey explained.

"What Erik did in that restaurant must have been so unbelievably hurtful," Irene said. "You must have felt—"

"We don't hold it against him," I told her. "Especially my Mom."

"Her only regret is that he didn't pull the trigger," Zachary said.

Irene beamed at Erik and patted the top of his head. "I know he would apologize if he could."

"Get out of here!" Erik shouted.

"What exactly is his problem?" Audrey asked.

"A lack of social trust," Irene said. "He seems to believe—and unfortunately I think he got this idea from Margaret—that something called the Administration rules the universe. It's older than God, he says, something even God, if there is a God, would have to obey."

"Freedom is a delusion, he told me once," Cathy said.

"Yes," Irene nodded sagely, showing the tips of her hamster teeth, "that's why they locked him up in here. Or so he believes—even though, in reality, he's not locked up at all. The straps around his wrists and ankles are solely for his own protection. He's as free as a butterfly."

Erik threw his head back and yelled at the top of his voice, "Get the hell out of here!"

All things considered, I'm glad Alex turned out to be a policeman so we didn't have to go through with what we planned to do at the Mall. I like to think I've outgrown that idea (I'll be 15 in February and everything seems different already). Life is good, even if it gets too complicated sometimes. I feel like I just woke up from a crazy dream and now I can see more clearly. Everybody seems like sort of a fool—not just Zachary, even my Dad—but I don't hold it against them. I still want a boyfriend, like Spencer only closer to my own age, and I'd like a special friend, but maybe the two of us could just text together or actually shop at the Gap instead of meeting there for you-know-what. I told Zachary about my change of heart and he agrees that I shouldn't be so self-centered. "If there's going to be a human sacrifice," he says, "I think it should be Stupid Butchie."

Obviously Zachary hasn't learned a thing from all this. Stupid Butchie—Curtis, I have to remember to call him—is part of our family, and we shouldn't make him a scapegoat. That's the way I feel now, just wanting to forgive everybody, including myself, and get on with my life. Yesterday I took the train into the city to visit my Dad. He says he loves living in the bus station and wouldn't live anywhere else. He made me follow him all over Chinatown with Cupcake tied to a shopping cart, supposedly collecting recyclables. I started to cry when I realized he was trying to sell Cupcake to the Chinese butchers (Zachary says he was probably trying to sell me too). I love him anyway, I even love my Mom, when she isn't out stealing stuff.

I'm starting back to school tomorrow.   I know I've got to concentrate on my classes (big test coming up in String Theory) and my rowing if I want to get into a good college.   It's exciting to think that tomorrow I'll be eating Tastykakes in the girls room and listening to Mr. Siegal talking about *No Exit* (that's next on our reading list) and Ms. Stebbins warning me about STDs (as if she ever had any) and the rowing coach yelling like a slave driver, and I'll be pumping back and forth on that fake boat with all my might as if it was a real boat and I was out on the river with the wind in my face about to set a new school record.

I'm really, really happy.

THE END

ABOUT THE AUTHOR

Bruce Hartman lives with his wife in Philadelphia. His previous books include *The Philosophical Detective* (published by Swallow Tail Press in 2014), *The Rules of Dreaming* (2013), *The Muse of Violence* (2013), and *Perfectly Healthy Man Drops Dead* (Salvo Press, 2008). For more information, please see his website and blog, www.brucehartmanbooks.com.

Kirkus Reviews awarded *The Rules of Dreaming* its Kirkus Star for Books of Exceptional Merit and selected it as one of the "Top 100 Indie Books of 2013." *Kirkus* called the book, "A mind-bending marriage of ambitious literary theory and classic murder mystery... An exciting, original take on the literary mystery genre."

www.ingramcontent.com/pod-product-compliance
Lightning Source LLC
Chambersburg PA
CBHW020243180626
46810CB00006B/2347